D0454383

Mollie Hardwick is the autho... ... ...
recently *The Merrymaid* and *Girl with a Crystal Dove*. She is also
known to television viewers as the author of *Upstairs Downstairs*,
By the Sword Divided and the *Juliet Bravo* series. However, she
has had a lifelong interest in detective fiction, which was
responsible for her knowing Dorothy L. Sayers, to whom this
book is dedicated. With her husband Michael Hardwick, she has
written many books and plays incorporating Sherlock Holmes.

The Hardwicks live in a fifteenth-century house in Kent, which
is also home to two cats, Hudson and Marigold.

MALICE DOMESTIC

Mollie Hardwick

CORGI BOOKS

MALICE DOMESTIC
A CORGI BOOK 0 552 13235 7

Originally published in Great Britain by Century Hutchinson Ltd.

PRINTING HISTORY

Century Hutchinson edition published 1986
Corgi edition published 1988

This book is set in Plantin

Corgi Books are published by Transworld Publishers Ltd., 61-63
Uxbridge Road, Ealing, London W5 5SA, in Australia by Transworld
Publishers (Australia) Pty. Ltd., 15-23 Helles Avenue, Moorebank,
NSW 2170, and in New Zealand by Transworld Publishers (N.Z.) Ltd.,
Cnr. Moselle and Waipareira Avenues, Henderson, Auckland.

Made and printed in Great Britain by
Hazell Watson & Viney Limited
Member of BPCC plc
Aylesbury Bucks

In affectionate remembrance of a great lady,
Dorothy L. Sayers,
who capped my quotations with such masterly ease.

1

'Two more deaths this morning,' Rhona said with relish, piling used breakfast pots on to a tray. Doran Fairweather continued to study the copy of *Collectors' Choice* which had arrived in the morning post.

'Oh dear,' she said, her pencil hovering over an item on the 'Any Offers?' page.

'Don't you want to know?' Rhona was disappointed by her employer's lack of response. She so much enjoyed starting the day with a nice juicy piece of local news and a chat about it, and here was Miss Doran being dreamy and not wanting to hear. Doran heard the note in her voice rather than the words, and looked up from the page.

'Flu again, I suppose? It seems to be going round the village.'

'Oh no, not flu.' Rhona put down the tray. 'Miss Beamish and Mrs Trott. Milkman thought it was funny Miss Beamish hadn't taken in her pint, not that she has it more'n twice a week, so he climbed up on the flat roof and looked in at the bedroom window. There she was, sure enough, half in half out of bed, poor old lady, and her eyes staring open, just like on the telly so of course he knew and rang up the police straight away, and it was Constable Eastry as told him that was the second case this morning.' Rhona paused for dramatic effect.

Doran's large hazel eyes widened with interest. It was certainly more interesting than flu. 'No, really?'

'Yes, well, seems he had a call about five o'clock at home from someone that was passing Miss Trott's cottage on his way to work and noticed her door was open, so thinking there

7

might've been a burglary he took the liberty of going in and having a look round.'

'And?'

Rhona's handsome face took on a portentous expression. It occurred to Doran that with her tall imposing figure and fondness for drama she would fit in very well should the Abbotsbourne Dramatic Society unwisely put on a production of *The Trojan Women*. Doran began to cast it mentally, putting shopkeepers and housewives into Greek robes, binding Rhona's dark hair up in a fillet – it would have to come down later, of course, because she would have to be Cassandra, prophesying everybody's doom and the Fall of Troy. . . .

'. . . down in the woods,' Rhona was saying, 'not far from St Chad's Well, that's where they found her.'

Doran came out of her dream. 'Why, was she lost?'

'You weren't listening. I told you, there wasn't nobody in the cottage, only the cats wanting their breakfast, so he started looking about and not finding anything, he phoned Sam Eastry. He went straight down there with that young constable, you know, the fair one, and they found her.'

'Dead?'

'As mutton. Been there hours, they reckoned, died of exposure, what with the cold and her bad chest. Must have been eighty-seven if she was a day. They said she'd taken to wandering. Fancy, going like that, not even in her own bed, and what I ask myself now is who's going to look after things, the funeral and that?'

'Not to mention the cats. . . . Oh, we'll sort it out somehow.'

'You and the Reverend, course you will, between you.'

'What with my brains and his beauty,' said Doran facetiously, though with no hope of getting a laugh. Watching Rhona, her tale told, piling up plates, marmalade-dish and toast-rack on the tray, she felt slight remorse at having hoped, just for the fraction of a second, that the tale had been one of sensational murder that would enliven quiet Abbotsbourne in its late February sloth. A time when the old village seemed to sleep in a sleeping countryside without colour or movement,

8

curled in its valley-fold, remote and secret from the motorway that ran to the south coast and the busy Channel port of Eastgate, fifteen miles away. Nobody came to it in these grey cold days for its own sake. Tradesmen's vans, transports strayed out of their way, farmers' wives doing their shopping, the postman, the Gas and the Electricity were its only visitors. At closing-time the cars of commuters came home to roost in the council estate beyond the village. The castle ruins and the Abbot's House which was the museum were unvisited, the shops in the cobbled square held perpetual sales. Winter days in Abbotsbourne were dull, boring.

Doran shook herself. Life at her dear, cherished Bell House was never dull, with Rhona Selling to bring home rumour, legend, speculation. Doran had been lucky to find her, a widow living on social security after the death of her farm-worker husband in an accident with a combine harvester. Rhona was a contradiction of the saying that those who ought to be grateful never are. She was grateful for her lodging in the gracious old house (too big for one single lady), grateful for the satisfaction of cleaning it and running it efficiently, grateful for the home it provided for her daughter Debbie, fifteen years old. Grateful for Miss Doran, who treated her like a friend, not like a servant, but never embarrassed her by being too familiar.

And, Doran reminded herself, there was the shop. In the antiques quarter of Eastgate, a popular resort, it attracted both the trade and visitors. When Doran had managed it herself she had made rather a mess of things, her taste and knowledge of antiques being considerably better than her business acumen. Now that she had taken on Howell Evans as a partner it flourished. He should be at the shop now.

She picked up the telephone, *Collectors' Choice* at her side with the marked 'Any Offers?' page.

'Howell?'

'Hmmm.' His voice was slurred. Hung over from a party, one of those after-hours gatherings of Howell's friends, all dealers, all male – depending what you meant by male. Sometimes it was wine, sometimes pot. This morning it sounded like pot.

9

'Oh dear, did I wake you?' Doran asked with mock concern. 'It's only half-past nine, after all. Do go back to sleep.'

'Don't be bloody stupid, girl.' He sounded even Welsher than usual. 'I been here this hour and more. Half killed myself fighting that bloody packing-case, nails in it like bloody marlinspikes.'

'I shouldn't think you'd know a marline-spike if it came up to you and bit your ankle. Listen, I've just been marking up *Choice*.'

'That rag.'

'That rag. I know you don't think much of it, but you must admit I've got some nice things from it, not just stuff dealers can't shift or granny's-attic junk. How about this? "Brass four-poster, probably by Winfield, twisted tubular pillars with cast double mounts, ornamental panels on head and foot rails with mother-of-pearl insets." Nice?'

'Has it got the pavilion and coronet?'

'Doesn't say so.'

'Stamped Winfield?'

'Again, doesn't say.'

'Odds it isn't, then. How much?'

'Eight-fifty.'

There was a silence. Doran knew Howell was thinking up an argument to put her off. It came.

'Where'd we display it, then? Beds got to be displayed to attract, not piled up against a wall. No floor room, see.'

'I could tell that man in Brighton, the one who goes for brass. He'd know what it was without seeing it assembled. Oh, all right, I can tell you're not interested. Well, what about a longcase clock? Sounds good – about 1780, eight-day, brass dial with painted dial behind, sun, moon and stars revolving, Corinthian columns, brass finials. Maker Roberts, Bedford. Eight-seventy-five. Seen Nottingham.'

Howell was tempted, she knew. He liked clocks. But he said, 'Nottingham. Hell of a way.'

'Rubbish. You'd go anywhere for a clock like that. And we're due for a Midlands buying trip. Oh, Howell, do wake up and pay attention! If I didn't keep my eyes open we'd never have any stock.' This was not true, but he needed rousing. She read out further items for sale, half-talked him into interest in a walnut davenport, and promised to be at the shop within an hour.

Her mind went back to the morning's casualties. She wondered whether there might just possibly be anything worth buying from the home of either old lady. Mrs Trott had lived in an attractive little cottage – might it not hold furniture to match, or a bit of good china, or even one or two of the fans Doran loved and collected? Then she was ashamed of herself for the thought.

'Ghoul,' she said aloud. Ghoul to be even thinking of making profit from the leavings of two old people who were dead, while she was alive: Doran in her twenty-sixth year, born and bred in North Oxford, a don's daughter, Doran tall and slim and strong. Doran whom a man had once called his Dryad because she was like a young tree, with green glints in the grey-brown of her eyes and soft fine brown hair that curled naturally like very young leaves. 'Apollo hunted Daphne so, Only that she might laurel grow. And Pan did after Syrinx speed Not as a nymph but for a reed.' Well, Apollo-Pan had caught his Dryad and much good had it done her, leaving her trembling and vulnerable and a failure in Finals, while he went on to pursue other nymphs and a successful future in banking.

After the disaster of Ian there had been a time she hardly remembered: aimless drifting from one temporary job to another, her self-confidence so eroded that the prospects of each one were poor from the start. When she worked in an Oxford bookshop she would let her attention be caught by some volume and become lost in it, oblivious to waiting customers. Two shoplifters got away with valuable hauls, in both cases when she was in charge of the shop, and she was sacked as being too expensive to keep.

The secretarial course she began proved to be beyond her in her then state of absent-mindedness. The hooks, squiggles, ticks and spiders' footmarks of shorthand were too baffling to recognize in the mass; she was used to amateur two-finger typing and found the ten-finger system impossibly hard. Half a term was enough to show her that she would never be anyone's super-efficient secretary, though the rudiments of book-keeping were not too difficult to master.

At this time her despondency led her into a new path, the pursuit of pleasure, and more particularly the pursuit of love. The past was dead, she would be a new woman, a hard bright creature who caught men in her glittering web, played with them and discarded them when her desire and her self-esteem were satisfied. The plan worked out rather differently. There had been Jeremy, a youngish Oxford professor who had shown signs of interest in Doran at parties, and who was married to a plain wife older than himself. Doran set out to fascinate Jeremy. Her new coming-on disposition certainly intrigued him, and there were meetings in the town, a daring drink at the Randolph where anybody could have seen them, a meal at a French restaurant when he was supposed to be coaching. And a head-on encounter with his wife, as they emerged slightly merry from a lunchtime session at a pub with a conveniently unfrequented rear bar.

There had been a short painful scene. The wife had said some emphatic things about the kind of woman Doran was, and Jeremy had stood by making no attempt to defend her. They had walked away arm in arm.

It was nasty, sickening, but it provoked Doran's pride rather than quelling it. She continued to buy far more clothes than she needed, silly, pretty after-six dresses and cobwebby lingerie and Dior tights, had highlights put in her hair and took to recherché expensive perfumes. The results pleased her, though her mother said she looked too old for her age and not quite *right*, darling, for our part of the world, do you think?

But no moths came to this luring candle: until William moved in as a lodger with their next-door neighbour, who boarded students in her sprawling Victorian house. William was younger than Doran, a fresh-faced youth with a doggy eagerness of manner, friendly, easily impressed, virtually alone in Oxford; just the person to fall for her sophisticated image and the hurt, mixed-up girl behind it.

They saw each other every day. William came to meals,

William took her to films, though it was obvious he found it a strain to pay for good seats, and Doran contrived to help him out without injuring his masculine ego.

What masculine ego she began to wonder? For he was only too ready to be helped out – to receive hospitality at the Fairweathers' without offering any return, and to treat Doran as the rather jolly sister she was not prepared to be to him or any man. He was nothing for her, he would not bring comfort or joy or love or consolation. And somehow that was the worst blow she had received so far.

Her new façade crumbled; unobtrusively, gently, she reverted to the looks and personality she had owned before. Trying to pay Ian out in his own coin – if that was what she had been doing – was a senseless waste of time. By chance she heard of the sort of job she had not tried yet, someone needed to help out in an antique shop. Doran liked old things, said the acquaintance, knew about pictures, collected objects – why not give it a try?

It worked. The owner of the shop was a tough old party with little about her to attract an extremely vulnerable young party. But Doran's empathy was with the things she sold, valuable furniture, china, silver, or old things valuable from their very age; things once prized, now thrown out, small people of porcelain, fragments which had been part of a whole, objects which had survived their owners – many owners.

'This is what I'm going to do,' she told her mother. Her father had died, quietly and expectedly, after a long illness, and things must change. 'We'll go away from Oxford altogether. We both need a different environment. Where would you like to be, ideally?'

'The sea. Oh, I would love to be able to breathe the sea again, after being in the middle of England so long without a whiff of it.'

'Then you shall. Leave it to me, I'll ask around.' Mrs Fairweather watched with relieved surprise as her recently apathetic daughter embarked on a search for their new home; so she had really got over it all at last, thank goodness, poor child.

The home they found was a villa in Eastgate, on the south coast, a pretty house built at the beginning of the era when the English took to the seaside in flocks. Eastgate had a flourishing antiques district, where Doran could usually find temporary work, such as looking after shops while the owners went away on a buying trip.

Their content lasted almost a year. Then Alice Fairweather quite suddenly became ill, and as suddenly died, leaving Doran comfortably well off with what her father had left and the proceeds from the sale of the villa, a little compensation for being quite alone in the world. The villa had been her mother's home, not truly hers, and Eastgate was not where she wanted to live, though ideal for work. She bought a small shop in Old Town and, for living in, an enchanting house in the valley village of Abbotsbourne, near enough but not too near to the shop. Bell House was everything she wanted in a home – particularly this morning, a fine late February morning, a pale bright sun shining, the blue-green spears of daffodils piercing the ground in the front garden, crocuses a dazzle of gold. Upstairs a cheerful pop number roared out from Rhona's transistor above the whine of the vacuum cleaner. Doran, pulling on her jacket and hunting for her car keys, sang with it.

The blue hatchback Volvo wove its way with dignity along Mays Lane, past the few small ancient houses and cottages that were Bell House's neighbours, into and round the square. Shopkeepers, gazing idly out of windows, nodded and smiled to her. Outside the greengrocer's there were flowers, small expensive bunches of forced blooms; Doran wanted to buy them, fill the car with them, and give them away to anyone she met on the road to Eastgate who looked in the least downcast. She contented herself with a bunch of freesias and another of tight-budded tulips.

'What's all this?' Howell asked when she unwrapped them in the shop, filled vases from the tap in the sink at the back, and placed them picturesquely in the bow window. 'Selling flowers now, are we?'

'No, no. I just thought they'd look cheerful. I feel very

14

cheerful myself, don't you? No, don't answer that. Look, why don't you go down to the front and have a breather? Treat yourself to a pint outside the Port Arms or something. I can manage perfectly well.'

Howell shot her a liverish look, the sort of look he would have given an alleged Tudor joint-stool with a spurious top and two 'wrong' legs.

'How do I know you won't sell us short?'

'How do you know I'll sell anything?' Doran retorted. 'We've had the regulars in already this week, so anybody else will be a lovely surprise.'

'Mmm. Well, don't part with that ebony table clock.'

'But it's nothing – just a shell.'

'Maybe, but I've got Pink coming to look at it, haven't I. He's mad on table clocks – I'll get the best price out of him.'

'All right. But I'm going to part with that bachelor chest if I get even the sniff of an offer. I hate the thing, it reaches out and snags my tights every time I go within yards of it. And I think I *will* ring about that bed, you know – Mr Steiner's got a customer that likes them bright and brassy.'

'Your funeral.' Howell cocooned himself in coat and scarf, and departed. In his absence Doran transferred to the window an Edwardian painting of what they called the Sunbonnet School, a lethargic-looking rustic maiden feeding chickens in the road outside a thatched cottage, watched by a smocked child clutching a kitten to the imminent danger of the animal's life. She disliked it, but the genre was very popular. In its place she hung a sailing ship on the high seas which was certainly not a Montague Dawson but might please someone who cared for sailing-ship paintings. Then she rearranged silver items on a table, set up and admired two charming Minton tiles of cupids, hesitated over a French fan she half-thought of keeping for herself, and made coffee.

The only customer was a man she recognized as an Eastgate resident, a retired civil servant who tried, pathetically, to pass himself off as trade. Doran knew that he went all round the district practising this try-on, with varying success. Today it was a Staffordshire lustre jug.

'What's the best you can do on this?' He was striving to sound dispassionate, keeping the collector's lust out of his voice, as he lovingly ran a finger round the shining edge, then stroked the tiny landscapes in gold and tender pink that circled its waist.

'Seventy-five.'

'But that's what it says on the ticket.'

'Yes. But there's a code-number saying we can't take less. It's a very good Swansea example.'

'Oh. There's a hairline crack in the lip, you know.'

'I did know. It's been taken into consideration in the price.'

Glumly, not looking at his jug again, he left the shop. Doran wished she could have dropped the price for him, let him pay what he could afford for something he very much desired. He was a tired, lonely man, used up by life, his only pleasure the inanimate objects with which he filled his flat whenever he felt his pension could stretch to another one. Doran knew all this without telling; it was her weakness as a dealer to be intuitive about people and too readily sorry for them. Howell despised such softness. Just as well, or they would have made a loss, as she had done when she ran the business on her own.

'You're even sorry for the goods,' he had thrown at her. 'Don't like them left on the shelf in case it hurts their feelings. There's foolish for you.'

'I know. But I can't help feeling they're people, in their way – some of them, at least. Just as I feel people are objects – I mean are like objects.'

Howell raised satanic dark eyebrows. 'What does that make me, then?' Doran thought that what he most resembled was a pit pony of thorny disposition. She said lightly, 'A dictionary of furniture. Because you're so maddeningly infallible.'

By lunchtime he had not come back. Doran decided to join him for lunch at the Port Arms, the pub down by the old harbour which was a favourite with him and his cronies. They were there, a gaggle of them, not breathing ozone on the benches outside, but clustered in the stuffy little saloon bar where fishing trophies shared the walls with faded photographs

16

of players who had appeared at the nearby Theatre Royal.

Yes, they were like Things. Arthur Hidley, big, beer-bellied, red-faced and grey-haired, with a shiny look to his cheeks as though he used butter instead of soap and it never quite disappeared from the surface of his skin: he was a large bloated imitation Sèvres vase, all loud colours and pictures of big opulent overblown people like himself. Victor Maidment, slight and pale, his mouth perpetually turned down as though in disparagement. He was a thin spindly torchère which would tip over and spill its potted plant all over you, just from spite. Peg and Meg, the married couple from Harbour Street: Peg, whose real name nobody knew, a loosely-built man with hot brown eyes and a wispy beard who affected nautical dress, Meg small and indeterminate of feature, dressed in what looked like a random selection of the second-hand clothes she sold. They were a pair of cheap Staffordshire flat-backs with blurred outlines and colours, representing nobody in particular.

Doran responded amiably to the invariable greetings.

' 'Lo, darling. How's the world?'

'Kiss kiss.' (This from Peg.)

'Wotcher, Dore.' A little Cockney dealer who spent a lot of time at Eastgate, where he unloaded a surprisingly large number of small collectables, gathered who knew where or how. Doran loathed his version of her name but liked him personally, seeing him as a fugitive from some dispersed monkey orchestra. She went to his side.

'One day, will you *not* call me Dore, Bill? Like on my birthday. It makes me feel so. . . .'

'Wooden, ha ha – eh? What d'you expect wiv a handle like yours? (That's a joke, see – door – handle.) Where d'you get a name like that?'

Doran explained patiently what she was tired of explaining. 'It was Dora Ann to start with. My mother liked Victorian names and wanted me to be called by them both. But people got lazy and slurred them together and in time everyone called me Dor'Ann, so I changed the spelling. I rather like it, as a matter of fact.'

'So do I, so do I, now you've put me right. You look

17

bobbish today, anyway. Lost a wrong 'un and found a Titian, have you?'

She laughed. 'Wish I had. No, I feel cheerful. Just cheerful. As if something exciting were going to happen.' She caught Howell's sardonic eye through the haze of cigarette smoke. Her words had found a moment of comparative hush in the babble and he was reacting to them, saying with a look: You silly cow, what d'you suppose is going to happen to *you*, then? She made a cheerfully defiant grimace at him. They had no illusions about each other, and that made everything very uncomplicated.

When she got home in the late afternoon Rhona was hovering in the hall, bursting with news.

'Mrs Haydon-Tree phoned. She's having a cocktail party on Saturday.'

'Don't tell me I'm invited. I've hardly spoken to the woman – or rather she's hardly spoken to me.'

'Well, she wouldn't have phoned to say you're *not* invited,' said Rhona sensibly. 'It's quite a big do, for this feller that's bought The Oaks. A Mr Mumbray, he's called, funny name, and it seems he's quite well off.'

'Ah.' That would certainly attract the interest of Mrs Haydon-Tree, whose tastes were reflected in the large expensive house she lived in at the edge of the village with her husband The Colonel. She always referred to him as The Colonel, never as 'my husband' or 'George', and others were expected to do the same. They were both large, pink and hearty, with two cars, two daily women, and a finger in every local pie from the golf club to the school board of governors. Doran had never received more than a social nod from either of them; she was agreeably surprised that her natural curiosity about them was at last to be satisfied.

'What does he do, this Mr Mumbray?' she asked.

'She didn't say. But she did say he was a single gentleman and she was getting as many people as she could together to jolly him up.'

I'll bet, thought Doran. With all the widows and spinsters

18

there are round here he ought to be as jolly as a sandboy in no time. Spinsters, in this day and age, sounded odd. But Abbotsbourne owned some. Her imagination began to run riot, seeing a queue of eager ladies forming up outside the Haydon-Tree home, herself, ludicrously, among them. She knew herself for an incurable romantic, a Gemini searching for its other half. With every new man who came into one's life came the question: Could this be He? That not impossible He that shall command my heart and me? The love of one's life, or an acceptable substitute?

Rubbish, said Doran's sterner self. Rhona was still talking.

'Vi's going to help wash up afterwards. Not but what they've got a great big dishwasher, but it doesn't fill nor empty itself, does it?' Vi Small, christened Violetta by a romantic mother, was Rhona's sister, a capable creature who multiplied herself as required into domestic help, baby- or granny-sitter, cook, sewing-lady and messenger. Doran thought of her in a phrase gleaned from some old film: Dogs Walked Out, Fourth at Bridge.

'And Debbie's going to hand round – aren't you, love?'

Her daughter hovered behind her, still in her school coat, smiling shyly. One of the nice things about having a girl of fifteen about the house was that she didn't behave in the way girls of fifteen frequently did behave, to judge by the daily papers. Debbie was quiet, studious, gentle, still sore from the wound of her father's death. It was impossible to imagine her getting prematurely pregnant or dyeing her brown hair pink and canary yellow, or using four-letter words.

'Mrs Haydon-Tree says I've got to wear an apron,' she proffered. 'And take my glasses off.'

'Nonsense! How will you see which guest is which?'

Debbie sighed, then smiled. 'When I've passed A-Levels Mum says I can have contact lenses.' She melted unobtrusively away towards the kitchen.

Doran felt she could hardly wait to see this hostess's establishment, complete with imitation domestics from the dear dead days beyond recall. She telephoned the Reverend Rodney Chelmarsh at St Crispin's vicarage.

'Doran – hello. I was afraid you were the estimate for the boiler.' His voice was baritone, clear and firm and musical, with a smile in it.

'No, I'm not the estimate for the boiler. Just inquiring if you're bidden to this hooley on Saturday.'

'The Colonel's Lady's debauch? Not 'alf. She wouldn't leave the Church out of it, not she.'

'And you're going?'

'Try to keep me away.'

'Isn't Saturday your sermon night?' They both knew it was not.

'I shall wheel out the one I'd roughed in for last Sunday, when the Guides thankfully took over and ran the service. Of course I'm going, out of curiosity, as I'm sure you are. What are you going to wear? I recommend a Little Black Frock with a diamanté spray on the shoulder, just the Colonel's Lady's style, I feel sure.'

'Thanks, but I sent my last surviving one to Oxfam. More to the point, what are *you* going to wear?' Rodney was well known for abandoning all signs of his calling whenever possible. He groaned.

'The blasted dog-collar with a lounge suit. They'll expect it, they shall have it. How I wish I were a bishop. I could knock 'em flat in gaiters and a chasuble and orphreys and a purple vest and a zonking great gold pectoral cross.'

'Rodney!'

'Sorry.' But no apology was really necessary. Doran knew him for a much deeper person than he made himself out to be in his fight against the sanctimonious image.

When they met three days later in the Haydon-Trees' drawing room, Doran was wearing not a Little Black Dress but one of pale honey velvet, figure-fitting and unadorned, her only ornament a pair of antique pinch-beck earrings set with coloured stones. As she shook hands with her hostess, massive in something very tight and very pink, she caught the Colonel's Lady's gaze on the mild twinkle of them as they swung against her neck, and knew they were being assessed as meretricious, tawdry, even. The lady's own pearl necklet was probably not real, but of an expensive culture.

'Miss Fairbrother. How nice. So glad you could come.' The hand that squeezed hers was painfully encrusted with rings.

'She called me Fairbrother,' Doran said to Rodney, who was lurking in a corner of the crowded room. 'Just think what I could call her if I chose to take that line. Haydon-Coffin, Haydock-Tree. . . .'

'Haddock-Treat . . . there's no limit. However, bear and forbear, that's what I always say.'

'You look nice.' He did, indeed, a slender elegant figure in casual grey, the dog-collar setting off a thin clever face that never seemed to yield entirely to winter paleness but kept the faint glow of summer tan. His eyes were something between brown and green, darker than Doran's, with an attractive downward slant at the corners of the lids, and his light brown hair neither straight nor curly, but pleasantly unruly. He was thirty-eight, and Doran's best friend. They had tacitly agreed to keep it that way.

'Yes, I do, don't I?' he agreed. 'What a perfectly awful, ghastly, pernicious room. The Abomination of Desolation.'

'The pit that yawns. Actually, it's not that bad, only dull.'

'Terribly terribly dull, darling,' said Rodney in his Noël Coward voice, the only one in which he ever called her darling. Sipping gin and tonic (at least it wasn't plonk, all most people ran to), they gazed round the large light room, papered in pale beige of an amorphous pattern, with expensive sofas and chairs, so deep that one would not lightly sit on them if one hoped to get up quickly. Their fabric was smothered in fashionable tropic birds, roses, camellias, and a great deal of bright green foliage. One, in a corner by itself, was covered in pale fur fabric, closely resembling car upholstery. 'High Tottenham Court Road,' murmured Rodney.

A large cabinet of display shelves was full of objects which shouted of foreign travel. Dolls of all nations, things carved from the bones and tusks of animals, two bulging Japanese wrestlers in combat, a terrifying Polynesian mask, a Dutch fisherman's cottage with native in costume smoking Dutch pipe: they ranged from West to East and back again. The mantelpiece bore a selection of what Doran called Nothings. Over it hung a large post-horn of blown glass, and in front of the fireplace lay a tiger-skin, with head. It had been a very odd tiger, Doran thought. She prodded at it furtively with the toe of one shoe, then touched Rodney's arm.

'Look.'

'What?'

'The fur. It's not real. It's fake fur, and the head's plastic.'

'How do you know?'

'I know.'

'Well, blow me.'

'Blow me, too. Just glance aside at that wall.'

The entire surface of one fireplace alcove was covered with weapons. Doran, who had yawned through many an auction of such things, recognized a militia infantry officer's sword, a Cromwellian musket, a Malay kris, a javelin head, an arrangement of Eastern daggers – it was an array as chaotic as the loading of the display shelves.

'Where would he have had to serve,' Rodney asked, 'to collect all that lot? He doesn't look exactly battle-scarred.' He nodded towards the plumply comfortable form of their host, his white moustache vibrating gently as he flirted with a pretty girl neither of them knew.

'In a factory, for one thing,' Doran said. 'The pistols are fibreglass, and the sword's Brummagem, if I'm not mistaken.'

'Oh. Fake tiger, fake pistols – how interesting. You know, you've got the perfect set-up here for a nice unorthodox sort of murder. Murderer snatches down pistol, finds it's a duff one, tries the other weapons one after another, finally pitches on a dagger that *does* work and impales his victim –'

'What was the victim doing while he was choosing his weapon? And what about fingerprints?'

'How do I know? You're the one that reads all the thrillers. Anyway, I'd be prepared to bet someone in this room would be an absolute sitting duck for a murderer with imagination. . . .'

'Hush. Look, the guest of honour.'

Both Haydon-Trees had hurried to the door to greet the new arrival, followed by a scatter of guests. As introductions began the two in the corner watched and noted, and exchanged thought-waves, then glances.

'Well?' Rodney asked, very softly. 'Which is Mr Mumbray – murderer or murderee?'

2

'Either, I'd say.'

'The Smiler with the Knife, or the Body in the Library?'

'Exactly. I can see him in both rôles.' Inwardly Doran was jeering at herself. That not impossible He, indeed! Mr Mumbray struck her as just about as impossible as they come, from a romantic standpoint. Not that he was absolutely ill-looking. He was apparently in his late fifties, perhaps older or younger, tall, imposingly built, solid rather than stout, and conventionally tailored. His very short colourless hair was cut *en brosse*, his face colourless too. From a distance Doran guessed that his eyes were of that paleness sometimes called grey.

She glanced at Rodney. His expression was impassive. His hand strayed towards the small gold crucifix he wore unseen round his neck, for he had felt a spiritual chill come into the room with Mumbray.

'A dead ringer for Erich von Stroheim,' he murmured. 'I bet the back of his head's absolutely straight. Yes, look, it is.'

'He's probably got a lovely nature.'

'Let's be having it, then.' Debbie Selling had been pushed towards Mumbray and was shyly offering him a plate of cock-tail bits. He took one without thanks, seeming not to notice the child.

'Correction, no lovely nature,' Doran said. 'Poor Debbie. Let's go and ask her to feed us and be nice to her.'

Debbie was relieved to see their familiar faces smiling at her out of the blur of featureless blobs, for her glasses were in her pocket.

'The pink ones are nice,' she said, 'and those with the little black bits. Auntie Vi made them.'

'Then they must be good. Thank you, Debbie, you make a smashing waitress.' Doran filled her mouth with something that might have been smoked salmon in aspic, precariously perched on a sliver of toast. 'Gorgeous. No, I'll keep off the vol-au-vents, they squash in the middle and send filling all down one's front.'

'I just wish I could see properly,' Debbie said wistfully. 'I did put my glasses on and look round, but she – Mrs Haydon-Tree made me put them away.'

'Worry not,' Rodney assured her. 'One can get by, however bat-eyed. Do you know, I once started to deliver a sermon without mine, turned over three pages and went straight on to "And now to God the Father. . . ." But nobody noticed, they were all asleep anyway.'

'That wasn't true,' Doran told him severely when Debbie had turned away.

'I know. But it made her laugh. Better is a white lie that doth good than a stalled ox and a dinner of herbs. Dr Levison's looking lost – excuse me.'

Colonel Haydon-Tree was at Doran's elbow, propelling her towards Mumbray. 'Come along, come along, can't let pretty girls hide in corners. Mr Mumbray, this is our young Miss Fair . . . er. . . .'

'Fairweather,' Doran supplied firmly, noting the false brilliance of Mumbray's smile, and the enveloping cold limp dampness of his hand around hers. The Colonel, his duty done, drifted away. He had obviously no idea what else to say about her, and he had got the form of introduction wrong – the gentleman is always presented to the lady, not the other way round. He ought to have learned that in the Mess, or preferably earlier.

'Are you settling in all right?' was all she could think of to ask Mumbray. (Yes, his eyes *were* colourless; chromium eyes.)

'Thank you. Reasonably.'

'You've got domestic help? It's a big house, isn't it?'

'I brought my housekeeper from Kingsbury.' So he had

26

come from the county town, thirty miles away. His eyes were on hers – assessing, analysing, disparaging? In the absence of any conversational lead from him Doran began to gabble, hearing herself with annoyance.

'I'm sure she'll need someone – a daily woman. I can recommend Vi Small – she's the aunt of the little girl taking round food – absolutely marvellous, she can do anything.'

Mumbray nodded. It looked like a nod of dismissal. Doran was instantly furious that she had made any attempt at conversation with him. She turned away abruptly, to find herself bumping into Mrs Haydon-Tree who was leading Rodney up to her prize guest. He was not going to be trapped, as she had been, into talking social rubbish; he smiled politely, spoke, shook hands, and moved away.

Caught in an impenetrable knot of chattering people, Doran could not help hearing Mrs Haydon-Tree's loud voice giving Mumbray a briefing about Rodney, 'our dear young vicar'.

'. . . seems younger than he is, I always think – such a quaint manner, really, the things he says in the pulpit sometimes, you wouldn't believe, quite naughty, I sometimes think . . . but then hardly surprising, putting a good face on it . . . such a sad story, lost his wife a few years ago, cancer, and his only child's a cripple in a wheelchair, quite bright I believe but such a difficult girl, I never know what to say to her, you have to be so careful not to seem sorry for them. Everybody thinks he ought to get married again – well, a clergyman should be, don't you think? And with a daughter like that. He's always about with that Miss Fairweather, the girl you met just now, lives alone and keeps a shop in Eastgate, in fact there's been quite a bit of talk but nothing seems to come of it. . . .'

Doran, her face burning, pushed her way through the crowd out of hearing. Horrible, vulgar woman – how dare she discuss Rodney and herself? It was impossible not to know that people did talk about their friendship. But whatever they shared was nobody's business but their own. Nobody knew of Doran's own past hurt, or of how difficult poor Helena, in her wheelchair, could be, intolerant of any rival for her father's affection. They were horrible people and she needed another drink.

Mumbray had advanced into the room and was being pounced on by various of the guests. *There* was a favourable reaction – Stella Meeson. Stella, single, of no known background, fifty if she was a day, with glittering silver hair and a thin cat-face that was still pretty. She was peeking up at Mumbray, tilting her small head this way and that, giving him her slightly wild smile and chattering. Did Stella hope to make a catch? If so, she was not getting much encouragement. She would need one of the love-philtres she was supposed to make from herbs and things.

But Marcia Fawkes, with whom Stella shared Laburnum Cottage, was not hopping in Mumbray's walks or gambolling in his eyes. (There, that was the second gin, starting one on Shakespeare.) She was standing apart, glaring with the small brown eyes that somehow looked wrong in her broad light-skinned face. Marcia was short, shorter than willowy Stella, yet managed to give the impression of being tall and commanding. It was partly to do with the loud staccato voice which got her a hearing on committees. If she had ever been attractive there was no sign of it now.

She was looking at Mumbray as though she had seen something nasty in (or out of) the woodshed, willing Stella to move away from him, Doran thought. Why? Jealousy was a possibility. Jealousy because a man was talking to Stella, or the other way round?

Dr Eli Levison was at her side. The village doctor was an orthodox Jew, and bore his race's badge of suffering and oppression in his face, dark disillusioned eyes and a moustached mouth with a sad droop to it. He could not be older than the late forties, yet Doran experienced a lightning fantasy of him as an Auschwitz victim and Mumbray as a jack-booted tyrant.

'Enjoying yourself, doctor?'

'Not a lot. Do you think they'd notice if I slipped out? Esther's on her own and Sharon's not all that well.'

'I'm sorry. Nothing serious?'

28

'Just this bug everybody's had. But it sometimes hits kids hard. Excuse me – I can see a path to the door.'

Doran watched him go, and wondered if he were ill himself. His sallow complexion looked even more waxen than usual.

Rupert Wylie, the younger partner in Dixter and Wylie, estate agents, was leaning on the grand piano in converse with Ernest Tilman, the bank manager.

Tilman was saying '. . . funny business altogether, those two old ladies going off like that on the same night.'

Rupert shrugged shoulders massively muscled by tennis playing. 'Funny perhaps, but nothing suspicious about it, according to the eyes and ears of the village.'

'Meaning who?'

Rupert nodded towards Vi Small. 'Our Miss Small. She'd have made a terrific Grand Inquisitor in the days when they had such things. I bet you she's been on a special mission to the police house, asking questions. Not to mention the post office and the doctor's surgery. Not nosey, just likes to know everything.'

Tilman laughed. 'There's one in every community. Well, neither of the old dears was murdered for her money – they didn't have bank accounts, and that's not giving away any secrets. Of course, they might have kept cash in stockings under the mattress – that could have been a motive for murder.'

'Aren't we all murder-conscious these days? Because there's so much of it about, I suppose.' Rupert sipped his warm and unpleasant martini, pondering. The local double tragedy might well have its brighter side for him. Old Miss Beamish had died in a small terraced house built around the soulless year 1900, of tinned-salmon brick with nasty stone lintels, poky rooms and no garden to speak of. If it came on to his books he could sell it, but it would hang about, hopefully offered as Always Popular Older Style Bijou Home with Some Modernization Required, Eminently Suitable for First-Time Buyers. If all else failed it might be given the Don't Judge a Book by Its Cover treatment.

For Mrs Trott's cottage, however, he was already composing

a flowery description: 'The Dream Cottage you've always wanted. We seldom get properties like this. Dating from the eighteenth century, set picturesquely on edge of woodland. . . .' Never mind the dry rot, worm, leaking roof, loo at the bottom of the neglected garden, primitive kitchen and all-pervading miasma of cats, somebody would snap it up and spend a fortune transforming it into something out of Disneyland.

If anyone set out to murder for gain, Rupert mused, who better motivated than an estate agent? Always assuming that Brett, Packer and Firkin didn't get their claws on the property first. . . .

Tilman recalled him to civilized thoughts. 'I suppose you were glad to have The Oaks off your hands?'

'Very. We'd given up hope of shifting it. Curious customer, though.' They were both looking at Mumbray.

'Yes. Retired solicitor, I heard. And speaking of customers. . . .' Tilman smiled and wandered off in Mumbray's direction. An introduction might bring the newcomer to open an account at his branch.

Rupert Wylie transferred his gaze to Doran, whom he rather fancied. Pretty, model figure, tempting mouth. But she seemed to be lost in a dream, and he remembered that she was not much good at parties. After another martini perhaps he would ask her to come for an evening run with him in the shining BMW he sometimes used for ferrying likely clients towards properties.

Mumbray was smiling; a curious smile, hard to look away from. He was bending his large head down towards Barbary Miles, a lovely dark creature of twenty-two, daughter of the partly invalid Major Miles, so badly wounded in the last war that he spent much of his time in bed, tended by the district nurse. Tonight Barbary was wearing an ethnic garment of scarlet-patterned cotton edged and scrolled in gilt. With her dark fall of shining hair and cheeks of deep pink she looked, thought Doran, like Rose the Red in the ballad. A little deeper pink than usual, those cheeks, as she listened to what Mumbray was saying? But someone had come between them and was leading her away: her boyfriend Bob Woods, tall and rangy and as fair as she was dark, with a square jaw like Garth of the strip cartoon, the terror of visiting cricket teams and tipped to play for his county. What a fairy-tale couple: they would make a delicious pair of Chelsea figures for a mantel-piece, except that it was hard to imagine Bob simpering or herding porcelain sheep.

Doran fell to her old game of comparing people to Things. Stella would be a pre-Raphaelite's Vivien or Morgan le Fay, Marcia one of those eighteenth-century portraits of women so hard-favoured that one wondered why they bothered to have themselves immortalized in paint, the Colonel a large veneered wardrobe. . . .

Rodney's voice interrupted her thoughts. 'So he's a D.O.M., is he?'

She started. 'Sorry – what did you say?'

'A Dirty Old Man. Making eyes at little Barbary. Likes the chickens but despises the hens.'

'Thanks. That puts me firmly in my niche in the farmyard. Why,' asked Doran in a voice fortified by gin and tonic, 'are they making all this fuss about a very ordinary sort of man, unless he's so stinking rich that. . . .'

'Ssh,' Rodney hissed in her ear. Mumbray had come up to them and was looming over her, like a liner over a tug.

'You mentioned a daily woman,' he said. 'Not the name.'

'Yes, I did, actually.' (Don't babble, you fool.) 'It's Miss Small, Vi, over there, with the tray of glasses. Shall I speak to her – ask her to call at The Oaks?'

'Thank you. Tell her to see Mrs Butcher. I hear you deal in antiques.'

'Er – yes. In Eastgate. I've a shop.'

'I'm short of a bookcase.'

'Oh. We don't get many – not worth having, that is. What kind were you thinking of? Glass-fronted? I know where there's a rather nice –'

'It doesn't matter. Just something to hold books.'

Aware of Rodney's sardonic eye on her, Doran nervously reviewed the contents of the shop and the storeroom where stock too big for display was kept along with repair jobs. 'I believe there's one that might do – it's nothing special, stained oak, about fifty years old. If you'd like to look at it we could get it out for you. . . .'

'Bring it up to the house, will you.' Unbelievably he had turned his back on her and was walking away. Doran gasped with rage.

'Of all the insufferable, rude, boorish, loathsome rotten bastards. . . .'

Rodney cast his eyes heavenwards. 'My cloth, remember my cloth.'

She fumed. 'See if I go traipsing up to his horrible house, just see if I do, that's all.'

'You will, you know. You'll be too inquisitive not to. Put that glass down, you've had enough. We'll go for a brisk walk round the churchyard and you can reflect on Change, the which all mortal things doth sway. If that doesn't sober you up we'll run four times round the cricket field, like school punishments.'

Doran shook off his hand. 'Do stop talking like a mixture of Peter Wimsey and a Wodehouse curate. It infuriates me.'

'Sorry about that. Come on.'

Doran had a moment of compunction. 'Oughtn't we to say goodbye to the Haydon-Trees?'

'She won't notice, she's got the MP in tow, and the Colonel's drunk. Out, quick.'

Howell was not pleased to be asked to go down to the store-room and fetch the bookcase. 'What do you want that thing for? It's rubbish.'

'I know. I've got a buyer who likes rubbish – understandably.'

'What?'

'Nothing. Come on, I want to close.'

Howell grumbled on the way to the storeroom two streets away, continued to grumble as they heaved cumbrous pieces of furniture aside to get at the bookcase, which stood against the far wall as being the sort of thing nobody in their senses would want to get at. It was not a thing of beauty. It had been made in the 1930s, possibly as a piece of office furniture. A sort of dado of secular stained glass over the top row of its dirty panes did nothing for it.

'Come on,' Doran said. 'We've got to clean it up a bit.'

'*You* clean it up – I'm filthy enough already.'

'Here, catch.' She threw a duster at him. By the time they had taken the top layer of dust off it the thing looked slightly more like a piece of furniture and less like a glazed filing cabinet.

'Now,' Doran said, dusting her hands together, 'we'll carry it to the door and you can bring the van round. If there's a warden about I'll tell it to expect you and that we won't take long loading up.'

'The *van*?' Howell's tone suggested that he had heard some unspeakable obscenity uttered.

'The   van.   Wheels.   We – have – to – take – the – bookcase to – Abbotsbourne. Got that clear?'

Howell swore, comprehensively, in Welsh and English. He hated leaving Eastgate at this time of day, when he was looking forward to shutting himself up in the cosy tarted-up cottage he shared with his friend Andrew. Seeing his protests unavailing, as a final trump card he brought out the reminder that Doran's Volvo was parked in its usual spot and would have to stay there all night if she drove to Abbotsbourne with him in the van.

She smiled. 'Not so. I'll go on ahead in the car and you follow. It's a house you don't know, so I'll guide you. And don't say that word any more – I know what it means and it's very boring.'

The Oaks lay just beyond the village, up a small blind lane. It had been built in the 1890s by a retired businessman with dynastic ambitions, but his large family had been decimated by two wars. After 1918 it had been lived in by two old people who in their turn had died, leaving it to the mice and invading tramps. Then it had been furbished up by the council and used as a hostel for walkers and cyclists; gradually they too had left it. In 1940 it had experienced a brief revival as an ARP station and first-aid post.

With peacetime it had fallen empty again, and remained so, a house nobody wanted. There was talk of pulling it down and building on the site, but even this project seemed to be under a curse of procrastination, and a rough survey had shown that the place was structurally sound. So it stood, the house-agents' despair, until very suddenly a SOLD notice went up, and workmen moved in with scaffolding, ladders, a cement-mixer and a great number of buckets and paint-pots. The front drive rapidly filled up with rusty iron baths, cracked wash-basins, cisterns and lengths of piping, butlers' sinks and decrepit light-fittings.

Now they were all gone, and The Oaks was inhabited again, curtains at the windows, the garden tidied up. It was as welcoming as it would ever be, which was not saying much. Doran and Howell stood by the van, surveying it.

'Crummy joint,' Howell said.

'Horrible. The bookcase should just about suit it.' They unloaded and carried it up the three front steps. 'Mind you get sixty for it, now. See you.' Howell turned to go back to the van.

'Howell.' Doran spoke urgently, out of a sudden impulse. 'Yeah.'

'Don't go, will you? I mean, would you very much mind waiting in the van for me? I shan't be long. No, I haven't gone mad and I know I've got the car – it's just . . . something.'

He shrugged. 'Okay.' If he was going to be late he might as well be very late, and his partner did look a bit defenceless standing there in front of that bloody great black-painted door in her jeans and her old purple sweater, with her hair mussed up from their exertions in the storeroom. He was not much given to chivalrous gestures, but she asked very few of him.

Mumbray himself answered the door. Unsmilingly he said, without a greeting, 'So that's it.'

'Yes. It isn't much to look at but it's perfectly sound and it does hold a lot of books. . . .'

'Yes, well, bring it in.'

She was startled. 'But – I can't carry it by myself.'

'How did you get it here, in that case?'

34

'My – my partner, Mr Evans, helped me. Perhaps if you took one end we could manage.'

Without any show of willingness he tilted the thing over towards himself while she grasped and lifted the feet. In the dark hall he said, 'That will do. Put it down here.'

Too amazed by the man's arrant rudeness even to be angry, she said, 'I shall have to know if you approve of it before I leave it. You'd better look it over, open it up and see the inside. It does lock – here's the key. Oh, and there's no worm.'

He opened the doors and glanced perfunctorily inside and at the back of the piece, though she wondered how he could see in such bad light.

'That will do,' he said. 'How much do I owe you?'

'Sixty pounds, please. The VAT. . . .'

For the first time his face cracked in a supercilious smile.

'That's a great deal too much, and I'm sure you know it.'

'Indeed it isn't! It's a fair price. I know it's not antique as such, but it's good craftsmanship and the cheapest you'll get if you want something substantial. You'd pay a lot for even a new whitewood one that size.'

'I'll pay you forty-five.'

'Sorry.'

There was a silence. Doran hated bargaining, unlike Howell who loved it, but she would not be done down, especially by a buyer who could afford to pay, like this one. What was he waiting for? Was she supposed to stamp her tiny foot or burst into tears or tell him she had six children and aged parents to support? She folded her arms and stared back at him. Suddenly his face blanked, as though he could no longer be bothered arguing – or as though, thought Doran, he was not getting some response he wanted.

'Fifty-five,' he said.

Howell would have to be satisfied to drop a fiver. 'All right.'

'I'll give you a cheque.' He led the way into a room to the left of the door, a huge high-ceilinged room with dark wallpaper from picture-rail to ceiling. Doran enjoyed rooms, but this one was only enjoyable for its grimness. The furniture looked as though it had been taken over wholesale from a run-down men's club – worn leather-covered armchairs, a Turkish carpet of ox-blood red and battleship grey, a huge partners desk, reproduction and clumsy, and a table of which nothing was visible but the legs because it was piled high with books. Hundreds more books were heaped on the floor, in front of empty bookcases which were just purpose-made shelfage. One of her irrational pangs of compassion hit her at having to leave her bookcase in that dreary place; it had probably been quite happy in the storeroom, among nice old furniture.

Mumbray was sitting at the desk, writing the cheque in a space cleared of clutter. 'The name?' he asked.

'D. Fairweather and H. Evans.'

Writing, looking at the cheque, he said sharply, 'Sit down.'

Doran didn't want in the least to sit down. But against her will she dropped into the upright chair at the opposite side of the desk.

'You live in Abbotsbourne?' he asked.

'Yes.'

'What is your house like?'

'Well, it's, er, mostly Queen Anne, I suppose, with a bit of Charles II and a Victorian kitchen bit built on. It's called Bell House.'

'And filled with antique objects?'

'Quite a few, of course. I tend to buy things because I like them, then live with them until I feel I can bear to part with them and bring something else home. . . .' Why on earth was she telling him all this stuff, which couldn't possibly interest a man who lived among such dreadful furniture himself? But the curious inquisition was going on, and the most curious thing about it was that in spite of herself she could not help answering the questions asked in that flat impersonal voice, little as she wanted to tell him anything about herself at all. It was almost as though she were undergoing an official interrogation in some unimaginable place – the office of a chief of police, perhaps, in an Iron Curtain country.

'You have had lovers?'

Heavens, what was this? The chromium eyes were fixed on hers, adequate substitutes for the glaring light they turned on to one in films of such interrogations. She could not drag her own away from them or stop her voice answering.

'Yes.' Did his face show a shade of disappointment?

'How many?'

'One.'

'His name? I want to know his name.'

Doran had always heard that a hypnotist cannot make the subject do anything outrageous to that subject's nature. Mercifully it was true. Ian's name would not pass her lips. She stared back at her questioner, feeling indescribable sensations all over her body; then realized that the eyes had shifted from hers and had wandered downwards, browsing from neck to breast, from breast to crossed knee, and that a force was being directed at her which was in part sex, and in part something else: the lust for power over her body and soul, an attempt at mental rape. She fought it silently with all her strength, this cold-blooded pass which was more insulting than the most brash approach any ordinary man could make. She wished she carried a little cross like Rodney's. . . .

Rodney! It was as though he stood beside her and told her what to do. In a flash she was out of the chair and at the window, banging with her fist against the pane. The van was a few yards away, Howell at the wheel, smoking and reading a newspaper. He heard her, and looked up.

'I must go,' she gasped. 'The van's waiting.' Almost out of the room she heard footsteps behind her and went cold with panic.

'You forgot your cheque,' Mumbray was saying, with an icy smile. Doran snatched it and ran.

Howell raised his eyebrows at the sight of her white face.

'You seen something nasty in there?'

'Very nasty. Can I have one of your fags?'

'But you don't smoke, gal.'

'I know, but I will now.' Fortunately it was an ordinary cigarette, not a joint, but even if it had been she would have accepted it and taken a few puffs before throwing it away.

They sat in silence for some moments. Then Doran said, 'Is he looking out of the window?'

'Can't see nobody.'

'Ah.' It was a sigh of relief.

'I don't want to rush you, but you were in there a bloody long time, and some of us like to eat,' ventured Howell delicately.

'Yes, I know, I'm sorry.' She climbed out of the van.

Howell leaned out to her. 'Sure you're fit to drive?'

'I'll be fine. You go on.'

Before starting the engine he put his head out again and called, 'Take care.'

Howell was nice, really, she thought as she heard her Volvo jump into life. Everybody was nice compared with Leonard Mumbray, who had brought something into Abbotsbourne which had not been there before: or not for a very, very long time, since dark gods ruled forests long cut down.

3

The bar of the Rose Reviv'd was always well patronized at opening-time on Sundays. It had only one bar, which was neither saloon nor public. Abbotsbourne's other inn, the Feathers, was the popular resort of people from the council estate, workmen, farm labourers, and the local cricket team and their opponents. They found the Rose, with its beams, horse brasses and old prints, too fancy.

The Bellacres, landlords of the Rose, welcomed all trade to their doors, and spared no effort to attract it. In the bar it was possible to eat a good lunch prepared by the little Swiss chef they had lured from the cathedral town where restaurants were plentiful. They also supplied coffees and teas, sold decorative and not so decorative curios, pomanders, little bags of lavender and pot-pourri, and postcards. Mrs Bellacre, handsome, smart and young-looking to have two grown-up sons, let four beam-striped bedrooms to travellers and cooked breakfast for them. She was generally known as Rosie, though it was not her name, and her large affable husband as Winnie, from a fancied resemblance to the late Churchill. Both had tireless energy and a keen business sense which matched their Manchester accents.

On a bright Sunday morning, two weeks after the Haydon-Trees' party, the bar was doing brisk business within ten minutes of opening-time. It was an understood thing in Abbotsbourne that to come out of church and go straight into the Rose did not necessarily mean that one was heading for damnation. The Rose was a focal point of the village, a meeting place, social centre, unofficial committee room. Its function as a seller of drink was purely incidental.

Doran had emerged from St Crispin's in the mildly beatific state which the service of Matins induced in her, a glow kindled by the small lovely building, where Saxon, Norman and Plantagenet mingled, and the stately measured language which had been spoken and sung in it for four centuries. 'In His hand are all the corners of the earth . . . O ye Dews and Frosts, bless ye the Lord; praise Him and magnify Him for ever.' And so on until the final prayer for grace, love and fellowship. It was unlikely that the rest of one's life thereafter would be pure and holy, as the Absolution wistfully implored, but at least one had tried.

'Draught special please, Winnie.'

The landlord, skilfully drawing the dark golden beer, eyed her slender figure admiringly. 'Pint as usual, love?'

'Of course.'

'Some are lucky. Our Rosie'd give an eye-tooth for a waist like yon.'

Doran patted the waist complacently. 'Yes, it does help to be able to drink beer. I'm a very cheap girl to take out.'

He winked. 'I'll remember that one night when I'm off the treadmill.'

'You never are. Thanks.' She turned to see Bob Woods and Barbary behind her. Bob's classic face was set grimly, and Barbary's lips were tremulous. A lovers' quarrel – what a pity on a morning made for lovers and their lasses. She greeted them. Both smiled, but not brightly.

'Got a drink, Doran?' Bob asked. She waved her full tankard at him. Curtly he ordered for himself and Barbary, and they drank in silence, the girl gazing unseeingly through the open door that gave on to the square. Suddenly she touched his arm – they had been carefully standing with space separating them.

'Daddy.'

'What? Oh. Right, come on.' He propelled her quickly away from the bar, towards a table in a shadowed corner, as Major Cyril Miles hobbled in. He was leaning on a stick, not crutches, so he must be having one of his good days. His right

40

leg had been shattered and his spine badly damaged on the Anzio beachhead in 1944, taking him out of the war at the age of twenty-five. The surgeons had patched him up into a semblance of wholeness, but he lived at the mercy of pain which could strike him down at an unwary movement or the blast of an east wind.

A good day it might be, but his face, lined like a much-folded map, was without a smile. Doran noticed that he ordered a double whisky, and winced to hear the price. The Major was known to be permanently hard up. He must need a bracer very much. The grey military moustache seemed to have a droop in it – how odd that facial hair could be expressive. Sensing that he was in no mood for conversation, she drifted away from the bar and became apparently absorbed in a print of Charles I's death warrant. But not before she had glimpsed the Major catch sight of his daughter, and turn sharply away, jolting the liquid in his glass.

A chorus of greetings at the door drew her attention. Rodney was there, a sporting, summer Sunday morning figure in the casual clothes he preferred to his canonicals, well-cut jeans and a light blue T-shirt. He seemed to bring light and cheerfulness in with him. Doran no longer felt alone in a crowd.

As he reached her she inquired in the Shakespeare Voice they used for quips nobody else would understand, ' "Are you at leisure, holy father, now, Or shall I come to you at evening Mass?" '

' "My leisure serves me, pensive daughter, now. Let's sit down, shall we? Do you want that topped up?" '

Doran put her hand over her tankard. 'No, thanks. Get your own.'

As he stood at the bar she studied him. He might have been any ordinary young man in any local, chatting to Rosie, saluting somebody at the other side of the room, laughing at something Winnie had said. Yet half an hour before he had been a grave figure of still dignity, a man set apart before the altar-rails, like a tall candle in the white cassock and golden stole he wore for the administration of the Eucharist.

41

Was that Rodney, or was this? A question she had no need to ask herself. They were the same, a person dear to her.

He came back to her table with his half-pint of bitter. It was all he ever drank in public, other than at parties. Clergymen attracted criticism.

'Everything all right?' he asked.

'Fine. You?'

'Never better.' But her sharp eyes could detect a shadow of trouble in his face. Helena again, the young daughter whose crippled state weighed so heavily on him. Doran thought he would prefer not to talk about Helena in his interlude of relaxation. She said, 'Looks like bother in the Miles boat. Bob's glowering like a thunderstorm and Barbary's been crying, and the Major's not speaking to either of them.'

'Oh dear.' Rodney studied the three. 'I thought the Major looked a bit glum in church, but it could have been my sermon – one never knows. Let's be very quiet and see if we can overhear anything. Shouldn't be difficult – Bob's shouting as though he was appealing against a run-out.'

The young cricketer's voice was indeed raised over the general buzz of chatter. '. . . bloody sacrifice. And what for? How do you know. . .?'

They failed to catch Barbary's answer, but her pretty face was a picture of misery. Her father's eyes were on her, brooding.

'Well, I don't like it,' Bob was saying, 'and I dam' well won't have it. Let him make do. The very idea of you and that. . . .'

Barbary stood up abruptly and walked out without casting a backward glance. Bob seemed about to follow her, then changed his mind and stalked back to the bar, brows knitted and mouth tight with anger.

'Viking in a rage,' Rodney said. Then: 'Look who's arrived!'

Barbary had almost collided in the doorway with Marcia Fawkes.

They exchanged glances. The formidable Marcia had never been seen in the Rose before, to their knowledge. As

42

churchwarden, church treasurer and prominent member of the Parish Council, as well as the local Brown Owl, charity collector and appeals organizer, she was well known to preserve jealously her reputation for probity. And now to sail boldly into what she would have termed 'a public house', on a Sunday: it was a phenomenon.

'Good Gordon Bennett,' said Rodney, who clung affectionately to pet television catch-phrases long after they had faded from the air-waves. 'She wasn't in church, I noticed. Is this the first sign of a descent down Sin's slippery path?'

'She might be collecting for something.'

'Hardly without a box.'

Marcia's small beady eyes darted round the bar, and came to rest on Doran and Rodney. Doran thought she detected the speculative gleam with which they were usually favoured. With a determined pushing aside of chairs, tables and people Marcia plodded towards them.

'Don't quote at her,' Doran murmured. 'She wouldn't catch on. Good morning, Marcia. Do join us.'

'I was going to. Good morning, Vicar.'

Rodney rose politely. 'Can I get you a drink?'

'Thanks. Whisky.'

Curiouser and curiouser, for it was well known that sherry and worse was all the visitor would get at Laburnum Cottage. On his way to the bar Rodney almost bumped into Major Miles, who was standing, leaning on his stick, his face uncertain and unhappy. Rodney paused, sensing that comfort or counsel might be needed.

'Morning, Major. You're better today – no crutches?'

'No. I. . . . Glad to see you, Rodney. Look, could we have a talk some time?'

'Of course, when you like. Shall I drop in after lunch on my way to Sunday School?'

Miles looked embarrassed. 'Er, perhaps not. I'm expecting a visitor. A bit later on, perhaps?'

'Let me see, I'm taking Evensong over at Henbury. What about before that?'

'Yes. Yes. That would be splendid. . . .' He seemed to be

43

struggling for words. Rodney felt the pull of the confessor to the penitent who cannot express his sin. He drew Miles gently towards an unoccupied corner behind the open door. Marcia's drink would have to wait.

'Come out of that racket so that we can hear ourselves speak. Something's troubling you. Can't you tell me what it is, even briefly?'

Miles seemed to gather strength. 'Well. Do you believe in – I mean to say, if a thing, a decision, is going to be the best for everybody, don't you think one should put aside . . . what can I say? Scruples. Of one's own, or somebody else's. If it's all going to result in good. . . .'

'I'm sorry, Major. If you could be a bit more specific. Is this something to do with Barbary – and Bob?'

'Yes, it is. She can see my point of view, and he can't, stubborn young devil. I've talked and talked to him, but – and now, when the thing's got to be settled, he's bullying her out of it. It's destroying me, Rodney, I'll tell you that. I'm not a fit man and I can't stand fights. Fights!' He laughed without mirth, tapping his wounded leg. 'That's good. An old soldier ought to be able to face 'em, eh?'

Rodney glanced across the bar and caught Doran's eye. She took in the situation, glanced towards Marcia, nodded, and beckoned to Winnie, who was collecting glasses. Message understood. She would order Marcia's whisky herself and he might go on talking as long as he wished. He bent down and said quietly, 'I feel you're very troubled. Shall we sit down, and you can tell me properly what the worry is.'

Miles hesitated. 'It's very good of you, Vicar.' Christian names tended to fall by the way in such situations. 'You see, it's not asking much of her, to do this. She knows I want only the best for her. She's my only one, you know. I lost her mother when she was born – Margaret was well over forty. She'll be bettering herself and there won't be the travelling, and the season-ticket money, and it'll mean comparative security for me. And it's only the work she's doing already, but in far better conditions. I know it's a bit, well, unconventional, but surely these days that doesn't matter.'

Rodney said patiently, 'You want Barbary to take a job that will bring in more money – is that it? But Bob objects, and perhaps Barbary isn't keen?'

Miles's lips were twitching with conflict. At last he said, 'I promised not to talk about it. Not yet, not until this afternoon. I shouldn't have spoken. Don't think any more about it.' Before Rodney could stop him he was hurrying out with his painful crab-like walk, into the sunlight, down the cobbled slope that led to the square. Rodney looked after him, troubled.

Marcia was telling Doran, 'I suppose it *does* look odd, my coming in here, but really sometimes I have to get away from Stella. She's quite impossible at the moment, quite.' She took a gulp of Scotch. Doran thought she might be more used to it than one would have guessed.

'Oh dear,' she said. 'And Laburnum's quite a small cottage, if – if things are difficult.'

'They are,' Marcia snapped. 'Always with her nose in some book or other about witchcraft, and very nasty pictures some of them have on the covers, quite obscene. And then bringing in all those weeds and cooking them in *my* kitchen – some of the best pans are stained bright green and a perfectly horrid yellow. I think it's downright unhealthy.'

'Not only unhealthy.' Rodney, who had been listening, sat down beside them. 'All witchcraft is dangerous.'

Marcia stared. 'You don't believe it *works*, Vicar, surely?'

'I know it can. Sometimes in very bad ways. We're not meant to meddle with it.'

'You're going to quote the Witch of Endor at me, I suppose?'

'No, no,' Rodney said mildly. 'I've no reason to believe she was anything but a perfectly respectable old party. But just tell Stella to leave it alone.'

'Try telling her yourself, Vicar. It's driving me to . . .' she glanced at her whisky glass and changed the end of the sentence, 'to thinking it's time I had a change of scene.'

Doran said, 'You wouldn't leave Abbotsbourne, surely? Not when you have so many interests – all your church activities, and the Brownies, and things.'

'Too many. I work my fingers to the bone for very little

45

thanks. Nobody would miss me. I shall find somewhere else, a nice little place where I can be quite free of – of Stella and her nonsense and her mess.' Doran was sure she had been going to say something else. Marcia drained her glass, banged it down on the table and rose abruptly. 'I must be going. Goodbye.'

'Well,' said Doran, when she was out of earshot. 'Well. What's bugging her, then? It's something besides Stella, I'm sure of that. They're really very attached to each other. What about the whisky? I think she may have had a wee yin already, before she came in here, don't you?'

Rodney's dreaming gaze was on a photograph of the hunt meeting outside the Rose.

'How delicious gossip is,' he said, 'and not even sinful, if you think about all the malice it enables one to get out of one's system, without doing the least bit of harm. I bet the other Apostles used to gossip like anything about Paul. . . .'

The church clock struck one, and Rodney looked at his watch.

'I must go. Nancy will be fretting over the roast or whatever it is. No good having a housekeeper and not turning up in time for lunch. Walk me home?'

'I'd like that.'

Strolling back to the vicarage they were passed by Sam Eastry, the village constable, riding the Honda he controlled like a spirited horse. Even the most languid of cats knew that he would respect its stately progress across the road. But groups of bored youths, busy carving graffiti on some inviting surface such as the interior of the bus shelter, scattered like startled birds at the putt-putt of the approaching machine. Sam was liked and respected, not least because he had chosen to stay in Abbotsbourne when offered the chance of promotion and transfer.

The offer had come soon after the death of his small daughter Jane in a road tragedy. He and his wife Lydia had not wanted to leave Jane alone in the churchyard of St Crispin's while they went to a place she had never known. It was irrational, and they knew it, but the feeling was strong. They stayed, and Sam kept Jane's grave bright with growing flowers, tending it like a garden.

There was another tie between Sam and Abbotsbourne. Campanology, the ancient and unique science of bell-ringing, fascinated him far more than criminology. St Crispin's had a famous 'ring' of six bells, all but one dating from before the Reformation, and Sam was the ringers' captain. He cherished the bells, his Ladies (for a bell is always feminine) like children, and was well known in his county and beyond as an expert. There were other rings in other towers, but to Sam his Ladies were irreplaceable, unrivalled. He would not leave them for a wilderness of promotional stripes. Lydia, their bright son Ben, and their comfortable modern police house, made up the rest of his reason for living.

Doran waved to Sam. He was one of her favourite men, a shoulder to lean on, authority and protection to a single female with a vulnerable house and shop. It was perhaps weak, wet and unfashionable to acknowledge oneself as a lone lorn woman enjoying dependence on men, but facts had to be faced. Sam was a shield and defender, a good person to talk to, and an invaluable source of information about everyone and everything in the village.

At the vicarage gate she left Rodney. It would have been nice to be able to invite him home for lunch, nice to lunch with him in the solid ugly Victorian house he lived in. But they both knew it was impossible.

His step was a little slower than usual as he walked up the path to the gothic front porch. In the hall he shouted cheerfully, 'Anyone at home?' thinking 'silly question' even as he shouted.

Nancy Kirton, his housekeeper, came out of the kitchen wiping her hands on her apron. She was small and spare and looked perpetually worried, which was the case. One of her worries was that her beloved Reverend would not get enough to eat. An orphanage child, she served, tended and guarded him and Helena, her substitute family, with obsessive devotion.

'Oh, *there* you are, Vicar. Lunch will be any time you want.'

'Meaning right away? Just give me two minutes, Nan.'

He went into the drawing room at the end of the hall. His daughter was lying on a chaise-longue in front of the french window. In the lofty-ceilinged room she seemed even smaller than she was, a twelve-year-old who had not grown much for the past four years. Her dead mother's vivid prettiness had not come down to Helena, the child so hopefully named for a saint-empress. A creeping muscular disease had stunted her growth, deformed her joints, cut her off from the normal life of childhood, and spoiled her temper. She scowled as her father entered the room.

'Where've you been?'

'Where do you think?' He kissed the top of the dark head, noticed the books that had fallen to the floor, the puzzle impatiently scrawled across with pencil-marks.

'Oh, *I* know. That place you won't take me into.' She turned her head sharply away.

'I've told you, chick, it's not me, it's the law. And you wouldn't like it if they did let you in, it's just people standing about talking.'

'Boring old people. What do you want to talk to them for? Oh, I suppose *Doran* was there.' The tone was unchildishly sarcastic. Rodney sighed inwardly. He would not let her get to him, tempt him into answering sharply. He was her buffer against the injustices of life, the only one she could take it out on, except for poor vulnerable Nancy. He had to stay reliable, firm, cheerful, an example to her, and that without preaching or scolding.

'Yes, Doran was there,' he said lightly. 'So were a lot of other people.'

'You didn't bring her back with you? She's not out in the hall?'

'Of course she isn't, what a silly idea.'

'You once *did* bring her.'

Yes, just once. It had been a disaster. Helena, jealous and balked of her father's sole attention, had been insufferably rude to Doran, who had taken it very well but had been unable not to show that it hurt. Nancy had burst into tears while serving the pudding, and Rodney had wished passionately that he had a normal, perfectly healthy child to smack soundly. He was not going to let her do that to Doran again. It had been the turning point in their relationship, forcing him to realize that marriage, which had been in his mind, was impossible while Helena remained as she was.

He said, not for the first time, 'Why don't you come to Matins with me? You wouldn't have to keep bobbing up and down – you could sit quietly and listen to the singing, and look at the window you like. Better than sitting here by yourself.'

A gleam of interest lit Helena's eyes. 'And would you push me home afterwards?'

'Why not?' he said unwarily.

She was triumphant. 'Then you couldn't go to that silly Rose and talk to all those silly people. All right, I'll come next week.'

'Next week's Sung Eucharist, not Matins.' But his heart sank. He had just been blackmailed into giving up a brief weekly half-hour of rare, pleasant relaxation in his duty-filled life. The alternative was to take Helena to the Rose with him and leave her outside, where she would make his pleasant interlude a misery with incessant relayed demands.

'We'll see,' he said.

She hunched a shoulder against him, thunder-faced. 'You always say that when you're not going to promise me something. Go to your beastly horrible Rose, then – see if I care.'

At another moment Rodney would have been amused to hear the inn described in terms of a particularly disreputable mistress, but he was not in the vein to be amused.

'Come on,' he said, 'lunch. Feel like walking, or shall I put you in your chair?'

'Walk.' He half-supported, half-carried her, an arm under her shoulders, her feet dragging, on a slow, laborious progress to the dining room.

Sunday school over (and he was relieved to be out of it, so many ordinary normal brats to contrast with the condition of his own unhappy child) he collected his cassock and set off in the Mini for Evensong at Henbury. It would be a pleasant drive through country lanes and over downland, one which might shake off the black devil perching on his shoulder. He was almost beyond the parish boundary when he remembered Major Miles.

At least there was plenty of time. He had started early to allow for driving at a saunter. He turned the car and made for Wicket Lane, which aptly enough bordered the cricket pitch. Major Miles liked to hobble out on a fine afternoon to sit in the sun and cheer on his prospective son-in-law's team.

Old Thatch was a picture-postcard cottage set in a garden which could have rivalled Anne Hathaway's, if the Major could have afforded enough help. As it came in sight round the corner of the lane Rodney admired the thick-blossomed almond tree by the gate, now in full early beauty.

Beneath it, at anchor, stood Sam Eastry's Honda. And beyond that, an ambulance.

4

'But he can't be dead.' Doran, on her knees beside a child's miniature chair which she was cleaning, stared up at Rhona and Vi. 'I saw him, before lunch today.'

'Death don't always get advertised beforehand like next week's film,' Rhona said sagely. 'Vi just happened to be at the Singhs', the old lady not being too well, and she saw the vicar's car and the doctor's, and Sam's bike, and stopped to ask.'

'True as I stand here,' confirmed her sister. 'It was Bob answered the door, all of a taking, and I could hear Barbary crying inside, sobbing her heart out, she was. "The Major's dead," Bob says. "Barbary come in and found him on the floor, and a few minutes after he died." Well, I said anything I could do, like, but Bob said Dr Levison was looking after Barbary and Sam had phoned Lydia to come round, so I didn't want to get in the way, and I come straight here.'

Doran shook her head, dazed with shock. 'But – what killed him? It couldn't have been his leg trouble, people don't die of that. Was it a heart attack?'

But Vi, having shot her bolt, was in haste to extract the last ounce of drama out of the situation in other quarters, Rhona excitedly in her wake; a pair of Trojan Women off to cry woe. They would have been shocked to the soul if somebody had observed to them that a sudden death makes a nice change in the daily routine. But it did, even to Rhona, whom sudden death had widowed.

'The vicar's car.' So Rodney had been there too. Doran telephoned the vicarage, to be told by Nancy that he was not back yet. She returned to the miniature windsor chair and mechanically resumed polishing it with a duster. Under the seat was a small cluster of worm-holes. She peered at them, but the worms had been long gone. There was something particularly chilling about hearing of a person's death when one had seen them alive only a little time before, alive and well.

But the Major had not looked well. Physically no worse than usual, but worried – grieved, anxious, angry? Doran sat back on her heels, remembering that among the customers of the Rose that morning several had seemed under a cloud. Major Miles, Barbary and Bob, quarrelling, Rodney (but that had been something to do with Helena), Marcia, behaving out of type. It was as though someone had carried plague to the village. Would it kill off the inhabitants, one by one, as plague had done in Eyam, three centuries since?

That plague had come in a box of clothes brought from infected London. How had this one been borne? Doran knew that she was being wildly fanciful, and hoped that she was not, yet again, letting her imagination feed vicariously on the troubles of others.

Yet it fed, during a night of fitful sleep.

Only the death of an elderly, ailing man, it made wide ripples in the calm lake of Abbotsbourne life. Rhona talked of nothing else while serving breakfast. The milkman had mysteriously heard of it at the dairy headquarters, and news of it had reached the postman at the sorting office. As soon as the shops in the square opened small knots of very early shoppers had gathered about their doors to talk about it.

So it had been with the deaths of Miss Beamish and Mrs Trott, and, as then, within two days the excitement had died down, except in those who would have enjoyed a first-hand account of the tragedy. Barbary had not appeared, and Dr Levison's car was to be seen every day outside the gate of Old Thatch. Vi brought a tasty decoration of the story to Bell House.

'Bob Woods has taken time off work, did you know?' she was telling her sister. 'He's there looking after her. I popped in, seeing Mrs Singh's better and I've a bit of time on my hands, and Bob answered the door, looking none too pleased to see me, and said there wasn't nothing to do what he couldn't do himself.'

'Ah, he did, did he.' Rhona made it sound like a profound comment on the wickedness of the world, thought Doran, hearing their loud clear voices from the hall.

'Myself, I don't think it's right, a young man there all day with his girlfriend.'

'Oh well. These days, it seems anything goes. Run along now, Debbie, you'll find your tea laid.'

Into Doran's mind, as Vi had mentioned Bob answering the door, had flashed a picture of a picture: a small jewel-like *St George and the Dragon with Princess Sabra.* Giorgione, was it, or Uccello? A valiant, slender silver-armoured figure brandishing a spear before the entrance to a cave, in the mouth of which hovered an enchanting doll-like princess. What had that to do with anything? But she knew, instantly. Shutting the door against the Cassandras in conference, she went to the telephone and dialled the vicarage.

'Well, I'll see, but he's having his supper,' said Nancy's disapproving voice. Then, behind her, Rodney's weary one.

'All right, Nan, I'll take it. Yes?'

'It's me, Doran. Sorry to bother you. But I've tried a few times and you were always out.'

'Yes. Sorry. It's been a bit hectic.'

He didn't want to talk even to her, she knew that, but there was something she must ask.

'I won't keep you. It's just that – on Sunday, in the Rose – do you remember what we heard Bob saying to Barbary, when they were quarrelling?'

A silence. 'Not exactly.'

'Well, I can, part of it. He said "bloody sacrifice" and "the thought of you and that. . . ." Does that tie in with what the Major said to you?'

'I suppose so, in a way. He said . . . let me think. That he'd talked a lot to Bob, but Bob couldn't see whatever it was. And something about having scruples. No, that doesn't fit in, does it? Sorry. I'm not at my best and brightest just at the moment.'

'You poor thing. My turn to say sorry. I was a fiend to ring you. There's only just one other tiny detail – did the Major have a coronary, do you know?'

'Levison says there was no history of heart disease, and the Major wasn't the type anyway. He won't know any more till the results of the inquest.'

'I see. Very interesting.' At Rodney's end she heard a shrill, peevish shout of 'Daddy!' and Nancy's voice, shushing. Thoughtfully she hung up.

Something was haunting her, a half-memory; something to do with a Chelsea pastoral pair, shepherd and shepherdess. She had not sold any lately or she would hardly have forgotten. The nearest thing to them she was likely to get were late-nineteenth-century copies, sometimes bearing a spurious gold anchor mark. Perhaps she was remembering not a real pair, but someone she had idly thought of as a Chelsea porcelain type, or types.

It came back to her, from more than a fortnight before. Barbary and Bob at the Haydon-Trees' party, dark girl and fair boy; and the pink cheeks of the shepherdess turning pinker, as the shepherd hurried her away from . . . what, or whom?

Leonard Mumbray, of course. He had been the wolf in the fold then. Was it remotely possible that he could still be? Since the party he had been seen only occasionally, going about his own concerns in his black Escort, never with a passenger. He had visited the hardware store, the coal-merchant, the electricity shop. Rhona, on her own shopping expeditions, had reported these errands. She had little comment on him, nor, oddly enough, had Vi, who was now working at The Oaks three days a week.

'Dull old house, I wouldn't give you twopence for it. Too many stairs and a lot of nasty corners for collecting dust. It's not a bad kitchen, I'll say that, though not what I'd choose if I had that kind of money. Him? Don't see much of him at all, he's mostly in that big book-room, study or whatever you call it.'

I'd call it the perfect prison library, Doran thought, but she said, 'What about his housekeeper? He does have one, doesn't he?'

'Mrs Butcher. Little skinny thing, thin as six o'clock. Looks to me as though she'd been very ill, some time – nothing to her at all.' Vi flexed her own muscular arms. 'Not strong enough to square up to a sparrow, I don't wonder they need me there. As for cooking, I'd have thought she could have done it herself, just chops and shepherd's pie, boiled and roast and greens, and nothing special for starters, though he likes his afters, treacle puddings, chocolate soufflé, he's a glutton for that sort of thing.'

'Does he drink?' asked Doran, who firmly believed that appetites reflected their owners.

'Not as I've seen, and I would. No deliveries of wine and that. Bottle of brandy in the sideboard, but it don't seem to go down. No cooking wine in the kitchen, and I like a dash in a casserole.' Vi sounded disappointed, as indeed she was, having hoped for a rich source of gossip in her new employer. As it was, there was nothing to say. A silent man and a mousy housekeeper in a featureless house, from which not even her imagination could create a Northanger Abbey.

Doran thought of these things while reviewing Mumbray's possibilities as a wolf in the fold. Intense curiosity, backed by an instinct she had learned to trust in her dealings, urged her to find out for herself. But investigation needed time. She made an evening telephone call to Howell asking him to mind the shop alone next day. He was not pleased, having planned a buying trip to some unspecified place to look at unspecified stock. Well, he could do that any time. Next morning, she made a luxuriously leisured breakfast, went for a stroll round the village, admired the new foal in the field adjoining the stud, nodded, though with reservations, to the kennel-hand exercising his fox-hounds, and finally arrived at the gate of Old Thatch.

Feeling snipe-nosed, she pulled the iron bell. If Barbary answered she would express sympathy and ask if there were anything she could do. Natural enough, surely.

But it was Bob who opened the door. His smile was not immediate and he did not step aside to let her in. Almost stammering, she asked after Barbary.

'She's better, thanks. No, there isn't anything she wants.'

'You're looking after her?'

'That's right.'

His hard blue stare challenged her to criticize. She decided that comparative frankness was the only policy if she were not to slink away feeling like a baffled Paul Pry. 'I didn't come to find out any gory details,' she said. 'I'm glad you're with her. She must have had the most awful shock and nobody could be better for her than you. If only you'd been there when it happened. She was alone, wasn't she?'

'Yes.'

'Look, Bob – the whole thing worries me and I can't get it out of my mind. Could I have a word with you – just ask you something? I promise not to be a nuisance.'

After a fractional pause he stepped aside and motioned her in. The door opened straight into the living room, which bore evidence of having been tidied by a masculine hand, cushions unstraightened and books and papers piled on top of each other. In a vase were wilting flowers, gathered days before. There was no sign of Barbary. Bob led the way through the room into the adjoining kitchen. The table and sink were littered with used crockery, a cut loaf, empty butter-dish, and other testimony to male occupation. Doran reflected that Mrs Woods, mother of three athletic sons, had almost certainly not trained them in the domestic arts.

'Coffee?' Bob loomed over the cooker.

'Er – is there any tea in that pot?'

Bob lifted the lid. 'Plenty, but it's gone a bit cold. I'll put some hot water to it.'

'*Boiling* water.'

'What? Oh yes.' A faint smile lit his heroic features.

The tea was awful, but just drinkable. Doran took a few token sips before pushing her cup aside. 'Where's Barbary?'

'Still in bed. I'm making her stay there till lunchtime. The book says that in cases of shock the patient ought to be allowed to come round slowly in the morning – get into the day gradually, sort of.' Doran was touched to see a large volume, obviously a *Family Doctor*, open on the dresser. 'I've taken the

56

TV up there so she can watch all morning. Today she had it on for the *Breakfast Show*,' he added proudly.

'Lucky Barbary – what a nurse she's got. Don't let your talents get spread around or all the invalids will be wanting you. Listen, Bob. I've got an idea Major Miles's death wasn't natural. And I *don't* mean it was anything to do with Barbary, or not directly, so you can stop glaring. He didn't die of a long-standing heart weakness, as you'd expect a man of his age to die – I happen to know that.'

'Go on,' Bob said grimly.

'I also happen to know that you and she and Major Miles were having a disagreement about something, and that it had upset you all very much.'

'*How* do you know?'

'I was in the Rose on Sunday. I should think the entire bar trade noticed the three of you – and Major Miles said something about it to the vicar. You'd quarrelled about some decision that had to be made, one you had scruples about. I think it was a very important one – important enough to lead to his death. You can throw me out now if you like, but I think you ought to tell someone.'

Bob appeared to be struggling with himself. At last he said, 'All right. Maybe I ought. It was that fellow Mumbray.'

Doran gave an uncontrollable start. 'Yes?' Yes, of course it was.

'He came round here, one night after that party, and asked her father if he'd let her go and work for him, at The Oaks. Confidential secretarial duties, he called it. Said she'd have light hours and good money. Then he told them what he was prepared to pay, and it fairly knocked the Major for six. Twice as much as she was getting from the insurance firm in Eastgate, and no train fares, and days off if her dad was poorly and wanted her at home. And lunches on the house.'

'I see. Practically an offer he couldn't refuse.'

'Well. At first he said no. For one thing he didn't like the idea of her working alone with a strange man – I should bloody well think not. And then when he put it to her, she didn't seem keen at first, said she wasn't sure she liked

Mumbray, though of course he was very charming.'

Very charming! Doran's mind boggled. That cold, flinty-eyed, insufferably rude creature – charming. Her face expressed her thoughts.

'That's how I felt,' Bob said. 'I loathed the bugger on sight. And I could see then that he was making up to her, smarming all over her like a big white slug. Of course, I put my oar in right away, said I wasn't having my girl working for the fellow. I lost my rag properly, and Barbary turned awkward and said who did I think I was, and she was twenty-two and free to decide for herself. I suppose I drove her to it,' he added miserably. 'Should have kept my great trap shut.'

'Not easy.'

Bob stabbed a scrap of butter with a knife, repeatedly. 'Well, it went on like that, then one night she met him outside and went for a drive with him. I don't know any more about that, she wouldn't tell me. But it made her mind up for her, and she told her father she'd go and work for Mumbray. It didn't take much to persuade him, either. He was always strapped for money, poor old chap, with a joke of a pension. He'd taken out a second mortgage on this place, and there was extra insurance to pay because it was thatched – fire risks. Bar had always given him the best part of her wages, so he felt guilty about that.'

'And . . .?'

'Oh God, it got so awful. He tried to talk me round and I shouted at him. At her, too, and that upset the poor old chap, badly. Then, last Sunday, he told us both that Mumbray was coming to see him after lunch, and he'd give him yes or no, finally. So I made Bar come out with me, and we went up to the castle ruins and tried to talk it out, but it was no good. She gave me my ring back.'

'Oh, Bob.'

'I know, that was the worst that had happened. Not that I could get her to name the day, before that. I don't think she ever would have done, while her dad was alive. But when we got back from the walk I marched off and left her, and she came in by herself.'

'And found him.'

Bob nodded, living it all over again. 'I never should have left her.'

'*Had* Mumbray been to see the Major?'

'I don't know. I haven't had time to find out, with looking after her. If he did, I reckon they had some sort of row and it was the end of the old man. And if that was what happened, I'll get Mumbray for it. I'll kill him.'

As he spoke he looked formidable enough to beat a visiting cricket team single-handed; or to do what he had just threatened. A cold chill pricked Doran's spine. Then he smiled, and was a different person.

'Now I've told you,' he said. 'I don't know why, because I don't know you very well. But you were right, I feel better. Want to have a look at Bar?'

'If you think it wouldn't disturb her.'

Barbary was propped up in bed, against rose-sprinkled pillows, in sheets to match, a rose among roses, though those in her cheeks were paler than usual. Her eyes were on the flickering screen, her face relaxed and childlike. Doran knew quite certainly that Bob had shared that roomy bed and its rosy linen, and that in their new relationship Barbary had drawn comfort and strength from him. A splash of colour caught her eye, red and brown stripes – Bob's club tie thrown across a chair.

Barbary, absorbed in the television, had not heard them. Doran touched Bob's arm and drew him away from the bedroom door.

Downstairs, in the porch, she said, 'Don't do – what you said. In fact, I wouldn't do anything, if I were you. Just leave it.'

'And what are *you* going to do?'

'I don't know – yet.'

She arrived at the police house with no very clear idea of what excuse she was going to give for calling. Fortune saved her from inventing one. Sam was working in his front garden, planting his son Ben on his knees beside him. An officious

59

robin was alternately perching on a spade stuck in the ground and flitting off into the lower branches of a tree.

'Hard at it, Sam?'

Sam got to his feet. He was, she thought not for the first time, like a teddy bear, not the modern aggressively yellow kind in fancy clothes, but a fine mature fellow, cherished by somebody from nursery days onwards, his fur slightly worn but dependable as ever. The smile beneath his fluffy moustache was warm. He liked Doran, his policeman's instinct sensing something that needed his best reassuring manner.

'That's right,' he said, 'getting the early summer stuff out.'

'Dad raises it all from seed,' Ben told her proudly.

'Good for him. Ozzy's supposed to do that, but somehow we never have the sort of display you do.' Ozzy was the jobbing gardener who looked after the half-acre that surrounded Bell House, when he was not detained at home by family misfortunes or the infirmities of his car, which he referred to as 'Me Mo'or' and which appeared to be a chronic invalid.

'Well, well. I'll drop you over some of these, I've got far too many. Like bachelor's buttons, don't you?'

'Love them. Sam . . . I wanted to speak to you.'

He interpreted that tone. 'Ben, there's plenty more of them in the greenhouse – run along and make up a nice box for Miss Fairweather, will you?' When the boy had gone he opened the gate.

'Come on in.' She followed him up the neat path into the neat little newish house filled with a warm smell of cooking. Lydia Eastry put her brown curly head round the door, sensed that she was superfluous and vanished again after greeting Doran.

'I expect you'll think this is silly, but it's something I've got to tell you.' She outlined Bob's story. 'Now I happen to know that Major Miles hadn't any heart trouble before, so why then, just after Mr Mumbray had been to see him? Why did he die just then?'

Sam filled a pipe, struck a match, allowed it to go out, and laid the matchbox, pipe-cleaner and pouch neatly out in a row.

'I don't know, my dear. Nor does anybody. We'll know more when the inquest's been held. Shall we wait till then?'

'You *do* think it's silly. I knew you would.'

'I think you're very clever. A lot cleverer than most of us in Abbotsbourne. I wish I'd your brains. But it's a very delicate situation, you know. There'd be a lot of proof needed before anyone could point the finger. You know me – the old copper, slow and steady. I wouldn't want to make moves, or report anything, not without something substantial to go on.'

'Yes. I see. Thank you, Sam.'

The post mortem showed that Major Miles had died of cardiac arrest, and the coroner's verdict was Death from Natural Causes.

'I don't care,' Doran told Rodney. 'I am bloody but unbowed – I still think there was something fishy about it. Everyone dies of cardiac arrest. But why did he? Why don't *you* go and see Mumbray? You might get some sort of clue from him.'

'Dear girl, I'm a parson, not a detective. There are people in three parishes in constant need of my time and advice and ministry who expect me to be open all hours. I only pay a pastoral visit if I think it will do any good, and from my one glimpse of Mr M. I doubt if he'd welcome me looming up on his doorstep. So just leave it, will you? Leave well alone.'

Dissatisfied, Doran drove off. There was a sale over thirty miles away, westwards, on the Sussex coast. She bid more indiscriminately than usual, acquiring a pedlar doll which proved to have many of its wares missing or substituted, a millefiori paperweight which looked too good to be true, and indeed was. It would be hard to shift again, even with its falseness acknowledged. So would the pretty little mantel clock she bought for Howell, a charming case containing the wrong movement. He was displeased.

'What d'you want to go buying for if you can't trust your own judgement?'

'That's right. I can't, can I? In future don't believe anything I say – nobody else does.'

She stood among the mourners watching Major Miles's coffin being lowered into the grave, reflecting: 'Here endeth Doran's First Case.'

5

Ozzy was de-heading the thick ranks of daffodils which bordered Doran's flowerbeds in spring. Now it was late May, time for iris and peony and early lilies and starry alliums and the first crimson and purple bells of fuchsia. Doran surveyed their progress with pride. She had had the utmost difficulty in getting Ozzy to plant any of them, or indeed anything of which he did not know the name, as though some kind of introduction ceremony was necessary before they would consent to be planted.

'Very nice,' she said. 'Much tidier.'

'Be even tidier if I could cut them daffs down.'

'But then the bulbs wouldn't be able to store nourishment from the leaves. You have to leave them for six weeks to die off.' It was the fourth year she had explained this, but Ozzy was no nearer to believing it. She knew that if she went away for a May holiday she would return to find the daffodils cut down to ground level.

She sighed suddenly and sharply, as though a cold wind had blown through the still garden. There had been a song somewhere in her childhood, a Blackbird's Song, high and shrill and haunting. 'True love I ne'er may meet, All the world through, Dim is the dawn and sweet, Deep is the dew.' It was ringing in her head now, in the garden where real blackbirds sang, and made her restless, longing for something unknown, something elsewhere.

Bell House was her beloved home. But should a person of twenty-six spend all day and every night in her home, however beloved?

63

There was Eastgate, of course. She was lucky to have a shop in another place, a busy town to offset sleepy Abbotsbourne. Eastgate, and Howell Evans, and Arthur Hidley and sour Victor Maidment, and Peg and Meg and Howell's boyfriend Andrew and all the other locals, and never a Not Impossible He among them.

With that mythical He, who should command her heart and her, there could be holidays. She was not tempted by the cruise ship, the Italian beach or Cretan ruins. Her beckonings came from the Cotswolds, honey stone and blue-green hills, the gentle Scottish lowlands, the fortress towers of Durham and the wild poetry of Lindisfarne. In imagination the garden vanished, Doran was walking along the spur of land that led to the high-perched castle and St Aidan's ruined priory, ranting lines of Scott to the dipping seagulls.

And to herself. The companion who walked beside her had been only a phantom. The last of the cherry-blossom petals floated down to rest on her hair like bridal confetti. Listen, O lost and dear, Come, for your love is here. Here in the hazel wood – waiting for you.

'Them things,' Ozzy was saying. 'Them what you like.'

'What things, Ozzy?' He had a constitutional inability to remember the names of even the commonest flowers, made worse by questioning. Part Man of Kent, part didikei, Ozzy's mind became as mixed up as his origins if pressed too closely.

'Them red things.'

'Roses?' Doran asked patiently.

'Naw. Little fat ones, shiny.' His large face began to turn an alarming purple. Doran racked her brains for a red, fat, shiny flower she liked, and after considerable effort came up with begonias.

'That's it!' Ozzy beamed. 'Them'd look nice over there where I hoicked out them . . .' Awful uncertainty crept over his features; he was going to have to remember another name. 'Them howsyerfathers.'

'Forget-me-nots,' Doran supplied. 'Yes, yes I suppose they would. Can you get some from the nursery – if I write it down for you?' she added hastily. He could. He could read printed letters, but only just. She left him in his favourite posture, leaning heavily on his spade, cap over eyes, contemplating the future home of the howsyerfathers.

A bedroom window beyond the small orchard was wide open, Debbie visible at it, her brown head bent over her schoolbooks, swotting for A-Levels. Seeing Doran, she waved and smiled. She would never be a beauty, but intelligence gave her something like comeliness when the effort of study was not contracting her brow, and Rhona had persuaded her at last to do something about her straight hair, now permed into a short crop of soft curls. Doran began to plan for Debbie's future. A word to an influential Oxford friend when the time came, introductions to people who would know how to look after a shy girl student; perhaps a firm offer of contact lenses to get rid of the spectacles which sadly confirmed Dorothy Parker's well-known lines.

So many people to think about, and never mind one's restless self, to hell with blackbird dreams. Last Saturday's wedding had provided welcome activity and excitement, the marriage of Barbary and Bob. It had been advertised as a quiet wedding (how exactly did you advertise a noisy one Doran wondered?) but somehow had not turned out quite like that, with half of Abbotsbourne turning up for the ceremony and afterwards drifting up to the Rose for a long, champagne-floated party.

Barbary was a bride of legendary loveliness. 'In white, I see,' Doran observed to Rodney with a gleam in her eye born of champagne.

'Why not?' he replied levelly. She knew without telling that he knew of the nights of comforting at Old Thatch, the doorstep slices of bread and underdone eggs offered up on tea-slopped trays by Bob to his love, the girl he looked on as already his bride.

The newlyweds were to live at Old Thatch. Now it would be maintained by their joint incomes, Bob's a healthy one from the big hardware firm he worked for in Eastgate. There would be no questionable job at The Oaks for young Mrs Woods now. Doran even speculated that young Mrs Woods's job would shortly be concerned more with pushchairs and nappies than with typewriters and calculators: a sort of bloom was on her that might well be more than bridal.

'I'm glad something good has happened,' Doran said, reclining with her glass on a medieval window-seat. 'Perhaps the hex is off now. But you said there wasn't one, didn't you?'

'Who says I denyed of it, Betsy?' inquired Rodney, in Gamp-like tones.

'Oh. I thought you did. But you remember how we both felt at that awful party, about Mumbray.'

'That party. . . . Which lambs could not forgive, nor worms forget. And if I were you I should leave the bottle on the chimney-piece, and don't ask me to partake of none, being as I've an example to set to the parish.'

He turned away and moved off towards Dr Levison, who was drinking orange juice and looking depressed, as though he had just buried a favourite patient.

The elation had gone out of Doran. Flat as a long-poured glass of champagne, she gazed gloomily round the Rose's bar, now beginning to empty. Some guests were still loudly enjoying themselves, notably Rupert Wylie and a dazzling blonde girlfriend. Vi was behind the bar, washing up glasses and talking nineteen to the dozen to Rosie, her eyes and ears everywhere, antennae. No sign of Stella Meeson, which was odd, with her fondness for parties, but Marcia Fawkes was present, which was odder. In a corner, sitting huddled together, were the Reverend Ravi Singh and his wife Greta, like nervous little brown birds. Both over seventy, they had found a haven of peace following a hard life of struggle against prejudice after the end of the Raj, poverty and the loss of several children in India. Bob was their champion and protector, the reason why Rodney had asked Ravi Singh to assist him at the wedding ceremony.

The bridal couple were leaving, and Doran, cold and pensive, watched them go.

That had all been a week past. Now it was Saturday again; no wedding to look forward to. The shop was closed for the weekend, the day hers to do as she liked with. Her back ached with gardening. It might be nice to walk round to the cottage that had been Mrs Trott's and see how the building works were going on. The executors' sale had been quick. Dixter and Wylie had put a good price on the place, and got it.

There were voices in the hall of Bell House, Rhona's and a man's. Doran opened the door from the garden to see Leonard Mumbray about to leave.

He stepped back into the hall. 'Good morning, Miss Fair-weather.'

'Good morning.' What on earth could he want with Rhona?

'Very pleasant today.' His voice held a warmer note than she remembered, and he was actually smiling. Someone had called him charming – had she misjudged the man?

'I hope you're – enjoying The Oaks.' She found herself stammering, to her annoyance.

'Thank you. Most satisfactory.' It was impossible not to meet his eyes, which were still chromium but had a piercing quality which was, in a very strange way, attractive. And of course it was Barbary who had said that he was charming. To her relief he was going, saying goodbye to Rhona, who nodded and smiled and watched him down the path before shutting the door.

'Well! What was all that about, Rhona?'

'You'll never guess. Mr Mumbray's offered Debbie his library to work in – isn't that kind? He's got all sorts of books there, he says, and she can have it all to herself.'

Doran had followed Rhona into the kitchen, where Debbie was watching a pan simmering on the cooker. She looked excitedly pleased.

Yes, she was, she said in answer to Doran's question. 'He's got encyclopedias and reference books and dictionaries, and paper and different marking pens and everything. It'll be super.'

'I see. But – how did he come to invite you?'

'Oh, Debbie's met him before,' Rhona said. 'When she's called at The Oaks to see Vi.'

'He was in the garden one day, and he asked me in to look at his books, and said had I got a proper place to work in, and I said my room was all right but I kept getting interruptions – '

Rhona grimaced. 'That means me.'

' – so he said I could be absolutely quiet there, it's at the end of a lane and there's no passing traffic.'

'Nor no telly,' put in Rhona sternly, 'so you won't get tempted to start watching when you shouldn't be.'

'Mm. It sounds all right. Only – Debbie, do you like him?'

Debbie's eyes widened. 'Oh yes! He's ever so kind. He gave me fifty pence just now, for myself.'

Never take sweets from a stranger. Doran looked hard at Rhona, but met only a complacent smile.

'Said he couldn't believe I was Debbie's mother, more like her sister, and was I going to give her a stepfather one of these days?'

Damned cheek, thought Doran. Aloud she said, 'Did he suggest himself for the rôle?'

'Good gracious no, of course not, Miss Doran.' But Rhona smiled secretly as she tossed her head.

In Doran's workroom was a stock of cleaning materials – soft soap, oil, polish, paint-stripper, rags. A compulsion she only half understood took her to the cupboard for the tin of soap and a sponge. Rhona, crossing the hall, stopped in surprise.

'Why, whatever are you cleaning the door for?'

Doran flushed, caught out. 'I, er, I thought I saw dirty marks on the paint. Fingermarks.'

'You never did, if you'll excuse me. Where there's white paint in this house it stays white. And there's no call to touch that knob – I polished it only this morning.'

'Sorry, Rhona.' But she was curiously relieved to have carried out the small unnecessary ritual of cleansing.

On a damp, close evening in early June Doran's absorption in a television serial was interrupted by a visit from Sam Eastry.

'Oh dear, am I stopping you watching?'

Doran switched off the set. 'I'm quite glad to stop, in fact. I don't know why I watch this thing – it's perfectly horrid and it gets worse. Don't you think there's something crawly about kidnap cases?'

'That's one way of putting it. I can't say I'm sorry we don't get a lot of it round here. Something to be said about living in a valley that doesn't attract the rich. And that's what I've come about, really.'

'The rich?'

'Well, getting on that way – for Abbotsbourne. You don't happen to have had a knife, a sort of dagger, offered to you recently, do you? At the shop, or here?'

Doran thought. 'Can't say I remember one. We had a very nice naval officer's sword brought in, but it went the same day. No daggers. Why?'

'There's one gone missing from Colonel Haydon-Tree's, and they're upset about it. Seems it was a very valuable piece.'

Doran snorted. 'If it was one of those weapons they've got all over a drawing-room wall, my guess is that it was something knocked up in Birmingham about ten years ago. One or two right pieces, but on the whole a lot of tat.'

'Seems this wasn't tat but the real thing, and worth a pretty penny, the Colonel says.'

'Oh. Astonishing. What was it?'

'Well, I'm not too great on history, Doran, but I understood the Colonel to say he thought it was Italian make and hundreds of years old.'

'You interest me strangely. Pray continue your narrative.'

'You will have your joke. I can't tell you any more, because I've not been told myself. Truth is, they didn't seem to know much about it themselves, which I thought was funny.'

'I think it's funny too. Would you like me to go round there with you and take some notes? I might be able to sort it out a bit.'

'I was hoping you'd say that. I'd be very grateful, Doran. Could you make it this evening? I've just left them, and I know they'll be in.'

'I could make it now. Don't thank me, I've absolutely nothing else to do. My practice, like Watson's, is never very demanding.'

Sam smiled dutifully and nodded sagely, in token that he recognized the source. He would never willingly be typecast as the thick village bobby.

They stood at the Haydon-Trees' front door, their hair and faces damp with moisture in the night air. The gardens around them steamed almost audibly, as though with gases from an underground geyser. Doran mopped her cheeks with a handkerchief.

'Lily Lawn. What a name for a house. Sounds like a black soul singer, doesn't it? Lily Lawn sings reggae. Lily Lawn and the Four Clefettes. Way Down in Dixieland with Lily Lawn. . . .'

'Shush,' Sam said as the door opened. Mrs Haydon-Tree greeted them with surprise.

'Constable Eastry, again! And Miss Fairbrother. Well, do come in.'

'Fairweather, please, if it's all the same to you.' Doran muttered under her breath as they entered. Mrs Haydon-Tree led them into the drawing room. The Colonel rose from his chair by the large, expensive electric fire, roughly Jacobean in design surmounted by an heraldic shield and filled with a cheerful blaze from fake logs.

'Well, this *is* a pleasure. My dear young lady. Sit down, sit down.'

'You both look soaked, you poor things,' commiserated his wife. 'Do have a drink, won't you. George, do the honours, dear.'

'O'course, o'course. What'll it be? Scotch, brandy, a nice glass of port?'

Both refused politely. 'Miss Fair*weather*,' Sam said with the flicker of a glance at Doran, 'kindly said she'd come along with me, because being an expert in these matters she'd know all about your knife and be able to tell you where it'd be likely to have gone.'

The Colonel cleared his throat. 'Yes. Hm. Yes. Very kind.' He looked across at his wife, as if expecting her to begin. Doran noticed that neither was looking their best. The lines of his face sagged like a bloodhound's and the whites of his eyes were yellow. His wife's figure was no less billowing, but somehow drooped more than usual, as did the corners of her eyes and her mouth. The determined blondeness of her hair had never been less convincing.

And all this for a lost dagger. 'What was it like?' Doran asked.

'Well. About *so* long. Here, you can see where it was on the wall.' He indicated the spot among the weapons on the wall, a faint white shape against the beige of the wallpaper.

'I see. Yes. European by the look of it. Can you tell me about its history? Had it been in your family long?'

The Colonel looked faintly shifty. 'Well, no. Rosemary and I bought it, as a matter of fact. Felt it'd look good among our own things.' He lit a cigarette, neglecting to offer the packet round. Five stubs already lay in the ashtray beside him.

'We liked it as soon as we saw it,' his wife broke in. 'It was in a little shop in one of those markets, the one near Lisson Grove, wasn't it, dear? And it had such a romantic story, at least the man said it had, Italian and old enough to have been used by one of the, er, Borjers. So I thought, no harm in putting it with all the precious bits and pieces The Colonel's picked up during his campaigns.'

Campaigns? Whom did he serve under – Marlborough? 'If you could just describe it,' Doran said. 'Was the blade of steel, and can you remember any decorations on the hilt? We shall need to know things like that to send its description round the trade.'

'That's right,' Sam confirmed. The unhappy owners looked totally blank.

'Was it insured?' Doran asked. 'If so, there'd be some kind of description in the inventory.'

The Colonel's face brightened. 'We never bothered to insure it, but the chap we bought it from gave me a receipt with some details on it. I think I've got it still – if you don't mind waiting I'll go and have a look in my den.'

Left alone with the visitors, Rosemary Haydon-Tree chattered. 'What a dreadful night, isn't it? Really, for June, I do sometimes wonder. My poor roses, all soggy. Oh, and Miss

Fairb – Fairweather, how kind it was of you to let me borrow your man last week to do that job on the pergola. Ours left *quite* without notice, really disgraceful and the thing was falling down. I was *so* grateful.'

You didn't pay him as if you were, Doran reflected. A measly three quid for a morning's work and Ozzy grumbling that I shouldn't have sent him.

'And how,' The Colonel's Lady continued, 'is the dear vicar and that poor little girl of his? I'm afraid we don't get to church as often as we ought, The Colonel likes me to go round the links with him on a Sunday morning, and then it's rather High, you know, I was brought up to something much simpler, and I must say I like that better. But such a nice young man, always a smile and a joke. I expect you see quite a lot of each other, with similiar interests?'

What similar interests, you nosey cow? Only you could make a phrase like that sound lecherous. Doran was saved from voicing her irritation by the return of the Colonel, with a piece of paper.

Dagger, mid-fifteenth century approx., Italian maker but unsigned, blade of flattened diamond section, iron hilt and original grip, faun mask engraved on pommel.

Glancing at the price she whistled softly. 'He certainly charged you, didn't he? But it sounds a nice piece. Can we keep this, please, for circulating?'

Mrs Haydon-Tree made an indescribable sound. 'Aeowgh! Not with the price on?'

'No, no,' Sam reassured her. 'Of course we wouldn't reveal that, just the details. It'll be sent to every antique shop in the area and some further afield within the next day or two.'

'It's an unusual piece,' Doran said. 'You ought to have a chance.'

'To go back to what we were saying when I called before,' said Sam. 'Are you quite sure no casual caller could have taken it? Somebody who was shown into this room to wait, possibly. A man asking to read the electricity meter? There's plenty of fakes about, on the look-out for an easy haul.'

'We've had nobody like that, have we dear?' The Colonel cast a look across at his wife which Doran could not interpret, and Rosemary said quickly, 'Certainly not, and I should know. I have to answer the door myself these days, rather a come-down when one's always had maids.'

'And no visitors, madam? A comparative stranger, that you don't know well enough to trust, who might have been a bit, well, light-fingered?'

'Nobody at *all*.' It was a snap, defying her husband to contradict her. But he kept quiet, throwing her another look, and this time Doran could have sworn it was one of conspiracy. Then the wife added, 'Of course, there was your gardener, Miss Fairweather. He was working on the pergola, just near the French window over there. And the window was open most of the time he was here, in that fine spell.'

'Ozzy? Impossible. He wouldn't dream of it.'

'Bit of a gypsy type, that's how he struck me,' put in the Colonel. 'Never know with gypsies, they'll pinch anything.'

Sam saw Doran's resentment, and said soothingly, 'Ozzy's all right, take it from me. He's been around Abbotsbourne for years, and never got into trouble to my knowledge. A bit simple, but as honest as bread. Well, if you really can't recall any visitor who might have slipped your dagger into a pocket, I think we oughtn't to take up any more of your time.' He rose, followed by Doran.

The Colonel saw them out. 'Good of you to come round. We wouldn't have reported it, you know, but for the money. It was such a lot to lose. I – if it's too much trouble, forget about it, Constable. Write it off.'

Back in the Scotch mist that veiled the lane Sam said, 'That was a funny thing to say. Sounded as if he'd started something he didn't fancy seeing the end of. And I reckon they'd had a suspicious caller, whatever they might have said.'

'I'm quite sure of it. The lady did protest too much. As to the money – they're loaded but mean with it. I'll tell you something else, Sam. Those weapons on the wall weren't the only fakes in that room.'

'No? You spotted something else?'

73

'Human fakes, Sam. I ought to have seen it before. Those two are ersatz, pseudo. Sham.'

'Oh.' Sam was thoughtful. They walked on through the damp haze, wet branches brushing their heads like questing hands. In the quiet a train hooted, rushing through the valley to the sea.

Sam broke the silence. 'Just a word on the side, Doran. I wouldn't get too deep into things, if I were you. There's something nasty about.'

6

Vi was going from house to house, with the enthusiastic haste of those bringing the good news from Ghent to Aix.

'They've gone! Vanished! Overnight!'

Doran, loading her car, looked up. 'Who, Vi?'

'Haydon-Trees. Two removal vans at the gate this morning, seven o'clock, everything out by nine. No sign of him or her, they'd gone off in the car. The moving men's gaffer locked up and left the key at Dixter and Wylie's, I know, because I asked him. And the Electricity and the Water's been to turn off the supply.' She paused for breath. 'And not a word to anyone, not a single word! Mrs Earp, that's their daily, she got a telephone call last night to say not to come again and there was a cheque in the post. What about that?'

'What, indeed? Good gracious. I was talking to them only ten days ago, and they didn't say anything then.'

'About the burglary, you was talking?'

'About the burglary.'

'Ah, well, if you ask me it's all connected. Where you get one funny thing you get another. Excuse me, I've got to tell Rhona.' She vanished in a whirl of summer frock and shopping basket.

Chiding herself for overmastering curiosity, Doran locked the car again and walked down to Dixter and Wylie's in the square. Rupert greeted her with humorous resignation.

'Don't tell me. You want to know about the Haydon-Trees.'

'Oh dear. It's no business of mine. . . .'

'Don't worry, you're the fourth person to ask. And the,

answer is that I don't know where they've gone, or why. We had a phone call two days ago to say they were putting the house on the market, and would we handle it and keep in touch with them through their solicitor. If you want to get in touch with them, I could give you his address.'

'No, thanks, Rupert, I don't. It was just idle curiosity.'

'You're looking very charming this morning, Doran. Tell you what, how about having a spot of dinner with me tonight? There's this smashing little place up at Elvesham – it's not much known yet, so we might as well go before it gets too popular. And the country's looking marvellous – '

'I'm sorry, Rupert, I've got a dinner date already – I really have, I'm not just saying it. Otherwise I'd have loved to accept.'

'Pity. Oh well, another time.'

A faint feeling of regret pursued her on the way back home. Rupert was a nice, amusing young man, good for the feminine ego, and such an outrageous flirt that one was in no danger of taking him seriously. But the dinner date was true; a rare, long-postponed dinner at the vicarage.

It was strange to be alone with Rodney in his own house, unmenaced. Helena was in bed with a headache and a high temperature, in the care of Nancy, who had apologetically served up a cold meal that needed no attendance. She appeared at the coffee stage.

'I think she'll do now, Vicar. She's asleep and breathing nicely. I've left the lamp on in case she wakens.'

'Fine. Call me if she should want me, though, Nan.'

Pouring coffee, he said, 'It's extraordinary. At times I feel exactly like the Viking's Wife with the Marsh King's Daughter.'

'Could you elucidate?'

'Sorry, Andersen – fairy tales. She, the Viking's Wife, was childless, and reared a foundling. By day it was a lovely young girl with a terrible temper and nasty habits, but at night it turned into an ugly great toad, with beautiful soft brown eyes. All it wanted was cuddling, poor thing. That's what I've got, you know.'

'Which did the Viking's Wife prefer?'

'The toad.'

'She would, wouldn't she?'

'Yes. I'm very mixed up, Doran. The child loves me terribly, and I love her, but sometimes. . . . Benny would have been able to cope. It wouldn't have happened if she'd lived.' Doran thought of the photographs all over the vicarage of his dead wife Benita, so pretty, so merry-faced, sometimes holding a healthy smiling baby. Benny would have been able to cope, but she, Doran, could not.

Through the open window the sound of bell-practice floated in on the night air, Sam and his ringers getting into form for Sunday. They were tolling steadily, a monotonous melancholy knell. Doran suddenly felt she could stand it no longer, and got up to leave.

'Sorry, it's time I went. Lovely meal – tell Nancy that watercress soup was fabulous.'

'Must you go? All right, I'll walk back with you. We might see some fairies, who knows? No, I'm not delirious. It's Midsummer Eve, the Eve of St John, the most magical night of the whole year. We might see the Wild Hunt, phantom horses chasing a phantom quarry. . . .'

'I hardly think they'll be doing that in the High Street.'

'No? All right, we'll go by Cow Lane.'

Cow Lane wound parallel with the High Street, but on a higher level, so that it ran just below the upper windows of the High Street houses backing on to it. Tonight they were either curtained and dark or warm glowing squares of light, impenetrable. Doran was faintly envious of that life behind bedroom windows.

'I do like people who leave their curtains undrawn,' Rodney was saying. 'It's a positive education. . . .'

He stopped abruptly, staring at one of the lighted windows. It was a bedroom of a terraced cottage, one of several substantial Georgian buildings fronting on the High Street and backing on Cow Lane. They were within a few yards of it, every detail sharp and clear, like a good television picture.

Stella Meeson was standing at a low table facing the window. Two tall black candles, one on each side of the table, threw her features into sharp relief, the mouth relaxed and soft, the eyes half-closed. Her puff-ball hair flew up from her brow like silver flames. She was draped in something dark which hid her arms, but they could see her hands busy over the table.

Another candle-flame sprang up. She raised a blood-red candle for a moment, then set it down with the others. Her lips were moving rapidly, her eyes now shut.

'We shouldn't be watching this,' Doran whispered. 'Why on earth has she left the curtains open? Unless it's part of the ceremony. Come on. Suppose someone saw us, staring into a bedroom window?' But she was too fascinated to make the move.

'We must. Be quiet,' he whispered back.

Stella bent forward and lifted what looked like a metal vase or cup, held it above her head, lowered it and drank from it before setting it reverently down. Then she picked up another object, kissed it, and held it upright, close to the window.

Doran gasped. 'It's the dagger – the Haydon-Trees' dagger. It must be!'

'Ssh.'

In one movement Stella cast off the dark cloak. Underneath it she was naked. A white, graceful, nymph-like figure, she stood unmoving, then brought the point of the dagger sharply down on her forearm. As the blood sprang and began to drip Rodney grasped Doran's arm and pulled her away. They walked rapidly along Cow Lane, not speaking until they had turned the corner that led to the High Street.

'What on earth was that all about?' Doran asked.

'Witchcraft. The Old Religion, *Wicca*. Very nasty – very dangerous – and I will not have it in my parish.' Rodney's voice was grim.

'But – Stella. I know she gathers herbs and things, and Marcia told us about the books. But this is something quite different – isn't it?'

'Entirely. It looked to me like black magic, not just the nutcase kind, and if so she's in with others. She didn't work that lot out by herself. That knife – wherever it came from, it was an *athamé* – something used to cut designs in the air,

78

and also for ritual sacrifice. It was black-handled, did you notice? And she had the altar, the chalice and the red fire candle.'

'What a lot you know,' Doran said admiringly. 'Where did you pick it all up?'

'By studying it, deliberately. A good bowler's got to know something about batting, and vice versa – if one's an agent of God it's as well to be thoroughly boned up on the Devil.'

They were walking down the steep lane that led to Bell House, between hedges where late hawthorn bloomed along with dog-roses and sweet-smelling wild honey-suckle. Doran said, 'I wonder if it's true, the story about the Oxford dean who told a divinity student that if he couldn't bring himself to believe in a personal God by four o'clock that afternoon he'd be sent down next day.'

Rodney laughed. 'If it is, it happened a long time ago. They don't make 'em like that now. I don't find the slightest difficulty in believing in a personal Devil. His spies are everywhere, even here. I can sense one when I meet it.'

'You did that night at the Haydon-Trees' party, didn't you?'

'Unless I'm kidding myself, yes. Mumbray.'

'Mm. I think the Haydon-Trees were frightened away. They were certainly frightened when Sam and I called on them. I wonder if Mumbray visited them, and threatened them, and took that dagger when they weren't looking? They were quite determined not to let me know they'd had a visitor. But threatened them with what?'

Doran halted suddenly, startling an owl which had been perching on top of a hedgerow, meditating on its next kill. 'Rodney, I know something.'

'Share it.'

'They were fakes, those two. I saw it all, that evening when I was there with Sam, and they were a bit off guard. The accents weren't right, the manners weren't right, the attitudes weren't right. It was like examining a piece described as Chippendale, and finding it was wrong all over. They weren't Chippendale, they were kitchen-table deal. He wasn't a colonel, he'd never been one. And Mumbray must have found out.'

'You really are uncommonly clever. Looking back, I believe you're right.'

'I am, I know it. He blackmailed them and they wouldn't pay – they were mean. They couldn't face exposure so they left. I bet the Colonel was a clerk in the Pay Corps who got rich somehow. I can check, you know – Army Lists. That's probably what Mumbray did, when he guessed they weren't pukka. And,' she went on, excited, 'he pinched the black-handled dagger for Stella, to get her started as a fully-paid-up witch. How about that?'

Rodney smiled for the first time. 'If you're not careful you'll be replacing Holmes as the last and highest court of appeal in detection. Don't forget what he said: "It is a capital mistake to theorize before one has data." '

'Possibly. But I'm sure. What are you going to do about it?'

'I don't know yet. It's one hell of a problem, no joke intended. I'm going to think it out. Here we are.'

'And Rhona's left a light in the hall for me, so you needn't come up the path. Rodney, what an exciting night!'

He looked down at her upturned face, ghostly in moon-light, his own graver than usual. 'Don't get carried away, Doran, Watch and pray. And I mean that.'

Doran worried at the quotation on her way upstairs. It wasn't the Bible. On the landing it came to her: 'Christian, seek not yet repose, Hear thy guardian angel say, "Thou art in the midst of foes – Watch and pray." '

As she came back from the bathroom at the end of the passage leading to her bedroom, a faint sound caught her ear. It came from the oldest part of the house, the Stuart part, a few steps down from the Georgian bedroom floor. It was the rhythmic sound of sobbing, muffled but unmistakable.

Doran went quietly down the steps and paused outside the door that bore a little painted sign, DEBBIE'S ROOM, deco-rated with a spray of flowers and a picture of a teddy bear. The sobbing was steady, unceasing, heartbroken, pitiful to hear.

Rhona had said something about Debbie being under the weather – studying too hard, not eating properly, and what a relief it would be when the blessed exams were over. She had said it more than once, backed up by Vi as Chorus. Doran had not seen much of Debbie for the past few weeks, and if the child had looked pale or harassed – as perhaps she had, thinking back – it was only to be expected. But this was something else.

Doran tapped on the door softly. Abruptly the sobbing ceased, on a gasping breath. The room was utterly quiet as she entered it. A pretty room, a young girl's room, rosebud-sprigged curtains, tiny glass animals on the mantelpiece, a frilly-skirted dressing table.

Debbie was a hump in the bed, her head covered up by bedclothes, rigidly still. Doran touched her shoulder.

'Debbie. What's the matter? Tell me.'

A choking sob was all the response. Very gently Doran peeled back the sheet, revealing a tousled head buried in the pillow. The head turned to show a face painfully swollen and distorted with crying. The swimmy, tear-blinded eyes hardly seemed to recognize Doran, who coaxed, murmured and patted, faintly surprised in one corner of her mind at how easy it was to feel maternal affection for the distressed child who had been until now only a sharer of her house.

'Tell me. I don't care what it is, I might be able to help. Is it school, Debbie? Are you worried about exams?'

'I'm no good,' whispered the hoarse voice. 'Couldn't answer the questions. I've got . . . a third-rate mind.'

'What absolute nonsense! I never heard anything so silly. Why, you're one of the brightest people I know. Everybody says so. Where on earth did you get such ideas?'

'He told me. Said I was human . . . rubbish.'

'He? Who?' But she knew the answer.

'Said I . . . thought a lot of myself. But I was wrong. Said I'd never make a teacher or get a job in computers. And I'm so ugly,' the voice rose to a note of hysteria, 'I'll never get a boyfriend. Never get married, either. That's why I . . .' The sobbing began again – tearing, agonized heavings of the slight body.

'That's why you what? Debbie, Debbie, don't cry like that, or I'll have to call your mother.'

'Oh no, please! Not Mum.'

'All right. But I'm not leaving you like this. Now try to calm down, and I'll bring you a cup of tea.' Doran padded softly back to her own room, listening for any indication that Rhona had been awakened. None came. Her bedside teamaker produced two good cups. To one she added sugar from the stock kept in the landing cupboard for guests' use, and stirred in two herbal sedative tablets. When she returned to Debbie's room the girl was quieter, and drank the tea eagerly.

'That's good,' Doran said. 'Now I'm going to sponge your face and shake your pillows up and make you comfortable. Then you're going to sleep. I won't leave you alone, I promise. Look, I'll sit in this chair and put my feet up.'

The bed re-made and the bedside lamp moved to where it would not shine on Debbie's face, Doran retreated to her chair. Through the open curtains she saw the sky change. The moon became the ghost of a silver coin, then faded as a rosy glow began to spread, like a slow blush. The rose turned to orange (the exact colour of the inside of a chocolate cream, Doran thought), the orange to a pure, glorious gold. Disjointed words and glimpses of scenes flitted madly through her brain as she struggled not to sleep, not sure whether Debbie was sleeping silently or still awake. The first cheeps of the dawn chorus started up, swelling to a frantic twittering. Now she could hear even breaths coming from the figure on the bed. Very quietly she got to her feet, stiff and chilly, and went back to her own room. Once in bed, and warm, she dropped into sleep.

Next morning, with a thick head, smarting eyes and a furry mouth, she went down to breakfast. Rhona seemed much as usual. Debbie had gone to school, she said, in a bit of a rush after a bad night. 'All that reading, she didn't ought to do it so late.' So Rhona knew nothing.

Doran began to tell her. 'Rhona, there's something you ought to know. . . .' Rhona glanced at the clock.

'If you'll excuse me, I've got a hair appointment. Got to be there on time, as it's a perm.' A few minutes later Doran heard her leaving the house. Well, bad news would keep, and she would have time to think how to put what she had learned from Debbie. As soon as it seemed decent she dialled the vicarage number. Nancy answered, rather pleased to deny her.

'No, the vicar's not in, Miss Fairweather. He was called out early, must have been an hour ago – old Mr Collins, dying. If he's back in time he's promised to look in at the Senior Citizens' Club, and then he's off to Barminster for lunch with the dean and a diocesan meeting. So I don't know when you'll be able to catch him.'

Doran had made up her mind what to do, with or without Rodney. Her plans were foiled by a telephone call from Howell, snuffling theatrically. 'Can't make it today, sorry. Come down with a rotten cold last night, stinkin' bad, it is. Andrew made me stay in bed.'

'But that man's coming – the Brighton dealer who wants the screen and the rosewood chiffonier. He's loaded and I think he'll pay our price – we can't afford to miss him.'

'Then you'll have to see him yourself, won't you, gal.'

'But Howell, I wanted not to come in today. . . . Oh, all right. Don't bother to sniff any more. But if I find you've been putting me on I'll kill you. Better stay away from the Port Arms, that's all.' She banged the receiver down. There was nothing to be done about it; she drove to Eastgate as usual.

Rhona was not back from the hairdresser's, so the night's events would go unreported until she returned in the evening. It could make no difference to Debbie; they could all three talk the thing over later, and that would be the most sensible way of dealing with the problem.

She would remember, long afterwards, thinking that.

The afternoon was so fine and warm, and Helena so much better, that Nancy decided to bring her down to sit in her wheelchair in the sunny front garden of the vicarage. There she could see people passing and talk to them, if she were in a good enough humour, and with luck she would not grow querulous if her father got back late from Barminster.

She drowsed in the sun, the book she was reading fallen to the ground. A voice roused her.

'I think you've dropped this, young lady.' A man stood beside her, the book in his hand. He was nobody she knew – a large, well-dressed man, smiling down at her, a smile of intense benevolence. Somehow Helena found herself smiling back, though she normally scowled at strangers, whom she suspected of getting into conversation with her so that they could ask her morbid questions about her crippled state. But there was something different about this stranger, though Helena was not sure what it was.

'It's a lovely day,' he said. 'Would you like me to take you for a ride?'

'In your car?'

'No, in your chair. Perhaps I should have called it a walk, not a ride. Would your father mind?'

Helena considered. Her father had never actually told her not to let strangers push her chair. Perhaps he would be jealous, and that would be nice, and would also pay him back for leaving to go to Barminster and the silly old dean.

'He's not here. No, he wouldn't mind anyway. I'd like that.'

'Good. Shall we go to the castle ruins?'

'If you like. We used to go there when I was little. Mummy took me.'

They talked hardly at all as he pushed her along Church Lane, then turned off along an unfrequented footpath between high hedges, through a gateway into a field where sheep grazed, out into a small country road which led to the empty shell of grey stones which had once housed a Saxon queen. It stood on a grassy incline, among trees and bushes which were slowly creeping up to cover its walls.

As they drew near to it Helena, who had been half dreaming, was suddenly pierced by the memory of the picnics there with her mother, when she had been younger and healthy and able to walk. A little sob escaped her.

'What's the matter?' the man asked.

'I was only . . . . thinking about Mummy. Wishing.'

'You should forget about your mother, now you're a big girl. Almost grown up.'

It seemed an odd thing to say, but the brusqueness of it stopped Helena's tears. When they reached the wall of what had been the keep the man paused, surveying it.

'I think we'll go inside,' he said. 'There are other people down there. We don't want to be bothered with them, do we?'

'No. . . . But my chair's too wide to go through that door. Anyway, it says Keep Out on that notice.'

The man smiled, a brilliant smile, showing white, small, regular teeth. 'We won't concern ourselves with notices. And if your chair won't go through, you can, can't you?' Before she could answer he had lifted her out of the chair and was carrying her through the doorway.

Many before him had ignored the advice to keep out of the ruin. The rough grass was littered with paper, cigarette packets, tins, odd shoes and even more sordid evidences of human presence. The man looked round with satisfaction, nodding. He laid Helena on a reasonably free patch of ground, propping her back against a block of fallen stone.

'I don't like this,' she said. 'It's dirty. And I'm not comfortable.' He ignored her complaint.

'I think we should have a nice talk,' he said. 'About your father. I believe he and Miss Fairweather are great friends. I suppose she often stays at the vicarage?'

Helena stared. 'Oh, no, never. I don't like her, you see, and Daddy doesn't ask people unless I like them.'

'Indeed. But surely that doesn't stop your father from visiting the lady?'

'Don't know.' Helena was sullen.

'Oh, I think he does. And stays all night, perhaps?'

'No, he doesn't. He always has breakfast with me.'

'Are you sure?'

Helena was not sure, when he asked like that, in such a mocking voice.

'Last night, for instance. I happened to see your father and Miss Fairweather going for a walk, very late at night. Now where do you suppose he slept? Not at home.'

'He was, he was! I wasn't well and Daddy came into my room twice to see I was all right. So there.'

The man seemed surprised and disappointed by her answer. Then he said, 'He has a lot of visitors, of course. Young people. To see him in his capacity of parish priest.'

Helena shrugged. 'Oh, confirmation candidates and all that. They don't come to see *me*.'

The questions came thick and fast. Were these young people alone with the vicar? Was the door locked? How long did they stay? Were there more boys than girls? Did he spend more time with them than with adult visitors? To all of which Helena snapped that she didn't know, didn't care, hated people who came to the house and took up Daddy's time. 'And my back's hurting and I think my temperature's coming on again. I want to go now.'

His manner changed. She had failed to be useful to him, and so must be amusing.

'Do you know, there's a torture chamber somewhere in the castle. I've heard that it's below this floor, in the old dungeons.'

'I don't care.'

'Oh, but you will when I tell you what they used to do there. Especially to little girls.' He proceeded to tell her, ignoring her frantic head-shaking and the fingers stuffed in her ears. What he said was partly founded on historical fact, partly the product of his own maleficent imagination. When the telling became tedious he began to demonstrate just how painful the tortures could be; especially to little girls.

Helena shrieked. She was an expert shrieker, finding it most effective as an ultimate form of protest at home. With practice her shrieks had acquired a train-whistle quality audible quite half a mile away, and deafening at close quarters.

'Shut up,' said the man in a savage hiss. He scooped her up, carried her through the doorway, still shrieking, and flung her into the wheelchair. A party of sightseers on the far side of the castle stared and conferred, but he was pushing the chair rapidly down the knoll towards the road.

Helena was now too frightened even to shriek. She clung on to the arms of the chair, trembling and gasping, expecting to be jolted out of it by the speed of its progress. At some point in the nightmare journey she drifted into a kind of swoon, so that her captor had to anchor her in the chair by her collar. A few cars passed them, and heads turned, but on the footpath and in Church Lane luck was with him, allowing him to reach the vicarage unnoticed.

The house was quiet, nobody on the look-out. He pushed the chair through the gate and left Helena where she had been earlier in the afternoon.

Doran brought her car to an abrupt halt in front of her garage. The doors were shut, which was odd – Rhona usually had them open for her to drive straight in. In her preoccupied state she could well have failed to notice and slammed the car into them, which would have been a fitting climax to a thoroughly unsatisfactory day. The Brighton dealer had turned up almost two hours late, and then haggled and chaffered over the price of the two items she had hoped to sell to him. Driven past her patience she had lost her temper, and that was another useful connection gone.

On the stretch of dual carriageway leading out of Eastgate the Volvo had developed a flat. After twenty minutes of perilous walking she found a roadside telephone, trudged back to the car, and waited to be rescued by the AA. Now at last she was home, almost two hours later than her normal time.

'Rhona!' she called, inside the house. 'Sorry I'm late, but it's been a perfectly awful swinish day. . . . Rhona, what's the matter?'

The housekeeper was sitting at the kitchen table, her head on her arms, dark hair spilling over her shoulders as though she had been tearing it. At Doran's entry she lifted a ghastly face.

'Debbie,' she said. 'She hasn't come home. She never went to school at all this morning. I think I'm going out of my mind.'

7

The story came out in gasped sentences from a mother too shocked to sound like her usual collected self. The staff at school had not thought it particularly odd that Debbie had not turned up that morning. She had been looking peaky, her teacher said, and they supposed she was having a day at home. Nobody had thought to telephone Bell House.

Half an hour after the usual time for Debbie's return that afternoon Rhona had started to worry. Even if the bus had broken down and she had had to walk from Downs Corner she should have been home by now. That was when she telephoned the school, got no answer, and tracked down Debbie's class teacher's private number.

'Not seen her all day. No idea where she might have gone. So Miss Raye sent round to Angela, that's Debbie's friend in Prospect Road, and she hadn't seen her since the day before. So what's happened?'

Rhona's fine dark eyes, gazing up imploringly, were the eyes of a hunted and cornered deer, the eyes of the despairing Hero in Leighton's picture. Doran busied herself making tea. Tea, the English answer to disaster: consolation brewed in a pot. Only a few hours ago Doran had been making tea for Debbie.

She joined Rhona at the table. 'Now what do we do first? Get Sam Eastry on to it.'

Lydia Eastry answered the telephone. Sam was over at the vicarage. There was trouble, it seemed.

'Oh no! What trouble?'

Lydia couldn't really say. She was expert at not really

saying what case Sam was on at any given time. Doran rang the vicarage, and spoke to a flustered Nancy.

'It's Helena. She's been – I can't really talk now, Miss Doran. I'll get Sam for you.'

Sam listened to the story, of Debbie's disappearance and distress the night before. 'You ought to have got me sooner.'

'Rhona was in too much of a state.'

'Yes, she would be. Right, I'll get on to Eastgate. Be with you as soon as I can. Don't panic, don't panic.'

While they waited for him Doran chatted soothingly to Rhona. Debbie might have had some accident – a fall that had knocked her out, perhaps. Or she might have taken a fancy to go somewhere by herself that morning, somewhere she could think without interruption, revise her work – she had her schoolbooks with her. Perhaps she had gone to Eastgate, or up to Barminster to stroll round the streets or sit quietly in the cathedral, a favourite place of hers.

Rhona nodded to every suggestion. 'Yes. Yes, she might.' But her eyes kept straying to the window, the door, the telephone.

When Sam arrived they went over all the points again while he scribbled in his notebook. Then he sat down at the telephone and talked to his superintendent. Doran heard him saying '. . . I wouldn't take action so early, as a rule, but she's a responsible kid, not the sort to play hookey for fun.' Rhona was straining to listen, eager to interrupt. Doran beckoned her out of the room.

'You know, I've just realized I'm absolutely starving. I had a sandwich at lunchtime and that was all. Could you rustle me up something, there's a dear? An egg and a slice of toast, anything. And I'll go and wash and change.'

Rhona was pathetically eager to oblige. When she had gone to the kitchen Doran rejoined Sam, who had finished telephoning.

'This business last night,' he said. 'Debbie was very upset?'

'Terribly. I don't think I've ever seen anyone more so.' But she had recognized the child's state of mind from her own memories of abandonment to grief, when Ian had left her and the world seemed to hold no more promise. That, too, had been the dark night of the soul.

Sam made her repeat all the disjointed things Debbie had said. He wrote them down in his notebook. 'Third-rate mind. Human rubbish. Somebody's been getting at her, trying to destroy her self-respect.'

'And succeeding rather well. "He", she said, "he". You know where she's been studying – by invitation?'

'I know.' Sam was poker-faced. 'If anyone did that – said those things – to Ben, I'd be very inclined to take the law into my own hands.'

Doran picked up some vibration from him. 'This trouble with Helena. . . .'

'Sorry, can't discuss it yet. *Sub judice*, you might say. Ask the vicar, but not tonight. Here's the patrol car. Good.' He went out, and Doran saw him talking to a sergeant and Glen Liddell, the blond Adonis who was community constable at Elvesham, up the valley. After a moment he was back.

'Right. The sergeant and Glen are going out searching in the car and I'm taking a different direction on the bike. We'll ring in if we find her. And tell Rhona to try not to fret too much, though that's easier said than done. Ninety-nine per cent of these cases are children running off because they're under too much pressure at exam time, and as a rule they're back in a matter of hours when their money runs out. I'm not too worried, myself. So long.'

'Good luck,' said Doran fervently. Dear Sam, being sensible and brisk, when his instincts as a father told him all too clearly how Rhona was feeling, and what were her imaginings.

The car and the Honda roared away, their lights swallowed up in the gathering gloom. The sunshine of Midsummer Day had been lost in cloud early in the evening, and with the dusk rain had come, growing heavier, pattering down now like a steady assault of tiny bullets. The women settled down to wait. Doran persuaded Rhona to eat a little supper with her, then, with intent, got out the whisky decanter and poured a stiffish measure. Rhona drank it without appearing to taste it, though Doran had never seen her drink anything stronger than sherry.

91

Apparently casual, she poured a second and a third.

'Wouldn't you be more comfortable on the couch?' she suggested. And Rhona, who would not have dreamed of sitting down uninvited in her employer's drawing room, meekly moved over and allowed Doran to raise her feet, so that she lay on the sofa. The television set babbled on, an inane sitcom with canned laughter followed by a news bulletin and an earnest arts programme. Doran gazing blankly at the screen, glanced aside and saw that Rhona was asleep. Stealthily she moved off to get a coat which would serve as covering, then settled herself down in an easy chair.

Another night of sitting up with a distressed person. Life was falling into a very strange and unpleasant pattern.

No news had come by morning. At seven o'clock Sam looked in to say that no sign of Debbie had been found. 'The rain made it impossible to search as we'd have liked. The odds are that she's found some sort of shelter.'

Rhona shuddered. 'Cold and wet. . . .'

'Yes, well.' Sam was still brisk. 'I'm sure she'll have managed. I'll let you know as soon as we know anything ourselves.'

Doran telephoned Howell. He had mysteriously recovered from his malaise, to judge by the chirpy voice in which he answered, but relapsed as soon as he heard who was calling.

'So you're still with us, are you,' she snapped. 'Look, we've got trouble here. There's a crisis, I can't get away. If you're not quite at death's door I'd be obliged if you'd go round and open up the shop. Okay?'

Snuffling, he agreed. 'Managed to shift the pieces yesterday, did you, then?'

'No, I didn't. He messed about so long that I got fed up and told him not to bother.'

'You shouldn' 'a done that, gal. I'd have got our price, all right.'

'I know you would, but you weren't there, were you.' Damn, damn, she thought, hanging up. Why did everything happen at once? That awful day yesterday, Howell malingering, the car playing up, a good buyer failing to bite, and a polite but firm note from Ernest Tilman about her overdraft. But none of the irritations would matter if only Debbie could be found. Meanwhile there was trouble, whatever it was, at the vicarage. Trouble at the vicarage: it sounded like an old-fashioned whodunnit title.

Rodney looked as if he had been up all night, as indeed he had. For the first time in his life he had taken the eight o'clock Communion service without shaving, and his hair was rumpled. Doran felt an unwonted impulse to mother him. But he had Nancy to do that, of course.

Tersely he outlined the events of the previous afternoon. 'Nancy had gone for a rest on her bed and slept longer than she meant to. When she came down she found Helena on the lawn as she'd left her, but in a fearful state of upset.'

'I can hardly believe any of this. You mean Mumbray virtually abducted her, took her to the castle, and behaved like that . . .? I'm speechless. How is she now?'

'A lot better. Levison came and gave her a sedative. Oddly enough, I think the shock did her good, in a way. She's brighter this morning than usual – people are, sometimes, after a sort of disaster. She told me the story all over again, without breaking down. I suppose it's a good sign.' He took off his spectacles and passed his hand wearily over his eyes. 'Now what's this about bother at your place? Sam said something before dashing off last night.'

'It's a bit more than bother.' Doran told him the story. 'Mumbray again – it must be. He's done something awful to that child, like hypnotizing her to break her spirit. And it's driven her to this – to running away.'

'Don't quote me on it, but I rather think that's the sin against the Holy Ghost. "Whoever shall say, Thou fool, shall be in danger of hell fire." He must have meant something like that, mustn't he? Well, if you'll excuse me, I've got to go out.'

'Finish your breakfast first.'

'Can't. Dust and ashes, never did care for the taste.'

'Where are you going?'

'To The Oaks. I couldn't leave Helena last night, and the place isn't on the telephone.'

'Let me come with you, Rodney.'

'No. I don't want you mixed up in this nasty business.'

'I rather thought I was mixed up in it already. It's my fight as well as yours, you know. I may have been just inquisitive about this wretched man once, but it's more than that now – not only Helena but Debbie. And there's strength in numbers.'

He sighed. 'All right. We'll drive – I want to get this over.'

The door of The Oaks was answered by a woman who must be Mrs Butcher. Small, almost undersized, thin and colourless, she made no impression on the eye. Doran could think of no appropriate comparison, except perhaps a plastic mouse.

'We'd like to see Mr Mumbray,' Rodney said.

'Who shall I say?' Mrs Butcher's voice was as negative as her appearance. It seemed incredible that even her dull eyes had not noticed Rodney's clerical collar. Given their names, she said, 'I'll go and see,' and shut the door on them.

'Well!' Doran exploded. 'Of all the offensive rudeness. . . .'

'The Watcher at the Gates.'

'Does she think we've come after the spoons?'

The door re-opened. They were summoned into the room on the left of the hall which Doran had been in on her first memorable visit. It was just as forbidding, even with all the books in place; she thought the bookcase she had brought from the shop looked at her pleadingly, like someone sold into captivity.

Mumbray was seated behind the big partners desk. He did not rise to greet them, only gave them a cool good morning.

'May we sit down?' Rodney asked. 'We both have some questions to ask you.'

'Certainly.' He motioned them to small hard chairs.

'This concerns two children.' Rodney's manner was quiet, his voice serious and measured, as Doran had heard it in his sermons. All trace of his light manner had gone. Nervous herself, she admired his calmness.

'I understand,' he said, 'that you took my daughter from the vicarage garden yesterday afternoon, pushed her invalid chair to the castle ruin, took her out of it and assaulted her; as well as frightening her with some very unpleasant stories.'

Mumbray's face remained impassive. 'Really? And where did you hear *this* unpleasant story?'

'From my daughter. She was badly shocked, but quite capable of remembering everything that happened.'

'Except for one small detail. Whoever was involved in this unfortunate episode, it was not me. I have never met your daughter.' Mumbray was looking Rodney straight in the eyes, his massive head erect and immovable. Doran was reminded of the celebrated heads of American presidents cut into the granite of Mount Rushmore. The flat denial took her aback, so loud, emphatic and believable, or almost believable. For a moment she wondered if Helena had been fantasizing. After all, the child had been feverish the night before.

'Are you suggesting that my daughter is a liar?' Rodney asked. Doran intuitively knew that he, too, had had a doubt. Mumbray lifted his shoulders.

'As I told you, I don't know the young lady, or she me. It's not for me to comment on her powers of invention.'

Rodney surveyed him, a long, slow, disparaging look.

'They'd have to be considerable, to invent someone like you.'

Mumbray smiled. 'I think I shall take that as a compliment. If you persist in this curious delusion, perhaps you'll be good enough to produce witnesses to my abduction of your daughter. In the distance you mention we must have encountered some.'

'I'll find them, and give their names to the police. Doran, your turn.'

Doran said, strangely nervous, 'My housekeeper's daughter, Debbie Selling. I believe she's been studying here.'

No flicker of expression. 'Yes.'

'She's disappeared. She didn't go to school yesterday. The night before I heard her crying, and she told me she – she was very unhappy.' She began to stammer.

'She – she – she. . . . It seemed someone had been g – getting at her. Destroying her confidence. She was . . . afraid of failing her exams. She mentioned "he" or "him".'

Mumbray smiled. 'Which naturally refers to me? Well,

well, Miss Fairweather. I congratulate you on your powerful imagination. Nearly as remarkable as the other young lady's. So I took the trouble to browbeat this schoolgirl – is that how you'd put it? – for some strange reason of my own. What would you say that could have been?'

'Evil,' Rodney said. 'Pure evil.'

The smile was broader, plump and benevolent. 'Have you two young people ever thought of taking up fiction? You seem to me to have a great gift that way – both of you. Consider that my constructive suggestion to you for this morning.'

Rodney got to his feet in a swift elegant movement and stood looking down at the man behind the desk. Pleasantly he said, 'If I weren't wearing my canonicals I'd be very tempted to knock your . . . perhaps I'd better make it by-our-Lady block off. But I am – such a pity. Doran.'

She followed him with relief, feeling panic still in her trembling knees. There was no sign of Mrs Butcher as they let themselves out.

'Right.' Rodney was not seeing her or the featureless front garden. 'We'll go back over the ground between my house and the castle. Get any report of a sighting you can.'

It seemed impossible to them by lunchtime that Helena, her wheelchair and Mumbray had been seen by nobody at all. A good part of their journey had been in open land, but the rest well within sight of houses or pedestrians. Only the stretch of road near the castle was impossible to check, since drivers of any cars that passed them would have seen nothing remarkable in the sight of a man pushing an invalid child.

'I give up,' Rodney said. 'The Devil's children have the Devil's luck, as Nelson remarked when things were getting tough in the Med. Either nobody *did* see them or he somehow erased it from their memories. I'm going to tackle Helena again.'

She was downstairs, on the sofa by the French window. Her face, which had lit up at the sight of her father, closed against Doran, behind him.

'Helena,' Rodney said, 'I want you to tell me some of it again. I'm sorry, but it's necessary. Describe the man.'

'Tall. Big head. Grey suit.' Helena was looking out of the window, away from Doran. 'Funny eyes, sort of like ice.'

'The voice?'

'Posh. Loud. Do I have to go through it? My head aches. I want you to come and sit with me. Just us.'

'Darling, I can't. But Doran will, won't you?'

'Of course. I'll read to you if you like, Helena.'

The plain little face took on the look of Queen Victoria hearing a doubtful joke. 'I don't like being read to. My head aches *dreadfully*.'

Rodney sighed. 'All right, I'll send Nan to you.' In the hall he said, 'I'm sorry, Doran.' His arm rested briefly around her shoulders.

'It's all right. She's feeling pretty spiky at the moment. But I wish she wouldn't look at me as if I'd been rolling in manure.'

Dr Levison was coming through the front door.

'Ah,' he said. 'Perhaps one of you could drop this prescription in at the chemist's. I've strengthened it quite a bit – she needs calming down. Tell Nancy the dosage will be different.'

'Thank you.' Rodney put the prescription in his pocket. 'Will you tell me something – do you believe the man was Leonard Mumbray?'

A curious look crossed the doctor's sallow face. 'Do you doubt it? I don't, for a moment. Who else could it be?'

'No. . . . But he denied it quite flatly.'

'He would, wouldn't he, and I quote.'

'And,' Doran put in, 'we can't find anyone who saw them.'

Eli Levison shrugged. 'That's life. But someone's bound to come forward. Don't tell me the entire population of Abbotsbourne went into a coma simultaneously.'

Curiosity prompted Doran to ask, 'Do you know Mumbray well, Eli?'

Again the odd look. 'No. Why should I?'

'I thought – from the way you said, "Who else could it be".'

'I must go,' Levison said abruptly. 'Tom Fullathorn's on holiday, I've got all his visits to do as well as my own. See Helena gets the new medicine today, and make her walk about a bit, keep her circulation going. You're too soft with her.'

Doran was tempted to ask outright whether he was worried about something – his wife Esther, perhaps, or Sharon their delicate younger daughter. But it would have seemed impertinent, and his manner did not invite further questions.

Rodney was telephoning Sam Eastry. But the constable was out, involved in the investigation of a serious road accident. It was mid-afternoon before his bike roared up to the vicarage gate. He listened patiently to Rodney's story and Helena's own account. By this time she was thoroughly enjoying re-telling her adventure.

'Well, it sounds like Mr Mumbray, all right. But if he denies it flatly and there were no witnesses it'll be difficult to prove. I'll go and see him, and if we still get nowhere I'll ask for a detective-sergeant to interview him. We've got to be careful – he knows the law, I'm told. Should do, being a retired solicitor. Funny – this is the second time there's been suspicion attached to him, without a shred of proof.'

Helena was listening, wide-eyed. 'Is that who it was? Mr Mumbray? The one who's bought The Oaks?'

'We think it might be, Helena,' Sam said carefully. 'I wonder – Rodney, would it be a good idea if I took Helena there with me? And you as well, of course.'

'You wouldn't be nervous, darling, would you?' Rodney asked. She shook her head vigorously.

'Course not. Not with you and Sam to protect me. Can we go in a police car?'

'If Glen doesn't want it. He's up at the hospital waiting for the chap that was involved in this crash to come round and give evidence.'

Helena was charmed by the panda car, the stares of passers-by, the novelty of being carried from it in Sam's strong arms and the importance of their arrival at The Oaks. She insisted on being allowed to claw her way up the front steps unaided. Mrs Butcher opened the door to them – this time Rodney thought he saw fear in her pallid face.

'You can't see him, he's busy.'

'I'm afraid we must, madam. It's a police matter, and urgent.'

98

She hesitated. 'I'll ask. But I'm not sure . . . he won't like it. . . .'

But Mumbray received them, this time in what passed in that house for a drawing-room, high-ceilinged and sparsely furnished. It had the air of being unused to company. Sam put Helena in the only chair that looked at all comfortable, her stick-like legs dangling above floor-level, her eyes fixed on Mumbray.

'That's him, Daddy,' she said before anyone could speak. Mumbray smiled his strange powerful smile like the turning on of an unshaded white light.

'Good morning, young lady. We haven't met, I believe?'

'Oh, but we have. You. . . .'

Rodney broke in. 'This is my daughter. Constable Eastry suggested that we bring her to see you and settle this thing once and for all.'

'What an excellent idea.' His eyes never left Helena's face. Rodney thought of the old poacher's advice to his son, 'Let the dog see the rabbit'. A very large dog and a very small rabbit were confronting each other, and the dog was winning. Helena seemed to shrink in the big chair, her thin hands twisting together and her face working. Rodney began to regret bringing her. She had seemed so confident before, and now she was beginning to wilt. Mumbray was addressing her.

'Your father has been telling me that you and I went for a walk together, Miss Chelmarsh. That must have been very nice. But I don't remember it, you know – and I'm sure I should have done, if I'd had the honour of escorting such a pretty young lady.'

Very far from pretty at this moment, she stared back, without speaking.

'Now tell me, where are we supposed to have gone, and what did we talk about? Just remind me, there's a good girl. Was it down to the shops in the square, or round the cricket field? Did I buy you an ice cream, as I'm sure I should have done? What was it – chocolate, strawberry, vanilla? Strawberry, I expect. What did we talk about, now?'

Helena's face was now ashen. Rodney moved to her side, a hand on her shoulder.

'That's enough,' he said to Mumbray. 'Helena, just tell me – is this the man?'

She answered in a whisper. 'Don't know.'

There was no more to be got out of her. Mumbray smiled and smiled. Sam tried a few questions, such as where Mumbray had been the previous afternoon and who could testify to his presence. But he had been here at home, he said, and yes, his housekeeper had brought him tea. Dissatisfied, Sam motioned to Rodney that they should leave, and picked up Helena. This time she buried her face against his shoulder as he carried her to the car.

More questioning would only be harmful. The new medicine had arrived, and Nancy gave her a dose before putting her to bed with her favourite toy, a hideous-faced monkey with orange fur.

'I can't do anything else but leave things for the present,' Sam told Rodney. 'We'll get nothing out of him, and – well, I don't like to say this, but Helena's not . . . quite normal. Oh, I don't mean she's mental or anything, but she's not been well. She may have caught a glimpse of Mumbray somewhere when she's been outside, and sort of. . . .'

'Woven him into a fantasy. I don't believe it for a moment, but you may be right.' Rodney spoke wearily and bitterly. He wished, as he so often did, that he had a wife beside him, that Benny hadn't died, or that he could marry again, someone who would tolerate Helena and be tolerated by her. Someone with soft brown untidy curls and a vulnerable mouth and a sense of nonsense that perfectly matched his own.

Doran switched on the local edition of the evening television news. Somebody was demonstrating a new breed of miniature goat. Two councillors were scrapping in public about the demolition of Eastgate pier. A royal princess, all smiles and hat, was opening a college of further education. Doran failed to hear the clang of the ancient iron bell at the front door.

Sam was in the room, Rhona behind him: he had his arm round her, Doran noticed with surprise. At the sight of his expression she switched the set off. 'Sam?'

'I'm sorry, Doran. Rhona, I don't know how to tell you. But – Glen and the sarge from Elvesham have been combing the woods. Up near the quarry. They'd have done it sooner if it hadn't been for the accident, and the hospital.' He was struggling, painfully unwilling to tell his news. 'They found Debbie.'

Rhona sat down heavily. Doran looked the question there was no need to ask.

'Yes. Dead, I'm afraid. I hate to . . . I wish I could soften it, but. . . .'

It was Rhona who asked tonelessly, 'How?'

'Hanged. From a tree. With her own belt.'

8

It was the first violent death to shake Abbotsbourne since a rejected lover called Gideon Lamb had jumped from the church tower in 1876. In the streets and the shops there was no other topic of conversation. But Bell House was a silent place, without Debbie's quick footsteps on the stairs, the faint music of Debbie's transistor radio playing as a background to her studies. Doran found herself listening for it, again and again.

Rhona retreated into some fastness where nobody could reach her. Vi's loud vocal grief left her unmoved, tight-lipped and expressionless. Vi was baffled, almost angry with her sister.

'I can't fathom it,' she told Doran. 'When Jim passed over she let it all come out, cried and carried on something awful. Well, I said to her, You've got to think of your little girl, she's going to be upset if you are, poor mite, it's bad enough losing her daddy like that, but I might as well have talked to the moon. . . .'

'But that was a different sort of shock, wasn't it?' Doran said. 'Accidents do happen to farm workers, but a school-girl. . . .'

'That's what I say, it's a proper tragedy, and she did ought to show some feeling, I mean to say, she'll do harm to herself, keeping it bottled up like that. . . .'

'Vi, I do think it's a mistake to go on at her. Underneath, she's feeling more than any of us can imagine. Try leaving her alone for a bit.'

Vi shrugged. She was not one for leaving emotions alone.

Poor Rhona, poor Cassandra, who had once revelled in other people's disasters. Cry, Trojans, cry. But Cassandra herself could not cry.

Doran offered to stay away from the shop so that Rhona would not be alone in the house. 'I can get someone else to look after it for the time being.'

'That you can't, not this time of the year, with all them tourists wanting to buy things.'

This was very true. An antique dealer is principally interested in selling to the trade, but the casual customer provides useful turnover money. Doran and Howell would not lower themselves to stock what Bernard Levin was inspired to christen ilth – leering comic animals inscribed A Present from Eastgate, faint and vulgar imitations of Dresden groups made in Taiwan, copies of a well-known Brussels statuette with which to delight your friends because it was also amusingly functional. But the shop-window display included modern horse brasses, strings of vaguely ethnic beads, brooches inscribed Mizpah, and small horrid ashtrays, saucers and juglets. They sold in quantities, and sometimes larger objects despised by dealers sold as well. Doran returned to Eastgate, leaving Rhona to go impassively about her usual duties.

Only once she spoke, sensing Doran's embarrassment.

'You'll have to excuse me if I seem to be callous, not crying or anything, Miss Doran. It was the second time it's happened to me, you see, and I can't go through all that again, being torn up.'

Doran nodded. She knew now the full meaning of the term Spartan.

The coroner's inquest was held in a hall once used for meetings of the Order of Oddfellows. Listeners were briefly harrowed by Dr Levison's evidence. Debbie had launched herself from the foothold of a branch growing low down a tree, which had snapped off under her weight, so that she could not have stepped back on it to save herself at the last moment. The headmistress of the school testified to the keen and conscientious work the girl had been putting in, both at school and at home. Rhona, poker-faced and flat-voiced, said that her daughter had been unwell and off her food for some time before her death, and that this had certainly been the result of work and worry.

Doran rose from her seat on the public benches and asked to be allowed to give evidence. Somewhat surprised the coroner agreed. Without embroidery she told of her vigil with Debbie the night before the disappearance, repeating the words she remembered so vividly.

'She said she'd been told that she was no good, human rubbish, unfit to teach or work or even get married. A man had told her this.'

The coroner, who had been scribbling notes, looked up.

'What man, Miss Fairweather?'

'She didn't say. But it can only have been Leonard Mumbray. She'd been studying in his library for several weeks.'

The coroner came from Barminster and knew few people in Abbotsbourne. Eli Levison supplied him with brief details about the owner of The Oaks.

'I see. Is there any confirmation of this?'

Nobody spoke.

'Well, then, has anybody reason to suppose that Mr Mumbray would be likely to speak in this way to a child?'

Doran glanced round the room. Rodney was not there. Vi and Rhona sat shocked. Stella Meeson was bending forward eagerly, her lips parted; Marcia, beside her, seemed about to speak, but stayed silent. Doran said, 'Yes, I have.'

'Please tell us what you know.'

'I don't know anything for certain. But I'm fairly sure that he was the cause of Major Miles dying so suddenly, and Colonel and Mrs Haydon-Tree leaving the village – and I know he took the vicar's young daughter away from home and frightened her badly.'

Amid a susurration of whispering the coroner looked thoroughly put out. He consulted Eli Levison, who shook his head and muttered something, and the Abbotsbourne solicitor, John Mandel, on his other side. The coroner banged on the table for silence and addressed Doran, frowning.

'Has Mr Mumbray been given the chance to answer these suspicions against him, Miss Fairweather?'

She began to stammer, cursing herself for it. 'Yes. Well, I – faced him with them – some of them. About Debbie. And Rod . . . the vicar took Helena to see him. Constable Eastry knows.' She caught Sam's eye, but he gazed placidly back.

'And what did Mr Mumbray reply to the accusations?'

'He – well, he said they were all nonsense. Naturally.'

'Naturally.' The frown was deeper. 'It seems to me there is absolutely no substance in what you tell me, Miss Fairweather, and I can see no reason to ask for a further inquiry. Whatever your own feelings may be, the jury must not be influenced by them. I'd suggest that you think carefully before airing your views in public. There is such a thing as the law of slander, you know.'

Thoroughly quelled, Doran sat down. She had made a fool of herself to no purpose. The jury's verdict was suicide while the balance of the mind was disturbed, and the coroner added a few words of his own on the pressures put on modern youth. The hearers dispersed, chattering; Doran felt herself being carefully avoided.

Disconsolately walking down the street towards the square she was aware of quick footsteps behind her. Eli Levison was at her side. If he had appeared tense at the vicarage he seemed on the edge of collapse now.

'Doran.' He was breathing heavily and there was wildness in his dark eyes. 'Don't repeat any of that stuff, will you? Not to anybody. Don't let *him* get to hear of it.'

'But – why? It's all true. You said yourself, to me and Rodney, that it must have been him.'

'That doesn't matter. Promise me you'll keep quiet in future.'

'What's the use of that, when they've all heard me? You know how Abbotsbourne people talk.'

'My God, yes. Listen – if it does get back to him and he says anything to you, tell him I was the one who advised the coroner not to follow it up. Can you remember? For my sake.' The brusque, opinionated doctor was pleading with her.

'Well, yes,' she said. 'I expect he will get on to me – I hope he does. But just tell me what this is all about, Eli.'

He shook his head miserably, like a dog which has taken a savage punch in the face. 'I can't. It's dangerous. Do as I ask you.' Swiftly he left her, got into his car and drove off, leaving her staring after him.

He's being blackmailed. The thought came to her so strongly that she almost spoke it aloud. Eli Levison had something in his background which Mumbray knew about and had threatened to reveal unless – unless what? Was he extracting money, medical services, drugs, from his victim? And if that was Mumbray's game, who else was being blackmailed?

Of course – the Haydon-Trees, she had guessed that already. But the persecution of Debbie and Helena had not been blackmail. 'Evil,' Rodney had said, 'pure evil.' Doran shivered.

She thought, walking home, what a dismal occasion the inquest had been. But at least the body had not been displayed on a table in an open coffin, as it would have been in Victorian days. Something to be thankful for. . . .

As she passed Laburnum Cottage, noticing Marcia's car standing in the road, Marcia herself bobbed up behind the hedge, startling her.

'Come in. I want to talk to you. Quick!' As she half-pulled Doran into the garden it was obvious, even in the open air, that she had been drinking. Doran found herself pushed on to an uncomfortable wrought-iron chair with Marcia almost knee to knee with her in another. Marcia was flushed and excited, her button eyes searching Doran's.

'You were marvellous, marvellous! To stand up and denounce him like that when nobody else had the courage. I do so admire you, my dear.' She stretched forward to put a hand on Doran's thigh, where it lay heavy and hot. 'I should have done it myself, I do know that, but I couldn't face it, all the scandal. . . .'

It was irresistible. 'All what scandal?' Doran asked gently.

Secrecy and drunken garrulity struggled in Marcia's face. 'I know you won't tell a soul. I can trust you, because you hate him too.' She clutched Doran's hand and held it tight. 'It was a long time ago, when I was a silly girl. I had a . . . I had a baby. I don't want to talk about all that because it was horrible. I was different then. Men – I hate them, do you? Oh no, of course. . . .'

'You had a baby,' Doran reminded her.

'Yes. The man wasn't going to do anything about supporting me, but I made him, of course, took him to court and filed a paternity suit, so he had to pay up. The beast, he deserved it.'

Doran waited patiently, as Marcia went to the open window and came back with a wine bottle and two glassess clutched between her fingers. She waved them invitingly.

'Like some? No? Mind if I do?' She helped herself to a glassful and sat down again.

'Do go on,' Doran said. 'Was this man. . . .'

'He was nobody, can't remember his name. I got the child adopted and never saw him again. Or the father. But I suppose my address stayed on the solicitor's file, and when I retired and moved here . . . well, it was easy enough to trace me, wasn't it?'

'Easy for the father?'

'No, of course not. For the solicitor. Leonard Mumbray.'

Doran felt like one who sees a great light. 'Ah. Yes.'

'I think he came here because of me, to torment me and soak me. I'm not a rich woman, you know, all I've got is my company pension and a nest-egg my mother left.' She drained the glass. 'And now this business with Stella. It was bad enough before, but I could have put up with it if she'd stayed . . . like she was. Now she's doing it because of him and everything's impossible.' She hiccuped and tears began to run down her flushed cheeks. Doran, whose hand had been captured again, detached it and stood up, murmuring that she must go.

'I knew you'd understand, a nice girl like you. I knew I could trust you,' Marcia gulped. 'After all, you've got it to face yourself, haven't you?'

'What have I got to face?'

'Well, scandal. All that talk about you and the vicar.'

Doran went quickly to the gate, not trusting herself to answer. Shutting it, she heard a soprano laugh behind her. Stella was framed in the open casement window, and she was smiling, a mocking feline smile.

Sam Eastry and his team were ringing a muffled peal for Debbie's funeral. The ball of the clapper of each bell was clothed with a leather muffler to produce 'a most doleful and mournful Sound', as the old manual instructed. They knew the business well. 'Ring one pull round and all stand but the tenor, but let her be rung one pull by herself, then ring two pulls round and the tenor two pulls by herself, then three pulls and the tenor three, then four and the tenor four, then five and the tenor five, then six pulls round and the tenor to be rung as many strokes by herself as the person is years old that is to be buried.'

Their voices rang out one by one – Evangelist, the treble, Sancta Maria, the second bell, Jacobus the third, Saint Paul the fourth, Jesu the fifth, and Great Harry the tenor. To Sam who cared for them and knew them better than anyone living, the old words inscribed around them sang in their tones.

'*Hic est historia Iohannis. Sancta Maria ora pro nobis. Jacobus Rex memento Regem coeli. Sancte Paule ora pro anima mea. Jesu est amor meus. Henricus Magnus 1540.*' Three had hung in the belfry since the rape of the monasteries, two since the star of Elizabeth Tudor had set. Now the second Elizabeth's star was shining, and another young life had gone out.

Sam had rung out the life of his own daughter Jane, and that had only been nine strokes of the tenor. Now he laid aside his rope and with his team went down from the ringing chamber into the church.

Doran sat in her favourite pew more than half-way down the nave. Seated there, she was not so near to Rodney that they were in danger of sparking thoughts off each other – he need not look at her unless he wished. At this service he was withdrawn behind his calling, and she would not meet his eyes to pull him back into her world.

109

The solemn phrases came and went in a sanitized version of the old service At the Burial of the Dead. Office-ese, Rodney called it; you addressed God as though he were the chairman of a company and Shakespeare wouldn't have understood a word of it. Rodney mounted the pulpit and gave a short, tense address mentioning none of the clichés about the deceased having gone to a better land, only that she had been cruelly cut down in her youth. He sounded, Doran thought, very angry. Then a hymn was sung, from the section For the Young.

It was not the hymn Doran would have chosen, the terrible avenging tune which marches through Verdi's *Requiem. Dies irae, dies illa, Solvet saeclum in favilla,* the generations consumed to ashes. The ashes of Deborah Mary Selling, soon to be interred in the section of the churchyard reserved for cremation burials.

Doran, Rhona and Vi walked home together, nobody saying much. We English, what do other nations make of us Doran wondered? Ozzy was working in the front garden, happily watering the beds. It was the wrong time of day, since flowers should not be watered in the heat of the sun, but it was something he knew how to do and could not make any serious mistakes over. He straightened up as they approached.

'Them clothes, as you put out for Oxfamine – can I 'ave 'em?'

'What do you want with children's clothes?' Rhona snapped.

'Oh, I'll find a use for 'em, don't you worry.' Ozzy's small eyes gleamed as his ancestors' had done when alighting on a heap of scrap metal.

'I suppose it doesn't matter. Take them if you want them.'

'Ar,' said Ozzy with consummate tactlessness, 'so long as you don't 'ave reminders, you don't notice so much, do yer. My old mother, she allus believed in making a clean sweep after a Passing. Oh, and I knew there was summink else, only my memory's that bad.' He beat his brow theatrically with his knuckles. 'Poor ole Ozzy, mind's goin'. That rabbit of Debbie's, you won't want that no more, will yer, so I'll take it off yer 'ands, and chop up the 'utch for firewood.' He beamed, the rabbit already simmering gently in the pan his

110

fancy provided for it, with onions and a few herbs, giving off a delicious old-fashioned savour.

Rhona's face changed suddenly, frighteningly, as though a mask of tragedy had been clapped on it. She screamed 'No!' and thrusting Ozzy violently aside ran towards the back garden.

Ozzy scratched his head. 'What's got into 'er?'

Vi snorted. 'You may well ask, you stupid old man.'

'Why, whatever did I do?'

'You Touched a Chord, that's what you done – isn't that right, Miss Doran?'

'Very probably. Ozzy, I shouldn't mention the rabbit again if I were you. Come on, Vi, lunch.'

The kitchen door was locked and bolted on the inside; thieves are well known to read funeral announcements. Rhona was outside it, the brown rabbit clutched in her arms, tears streaming down her face. Wordlessly she dashed past Doran towards the stairs. 'Thank God,' Doran said to Vi. 'You were right, Ozzy did touch a chord. Mopsy's the last living link with Debbie for her.'

Vi pottered about the kitchen wearing a set expression which Doran knew well. Not looking up from the salad she was washing in a sieve, she said, 'You didn't ought to have come out with all that about Mr Mumbray, in front of all them people. It wasn't nice.'

'Perhaps not, but I'm afraid it was true.'

'The coroner didn't seem to think so. And I never saw nothing like that at The Oaks. If he was that kind of man there'd be some signs, stands to reason.'

'What signs? Riding-whips over the mantelpiece? Framed prints of the Inquisition? How does he treat Mrs Butcher, by the way?'

'Hardly speaks to her – she seems to understand what he wants, without. Anyway, like I was saying, you didn't ought to have said them things. It upset Rhona, I can tell you, when she'd thought it was only the exams that was worrying Debbie. Upset me, too.' She chopped parsley, with angry thuds. 'You want to be careful what you say.'

Doran sighed. 'Oh, well. I wish to God I'd told her myself,

111

that morning. I suppose the whole of Abbotsbourne and district knows about it now, so we'll see how the gentleman takes it when he hears.'

'He won't be hearing, not yet. They've gone away. She told me yesterday. I've got the key to go in and see to things.'

'How long are they going to be away?' Doran thought of the key and its possibilities.

'Didn't say.'

Rhona did not come down to lunch. Doran's spirits were weighted by flat depression and the uncomfortable awareness of being criticized. Perhaps she should not have spoken out at the inquest. Perhaps the whole thing was delusion. Suddenly the atmosphere of her home was unbearable. Leaving Vi in charge, she drove to Eastgate. It was early-closing day, but she would open the shop and try to erase the unpleasant impressions of the morning. Keats complained that other people's identities rubbed off on him, and so they did, eyes and voices and feelings all round one like a cloud of witness for the prosecution.

Few customers came to the shop. An American couple in search of an old mechanical toy for grandchildren back home were unable to believe that such things were only to be found in the shops of specialist dealers and cost the earth when found. A student riffled aimlessly through a job lot of prints cut from books, examined every volume on the shelves, and left without buying. Young parents brought in an infant in a pushchair and a toddler who ran about clutching at everything within reach, finally demolishing a Dresden-type vase which Doran had rather liked.

'Don't see why we should pay,' said Father aggressively. 'You leave things about like that, kids'll get at 'em.'

'That's right,' confirmed Mother.

'If you'd kept him under control he wouldn't have got at it, and there *is* a notice in the window,' Doran pointed out.

'Don't expect a little kid like him to read it, do you, miss?'

'No, but I expect you to.'

They left without paying. Short of summoning the police there was nothing Doran could do to enforce her rule about breakages. By the end of the afternoon she felt as fragile as the vase had been. Driving back to Abbotsbourne with the car radio loud, to drown her thoughts, she knew that she was reluctant to go home. When she reached the square Winnie Bellacre was opening the front door of the Rose. On impulse she parked and went in.

'Evening, Doran. Not often we've the pleasure of seeing you this early.'

'I know. Suddenly I felt like bright lights, sweet music, strong wine. Or something.'

Glancing at her curiously, Winnie started a tape that played an inoffensive selection of classical works arranged for less purist ears, and switched on the string of fairy lights over the bar. In his fatherly heart there was a soft spot for Doran. He had sized her up as a lonely lass with none of these daft ideas about women doing without men. What she needed was a husband, the sort of supportive husband he was to Rosie. Might be old-fashioned, but he knew he was right. Serving her with the beer she asked for, he meditated on the young men who came into the Rose, and their suitability for the job. He was all the more pleased when his next customer proved to be Rupert Wylie. A bit of a Flash Harry, Rupert, but a nice enough lad underneath, when you got to know him, and well off with it. Winnie watched approvingly as Rupert made straight for Doran.

'Well, well, surprise, surprise! What are you doing propping up the bar at this hour?'

'Drowning my sorrows. What are you, come to that?'

'Well.' Rupert turned on her his special smile, kept for pretty women and clients with cash in hand. 'If you must know, I saw your Volvo outside. Just for once, I thought to myself, I'll get that wench to myself, without the usual mob surging round.'

'And now that you have, what are you going to do with her?'

'Did I mention to you a little place I've found up in the Downs at Elvesham – the Oast House, sort of wine bar and restaurant?'

'Yes, you did. You asked me to have dinner with you and I couldn't.'

'Then I'm asking you again. Come on, Doran. It's a beautiful evening and the BMW's just had her million-mile service. You look as depressed as hell – come out and be done good to.'

'All right – I will. Just for once. In fact I'd like it.'

'Good girl! Winnie, give her a Scotch to go with that and another for me – we're taking to the hills. Better phone. Right.'

Doran heard him telephoning for reservations, polite, assured, wholly in command, and smiled, suddenly lighter of heart. Angels often come disguised, this one more handsomely than usual.

The shining, sleek car flashed through the narrow steep lanes like a powerful fish intent on its next meal. The plump faces of pink dog-roses brushed its windows, swallows swooped in a clear blue sky and Rupert sang. Occasionally they met a farm vehicle, retreating into the nearest space to let it pass, while Rupert exchanged courtesies with a grinning driver. The inn was at the summit of a wider lane ending in open meadows starred with grazing sheep. Between the twin round oast towers someone had built a comely house of Queen Anne design in the same brick, now the colour of fading red roses by the light of the setting sun. Cars sporty and substantial were ranged in the side park.

'I told you people were getting to know it,' Rupert said as they waited for their aperitifs in a room full of exotic indoor plants, huge soft chairs and sofas, and low tables covered with glossy up-market magazines. 'Pity. One used to have it more or less to oneself.'

'One?'

'Well, one and one's party. You'll probably hate the dining room, all country oak repro, but it'll be a change for you, living in a world of genuine period pieces as you do.'

They drank large cold martinis in Stuart crystal glasses, and Doran began to feel expansive.

In the restaurant, which as Rupert had said was full of settles, love-seats, court-cupboards and chairs with gothic carvings rioting all over their backs, a waiter of uncertain nationality led them to a corner table draped in blossom-pink linen. The waiter seemed to know Rupert well.

A crisp chilled white Burgundy came with the hors d'oeuvres, an urbane Châteauneuf with the *boeuf en croute,* and with the ice *parfait* a delicate Muscadet. Throughout them, Rupert talked. He had a repertoire of house-agency stories varying from the ludicrous to the scandalous, and another one of what he termed conspiel, used to pull the customers in.

' "Investment potential" means it's too big to live in, you'd have to let it off. "Realistically priced", they couldn't shift it so they've come down to what it's actually worth. "Super starter home" means a crummy two-up-two-down just by the station. "Ideal for the commuter" means actually *at* the station. "Beautifully modernized", a DIY man's done it up in polystyrene. . . .'

'Enough, enough.' Doran waved her glass. 'All men are liars, but estate agents are the biggest liars. Are *you* a liar, Rupert – I mean personally?' His outline was wavering curiously against the rosy curtain behind him. He leaned forward.

'You've got a mermaid's face, Doran – did you know? Eyes like that special grey-green waves go in sunshine, and a pink coral mouth, and hair like that very pretty sort of curly seaweed.'

'I'm not a mermaid, I'm a . . . a tree-spirit. A Dryad, that's it. Someone told me. There, I said you were a liar. Didn't I? What's your birth-sign? I'm Gemini, we're terribly inquisitive and always looking for a kindred spirit. I should think you might be Taurus, you've got that sort of head. . . .'

'Well, I'm definitely not Virgo, and I didn't imagine you were. Come on. Let's not bother with coffee, unless you want it awfully.' She would never be more compliant than she was now, all the wryness and wariness gone from her, washed away in wine. He half-supported her to the car, settled her comfortably and drove to a shadowed glade where there was cover from the road.

The rear seat of the car could be pushed back to afford extensive room. Doran watched Rupert preparing it. ' "A bed",' she murmured, ' "a bed, cried Clerk Saunders, A bed for you and me." ' Rupert, unfamiliar with the balladry of the

115

Scottish Border, pushed her in briskly and followed her.

His hands and lips were persuasive. She began to respond, tentatively at first, then enthusiastically. Wild pleasure at relief from long starvation swept over her, yet even as it mounted she was aware of a small, ghostly Doran perched somewhere in the corner of the car roof, watching and shaking its head.

They drove home almost in silence, Rupert vexedly conscious that something had gone wrong, in spite of the success of his foolproof seduction plan, Doran staring out of the window at the gathering dark and the pin-points of yellow light springing up in the windows of farms and cottages.

Howell Evans and Doran descended the steps of the house where they had been viewing the contents of an executors' sale. Eastgate was not looking its best in sea-mist which had failed to clear and a light but steady drizzle. The castle had faded on its height into surly cloud, seagulls mocked harshly. Only the shops on Marine Parade, offering garish souvenirs, postcards and ice cream, made any show of cheerfulness.

'Well, that was a right load of old rubbish,' Howell said. 'Wouldn't give twopence for the lot, not with a Knibb longcase thrown in for makeweight.'

'Oh, go on, you would. Anyway, I thought you'd have liked that cruet set of the three Welsh ladies in steeple hats,' said Doran nastily. He glanced at her, huddled in a drab blue hooded macintosh. Her cheeks were pale and her lips drooped. Grabbing her arm, he directed her towards a revolving glass door. 'Come on, we're going in here.'

'It says Crab and Lobster House. I don't want crabs and lobsters.'

'It also says Best Bitter and Real Ale Bar.'

Doran shuddered. 'Don't. I couldn't touch drink in any form.'

'Yes, you could, just what you need.'

Seated at a table in the quiet bar decorated by fishy murals, Doran found that after all the cool golden beer went down well, soothing her outraged digestion.

'Better? Thought so. Your old Uncle Howell always knows. Let's have it, then – what's the gripe? Boozer's gloom it looks like to me.'

'Alcoholic remorse sounds nicer. Game for a page or two of *True Confessions?* I don't really care whether you are or not, I'm going to confess truly. Then you can take me down to the beach and give me a good kicking – I'd enjoy that, I honestly would.'

'Masochist.'

'That too. Howell, last night I went out with a man I hardly know and let myself be conned with an over-priced meal in a plastic restaurant made over from an honest oast house, repro. Jacobean and pink light-shades, you know the sort of thing.'

'And?'

'And I drank far too much, knowing I was and shouldn't. You don't need to say "and" again, because it finished up just the way it was meant to, in the back of his car. The back of a car, I ask you! How low can one sink?'

Howell pondered. 'Could have been the floor. This guy, did you fancy him?'

'Yes and no. I quite liked him, and now I never want to set eyes on him again. That's what it's done to me. And I don't blame him a bit, don't think that. He thought I was an easy lay, a pushover, and I was. Anybody's for the price of a drink – I deserve to feel as if I'd eaten a can of worms, which I do. I suppose it shouldn't have mattered. Everybody does it, after all. I just know it did matter – for me. God knows why. Howell – I expect it's different for you, but do you – have you ever, well, taken up with somebody who wasn't right, just because . . . I don't mean like you and Andrew. . . .' She floundered and halted, embarrassing herself into silence.

Howell let a small serpent of ash fall slowly from his cigarette, watching it thoughtfully. 'Two things my old mam used to tell me. Always count your change – and keep your trap shut when need be. It sounds better in Welsh.'

'Oh, Howell, I'm sorry. Don't mind me, I'm just babbling.'

He gave her his rare smile. 'Trouble with you, gal, you're too bloody romantical. You're no fairy nor no angel, nor is any of us, and I speak from longer experience than you've had, you with your university education taking up the time you ought 'a been living.'

118

'You can do a lot of living at university.'

'That part of the trouble?' He cocked an eyebrow.

'Yes. You're very shrewd, Howell, and quite right. I *am* too bloody romantical and it's time I grew up. Of course it was all perfectly normal and I've been making a fuss about nothing. Now I feel better.' She drained her tankard. 'Do you know what I'm going to do this afternoon? Strip all that furniture in the storeroom, all that pine stuff with nasty varnish on it. I'll get nice and tired and possibly blister my hands with stripper. Sorry to treat you to a dose of Our Readers' Problems.'

' 'S all right. I tell you what, gal, you been thrown by all this Abbotsbourne business, the kid and that. Stands to reason you don't feel normal, murders and suicides every few minutes, well, it's a bit of a facer, in a place like Abbotsbourne, good works and chapel bun-fights like. Not exactly Dallas, is it?'

'Bun-fight . . . I prefer muffin-worry, myself. But you're right again – nothing's normal there this summer. I can't remember how it was before – nice, probably. Why did one ever complain?'

Out in the street the rain still fell persistently. As they walked down Harbour Street they encountered Peg and Meg, huddled into anoraks, Meg's long patchwork skirt trailing on the shining cobbles.

'Kiss kiss,' she greeted them automatically in passing.

'There's coaches in,' called Peg. 'Funny how they come, even this weather. They're round the shops like flies.'

'Ta, mate.' Howell gave Doran's side a shove. 'Come on, we'd best open up.'

A grey languid August drifted by, bringing no more calamities to Abbotsbourne and a horde of undaunted trippers to East-gate. It was the nearest the town got to a high season, and Doran was dismayed when Howell announced that he was departing with Andrew for a fortnight's package tour holiday in Corfu.

'But you can't.'

'I can, too. Watch me, baby. Bring you back a bottle of olive oil.'

'You can drown in olive oil for all I care, you rat.' She resigned herself to the prospect of manning the shop single-handed, for the benefit of the visitors who crowded Eastgate's narrow streets. The foreign day-trippers, most of them youths and girls from France, spent their time and money wandering inter-twined with cans of Coke or ice lollies at their lips, shooting suspicious looks from dark eyes. Trade, or at least interest, came from the coachloads of elderly folk, short fat men self-conscious in open-necked shirts and short fat women with meticulously waved and curled white hair, addressing Doran in Northern voices as 'Luv' and in search of a nice little bit of something to take home. More often than not they failed to find it, settling with uneasy giggles for samples from Doran's prized stock of old postcards depicting large men in striped bathing-drawers complaining that they couldn't see their Little Willies, or saucy mini-skirted chambermaids pausing at hotel bedroom doors to inquire, 'Are you up, Sir?' Doran enjoyed serving such customers, sending them away with a spice of innocent lascivious fun to brighten their lives.

One day brought a surprise. Tall, bronzed and gilt-haired, Bob Woods with his bride on his arm, blooming like a deep red rose in early pregnancy. Doran kissed them both, venturing to comment on the impending baby.

'Thanks,' Bob said. 'We couldn't be happier. Barbary's not been too well, have you, pet, but now the three months is up she's going to be all right.' He touched her hair and brushed her shoulder with his hand. Can't get enough of her, thought Doran. Heigh-ho.

Bob wandered round the shop, picking up and putting down. He paused at a small picture on the wall, a watercolour group of stiffly crinolined ladies and furbelowed children being waited on at tea in a garden by turbaned servants. 'This. Indian, isn't it?'

'That's right. Primitive. A European family, done by a native artist, not long before the Mutiny. Very sad, if you think about it. They probably all got murdered.'

'Greta would like it – don't you think so, Bar? Her people came from near Delhi.' Doran, with an effort, identified Greta as old Mrs Singh.

'Yes, I expect she would like it,' she said, 'but it's a bit expensive. It really belongs to a set that got broken up – if I had the lot they'd be worth a fortune.'

Bob whistled softly at the price-label. 'Lot of money.'

'I could come down a bit, for you. It's usual.'

'Well, thanks. Can I have a think?' Knows about plastics, Doran thought sympathetically, nothing about pictures, but natural good taste. Barbary was rambling gently on about her baby.

'If only Daddy could have seen him, or her . . . I think he'd have liked a boy. But then again, grandfathers are supposed to favour girls, aren't they? Oh, Doran, if it hadn't been for that – awful business, he wouldn't have died, I'm sure of it.'

Bob was at her side, holding her. 'Steady, darling. Don't upset yourself. Dr Levison did warn you.'

'How is Eli Levison?' Doran asked. 'Last time I saw him I thought he could have done with some of his own sedatives.'

'Yes, he was dreadfully jumpy when I started going to him,' Barbary said. 'He's not so bad at the moment, though.'

I wonder, Doran thought, if that's anything to do with a certain party being away from Abbotsbourne, and if so, how many other people are feeling calmer? Like a black cloud being lifted.

Bob handed her the picture. 'I'll take it. How much, then?'

'Five pounds off,' Doran said magnanimously. 'I'll wrap it nicely for you.' Into tissue paper went the pink cheeks and white muslins of the memsahibs, the brown profiles and handlebar moustaches of their attendants. 'I hope Mrs Singh enjoys it. Let me know.'

She had not long to wait. Reading in bed that night, she was roused by the frantic clangour of the front door bell. She unlocked and unbolted the door, keeping it on the chain. On the step Bob loomed, thunder-faced.

'Good heavens, Bob, you look like the wrath of God. What on earth's the matter? Come in.'

He thrust a piece of paper at her, covered with scrawled handwriting. 'Read that.'

Doran peered at it. ' "Eastgate Borough Council . . .

121

Planning Authority . . . an application has been. . . ." Sorry, I just can't make this out. Can you tell me what it says?'

'Right. It's a notice of application to build an estate of twelve houses on the cricket field and the acre containing Willow Cottage.'

'Willow Cottage? But that's the Singhs'.'

'Of course it's the Singhs'. These bastards want to demolish it to build their blasted houses. I saw the notice on the fence at the end of Cricket Path when I took Greta the picture. Read it by my bike lamp. I couldn't believe it at first. I copied some of it down and read it out to Ravi and Greta.'

'Oh, Bob, you shouldn't have done. Weren't they terribly upset?'

'Upset? You're joking. The old man went a sort of green, and Greta . . . poor old thing, she cried all over my jacket shoulder. And Ravi said, "Terrible for us to lose our home but terrible for you, too, to lose your field." He could even think of me and the lads, at a time like that. And the village – what's the village going to do without a cricket ground? The nearest's at Deerholt, and it's too small for a decent match. It's awful, it's unspeakable, it's bloody unheard-of. . . .'

'Bob, please don't shout so, you'll waken Rhona, and she sleeps so badly. Come into the kitchen and sit down and have a drink or a cup of tea or something, and we'll talk about this calmly.'

They sat over tea until the small hours of the morning, Doran arguing that the situation could not possibly be as bad as it seemed. There must be a mistake, the cricket ground was public property, not to be sold. She promised to see their local councillor next day – or rather in the day that was just breaking. Yawning and gritty-eyed, at last she let Bob out. At the door he turned a haggard face down to her.

'I hope it's true what you say, and the best of luck, Doran. But I tell you what – if they can do this thing, and I find the sod who's responsible, I'll kill him. That's a promise.'

The councillor, run to earth at his office, was prickly and evasive. Doran left him having learned exactly nothing, and drove to the vicarage.

'I know,' Rodney said. 'Nancy heard it at the shops this morning. The notice must have gone up yesterday. Well, it's iniquitous, of course. Abbotsbourne without a cricket ground would be like London without Hyde Park – worse. As for turning the Singhs out and pulling the cottage down, the mind boggles.'

'But they can't do that, surely – it's theirs, isn't it?'

'Not so. It's rented, and I know the . . . oh dear.' He groaned. 'I know the firm that owns it – a very minor building society. It could be they own the field as well, in which case they're entitled to sell it.' The telephone rang. Rodney answered, and spoke aside to Doran. 'Leave this with me, will you. I've got a contact on Eastgate Council. I'll come back to you this afternoon.'

But it was mid-evening when he rang, and his voice was weary.

'Sorry, not good news. The building society's owned Willow Cottage and the field for forty years or so. The council treasurer says they, that's the council, pay 'em a peppercorn rent, so small nobody's ever really taken it seriously. It's paid every year by direct debit and most of the councillors don't even know it exists.'

'And?'

'And I tracked down the building society on the blower, in Birmingham, and got a chap who actually knew something. He said yes, they'd had a very substantial offer from a private buyer and he expected a vote in favour of selling to be passed at the next meeting.'

'But . . . Rodney, the council must have powers to stop this.'

He sighed. 'I doubt it. My friend thought they'd let it go through with only a token protest.'

'But why? Aren't they proud of that lovely field, and their teams?'

'My dear, they're Eastgateians, not Abbotsbournians, and they have no soul above amusement arcades. If you look at what used to be green and pleasant land round Eastgate, you'll get a fair picture of what they'd like to do to

Abbotsbourne. More rates, more trade, a nice big super-market in the square, a better bus service, make Abbotsbourne a Growth Village. Who wants to live in a museum they'll ask? And cricket, well, that's an élitist game, isn't it, yer actual cricket.'

'It's not! Rubbish!'

'That's the way they think. Serpents, there's no pleasing them. They'll get that land, as sure as ferrets are ferrets.'

Doran's rage was not to be diverted by excursions into *Alice*.

'It's all very well, you making a joke of it. I'm furious. I've never been so furious.'

'So am I. No joke intended. Blame it on my unfortunate manner.'

Within two weeks his gloomy forecast proved justified. The planning authority recommended, and the general body of the council passed, a resolution that the buyer of the cricket field be granted planning permission and the right to demolish Willow cottage, an unlisted and structurally unsound dwelling. Doran was horrified to find support for them among the villagers she had confidently expected to back up the petition she had organized. Abbotsbourne needed more young people, some said.

'But there's the Prospect Estate – there are masses living there.'

'Well, not right *in* Abbotsbourne, is it? What we want is new blood in the community. Too many old folk about.'

'Then I suppose you'd have Mr and Mrs Singh taken along to the vet's and put down when they leave their cottage?'

'That's not a nice thing to say, Miss Fairweather. Not nice at all.'

She screwed up her courage and called at Dixter and Wylie's. Only Rupert was there, not the senior partner. Attending to a customer at his desk, he glanced up. Instantly his face shut down. It was their first confrontation since the Oast House evening. When the customer had gone she sat in the vacated chair. Rupert regarded her coolly. His male vanity had been dented, and he was not used to that.

'This cricket field business, Rupert. Isn't there anything your firm can do to stop it?'

'I really don't see how. What had you in mind?'

Nothing constructive, now she came to think of it. 'Estate agents,' he pointed out, 'have no control over local building. We might sell some of the houses, of course, when they're built. I hear they're going to be private-estate type, up-market price.'

'Where did you hear that?'

'Inquiries.'

Doran chained his straying eyes with hers. 'Rupert, you know something, don't you? Who's buying the land?'

'Well. I don't think it's a secret any more. Mr A. P. L. Mumbray.'

This time there was no room for suspicion or doubt. Abbotsbourne had its resident ogre, whose trail of destruction had just been widened by acres. Doran, in a state of pure rage, went home and told the first people she encountered – Rhona and Vi, busy at the kitchen table with measures of flour, sugar, nuts and dried fruit. They listened in silence. She ended, 'So you see, Vi, I was right about that man.'

Vi nodded. 'That's it. All them things you said was true. Mind you, I've thought as much since – since Debbie. And I know our Rhona has, haven't you, love?'

Rhona's tone was casual. 'I've known it. I knew at the inquest, after you'd said those things. I've worked out some good ways of killing him.'

Vi gave a shocked gasp, but Doran said, 'So have I, in the last few minutes. Vi, can I rely on you to tell as many people as possible? I'll do the same, and perhaps we can get some concerted action.'

'I'll tell 'em, don't you worry. I've got to get round every house with the Crispin Cake, now we've put our little lot in it.'

The Crispin Cake was by ancient tradition made every year in honour of the church's patron saint, Crispin, to be shared out after morning service on the nearest Sunday to his feast,

25 October. Each household was supposed to contribute ingredients, though many thought it a load of old-fashioned nonsense and some non-churchgoers flatly refused. Rodney permitted himself a mildly jokey sermon on every anniversary, based on the story that the saint's remains, cast into the sea at Cayeux in northern France some time in the eighth century, floated across the Channel and came ashore in Romney Marsh. This year's cake as yet existed only in the form of groceries in Vi's basket, to be baked by her when enough had been collected. The business of collecting, with its accompanying gossip, gave her immense satisfaction.

Doran began her personal tour of news-relaying at the vicarage. Rodney was in the garden picking late apples, while Helena, in her wheelchair, nursed a basket. He gave a long, expressive whistle.

'Mumbray. Well, well. I did wonder, but it seemed fantastic. Well, now we know.'

'What's he done?' asked Helena. 'Something awful?'

'Fairly awful – bought up our cricket ground.'

'I hate cricket, boring thing. But I hate him worse, and don't you tell me a good Christian child doesn't hate people, because I do and I always shall, always, always, so there.'

Doran said quickly, 'So I'm going round spreading the news, in case there's something we can do now we know who it is. I feel like a Highland carle carrying the Fiery Cross.'

'Skiddaw saw the blaze that burned on Gaunt's embattled pile,' offered Rodney.

'And the red glare on Skiddaw fired the burghers of Carlisle,' Doran responded automatically. 'That was something else, actually, beacons, I think. Anyway, this cross is going to be pretty fiery, the way I feel.'

'You two,' Helena growled, 'with your silly poetry nobody understands. They think you're cracked, I heard someone saying that to Nan. Think you're very clever, don't you?'

'Not always, only sometimes,' Doran replied, facing the scowl.

'Oh. I thought you always did.'

'Shut up!' Rodney almost shouted at his daughter. She

126

subsided visibly in her chair, an apple rolling from her hand to the ground. To Doran Rodney said, 'Good luck. But you'll get some funny looks, I fear.'

Neither the looks nor the responses Doran got were very encouraging. On the whole her information was received politely, but with the unspoken comment that it was really none of her business. Her fiery cross failed to ignite anyone's anger, except that of old Mr Thompson who never missed a cricket match. 'You can tell that bugger I'll sue 'im, miss. Take me money out of post office and go to law with it, that'll make him sit up.' I doubt it, you poor old man, thought Doran. With a certain relief she entered the Rose, warm from its crackling log fire. Several locals were there, including a couple with a dog the size of a pony which seemed to fill the floor with its benevolent presence.

But Doran's eyes went to a corner table, where a woman sat slumped, head on arms. The fur-fabric hat and coat of large checks identified the wearer as Marcia Fawkes.

Rosie Bellacre, seeing Doran, came swiftly out from behind the bar.

'Doran, thank goodness you've come in. I was thinking of phoning Sam Eastry to give me a hand with her, seeing I'm on my own. Just look at her!'

Doran looked. 'Dear, oh dear. Like that, is she?'

'Brahms and Liszt. As a newt. She'd been at it before she came in.' Rose lowered her voice. 'I don't want to cause a disturbance, but I really can't have it, 'specially at this time of day, practically lunchtime. What are we going to do?' Rosie pushed her cheerfully-tinted auburn curls on end.

Doran lifted Marcia by the heavy shoulders and tilted her backwards in the chair. She was snoring slightly. 'Give me a siphon, Rosie.' Standing between Marcia and the rest of the company present she gave Marcia a short blast of soda water in the face, bringing from her a sharp cry. The dog rose and padded towards them, smiling and slowly wagging its great tail. 'Good boy,' Doran said to it, and to its staring owners: 'My friend's been taken ill. Nothing to worry about, but we're trying to bring her round. Please take no notice. Rosie, I haven't my car with me, but I see yours outside – if you'll give me your keys I'll get her home and bring the car back.'

'Don't bother, I'll come and fetch it. Are you sure you can manage? Thanks ever so much, you're an angel.'

Using strength she had not known she possessed, Doran half-dragged the semi-conscious woman out to the car and pushed her into the back seat. Half her life seemed to have been spent in encountering a drunken Marcia, but never so strenuously. At Laburnum Cottage the process was reversed and Marcia propelled to her own doorstep.

Stella answered the door in a drifting caftan with her hair down. Doran cut her exclamations short. 'Marcia's dead drunk. Help me get her to bed or on to a sofa or something. Get some cold water, ice, if there is any.'

'I could call her spirit back – there's a spell for it. . . .'

'Don't bother. Just fetch the ice.'

Some twenty minutes later, in a sorry condition of mess, Marcia was in her own bed. Stella had given up trying to help. She vanished, and a door slammed – presumably that of the bedroom from which a scent of incense drifted. Doran looked round Marcia's plain, impersonal room. On the dressing table lay a piece of paper, obviously a letter. Doran unashamedly read it.

It was typed on the official notepaper of the youth organization for which Marcia did unpaid work in Barminster: a cool, not unfriendly note asking Miss Fawkes to drop in next time she was in the town, so that they could discuss a rather curious communication concerning her which had been sent to them.

Poor cow, poor lonely stupid cow. She had let Mumbray bleed her of her small income and frighten the life out of her, to keep quiet a secret which nowadays would hardly cause an eyebrow to lift. The people at Barminster probably meant no action against her, merely wondered who was writing nasty things about one of their workers. As for the parish council, so far as Rodney cared any member of it could be the unmarried mother of seventeen children of assorted paternity, if he approved of them in other ways.

Mumbray had got tired of playing with his mouse, and had laid it low with a swipe of the claw.

Marcia's face was a very unhealthy colour, and her breathing was shallow. Doran went downstairs and telephoned the surgery. Tom Fullathorn, Eli Levison's partner, arrived within half an hour and pronounced that Marcia was almost certainly suffering from alcoholic poisoning, and that he would arrange for an ambulance.

'Keep her warm,' he said on his way out. 'Don't give her anything. Sorry to rush off, but I'm doubling for Eli today.'

'Not ill, is he?'

'No, but he's had a bit of a shock – letter with some sort of bad news. I'm keeping him quiet. See you.'

Doran watched him go. The arrows were falling on those who had fearfully waited for them. Who would be the next?

Three days later the ambulance was summoned again, this time to Cricket Path. Ravi Singh had suffered a massive coronary.

10

Mumbray had returned, had been seen driving his car and in the garden of The Oaks. Doran called there as soon as she heard of his presence. Waiting for him in the familiar forbidding room she was conscious of being more nervous than she had ever been in her life. Last time she had been in this room, she remembered, she had broken into a stammer. In spite of the October chill of the morning she felt a cold sweat breaking out on her scalp and upper lip.

It seemed like an hour before he appeared, though it was only minutes. He remained standing, surveying her without expression. Her mouth went dry. When she opened it to speak the stammer came on again.

'I – I've come to ask you not to – not to do what you were going to.'

'And what might that be, Miss Fairweather?'

'The – the cricket field. Don't build houses on it.'

'May I ask how you know that is my intention?'

'Everybody knows.'

'Then perhaps you will kindly ask everybody to mind their own business – and that includes you, Miss Fairweather.' He was still standing, looming over her. She jumped to her feet and faced him, at bay, as though he might lower that great head and gore her with suddenly emergent horns.

'You're doing a terrible lot of harm. Mr Singh's dying and his wife's nearly out of her mind. And it's going to ruin Abbotsbourne, I mean the houses are.' She heard herself being totally inept. 'And then the letters – you've been writing letters to people, I mean about people, upsetting them. . . .'

He let a silence fall, increasing Doran's nervousness, before saying, with his shark's smile, 'Have you ever heard of the law of slander?'

'Yes, of course.'

'Then I suggest you refresh your memory on its details. I assume you have uttered accusations of me in the hearing of others?'

'Well. . . .'

'Good. Defamatory words, designed to arouse hatred or contempt, uttered before a third party. Decidedly actionable. And I have a strong case for libel, in this – ' He took a letter from its slit envelope and held it out to her. With a sinking heart she saw the heading: St Crispin's Vicarage.

'A solemn indictment of me by your clerical paramour.'

'He's not my paramour!' Doran flared.

'No? I rather think otherwise, and so will many people before long, I believe.'

'You're not going to write letters about Rodney – make trouble for him?'

'Now I wonder where you two young people meet? Under the sacred roof of the vicarage, where little Miss Helena can't hear you? Or in your neat little house? I understand you sleep in a Jacobean four-poster, delightfully spacious. Or you may prefer the woods, with a spare cassock these damp evenings . . . How do clergymen disport themselves? I wonder if you and he practise . . . would you prefer the Latin or the Anglo-Saxon?'

'I won't listen to you!' She knew worse was coming and made for the door, his raised voice following her.

'It may interest you to know that your hot-blooded clerical friend has announced his intention of holding a Service of Commination against me.'

'A Commination,' Rodney explained, 'is a recital of divine threats against evil-doers. It's the strongest weapon the Church has – a denunciation of sinners and the expression of God's anger. Supposed to be said on Ash Wednesday, but may be used at other times, on occasion. This is an occasion.'

'I don't know anything about it. I think I've noticed it in passing in the Prayer Book. Is it often used?'

'Very seldom, thanks to widespread Church pussyfooting. The Book of Common Prayer recommends it for the punishment of notorious sinners, that their souls may be saved in the day of the Lord.'

'Punishment – what sort of punishment?'

'That's up to the Lord, isn't it? I heard the service said once, when I was a boy, by an elderly vicar who thought it might be a deterrent to the activities of Certain Foreign Powers.'

'And was it?'

'No. But it was jolly impressive – frightening, in fact. I used to lie awake at nights afterwards, wondering if I came into any of the "Cursed is he" categories. Well, I'm going to try it, and I've asked Mumbray to come and listen. The odds are he won't, but the fact that he knows it's happening might have an effect, on the principle of the witch doctor letting the native know he's having the bone pointed at him. Sympathetic magic.'

Doran laid her hand on Rodney's arm, an intimacy she seldom ventured. 'Rodney, have you really thought about this? He's a dangerous man and he hates you already. I've got the nastiest feeling that if you go ahead with it something awful will happen. Have you asked anybody's advice?'

He moved impatiently, and she hastily withdrew the hand.

'Why should I? As priest of this parish I can hold what services I please, go out in the fields and bless the crops, or invite everyone to bring their pets to church, piranhas and gerbils included. I suppose I'm allowed *some* compensation for having to use the Alternative Service Book?'

'It's not like you to be arrogant.'

'It's not like me to be harbouring a monster in my parish and doing nothing about it. As for asking anybody, I've *told* my churchwarden and the secretary of the parish council. That's all.'

'I see. Can I come?'

'I was counting on it. Bring your friends. Next Sunday after Matins.'

Sunday was cold and cheerless. Bare branches tapped at the

Perpendicular east window and rain-pools formed on the paths between graves. The church interior seemed cold, even though two services had been held in it that morning. Doran, alone in her pew, looked round at the others, thinly but significantly populated. Marcia, where she had sat during the earlier service. Vi and Rhona together, both in black, wearing expressions which would have graced the foot of the guillotine. Bob Woods, without Barbary, sitting with folded arms and grim mouth. A journalist from the local paper, eager for clerical scandal. Mrs Lewes, a widowed *dévotee* who hardly missed a service, week in, week out. Nancy Kirton from the vicarage, keeping an anxious eye on Helena, whose wheelchair was beside her pew in the aisle. There was colour in Helena's cheeks and something like an anticipatory smile hovering round her mouth, her eyes following every move made by her father.

He wore over his surplice the purple stole usually reserved for funerals. The silent congregation watched as he removed the flower vase from the front of the pulpit, covered the altar with its Lenten pall of black velvet, and knelt before it for some moments before going up into the pulpit. As he spoke the opening words of the service he looked slowly, deliberately, at each one in turn of the little congregation. 'Brethren, in the Primitive Church there was a godly discipline, that, at the beginning of Lent, such persons as stood convicted of notorious sin were put to open penance. . . .'

Doran shut her Prayer Book and listened and watched, hypnotized by the words and the speaker, a pale grim-faced stranger to her.

'Cursed is he that removeth his neighbour's land mark.' That brought a fervent, concerted Amen.

'Cursed is he that smiteth his neighbour secretly. Cursed are the unmerciful.' The chilling phrases rolled on. 'For now is the axe put unto the root of the trees, so that every tree that bringeth not forth good fruit is hewn down, and cast into the fire. It is a fearful thing to fall into the hands of the living God: He shall pour down rain upon the sinners, snares, fire and brimstone, storm and tempest; this shall be their portion to drink. . . .'

The words sank into Doran's mind, throwing up images, as she gazed at the stained glass backed by dull October light: pieced-together fragments in an unplanned mosaic, a little gold crown, an angel's wing, a baby's foot, a Magdalene with yellow crimped hair falling to her waist. She remembered noticing none of them before. The setting seemed not to be her church, any more than the man in the pulpit seemed to be her friend. Evil had changed it all.

'O terrible voice of the most just judgement, which shall be pronounced upon them, when it shall be said unto them, Go, ye cursed, into the fire everlasting, which is prepared for the devil and his angels.'

Doran hurried out at the end of the service, reluctant to encounter Rodney in the porch, where he always stood to greet the congregation as they left. But he was not there. Bob Woods was already striding down the path; Doran ran to catch up with him.

'Well? How did it strike you? I feel quite drained, personally.'

He laughed shortly. 'I reckon the Reverend's gone potty. Thought so as soon as I heard about this lot, but I wanted to come and hear whether he mentioned that bastard by name.'

'Do stop, Bob, I can't keep up your pace. So you don't think it'll do any good?'

'I don't think anything'll do any good except a thrashing that'd land *him* in hospital.'

'It wouldn't work, you know. The cricket field sale would go on and he'd have you for assault.'

'Let him. Be worth it.'

'Then why don't you do it?'

'Think I haven't tried? I can't get near him. The bugger's walled himself up there like Fort Knox, chains on the doors, windows tight shut. I've stood and shouted in the garden, told him to come out and face me like a man, and I've never even caught a glimpse of that mousy housekeeper of his. I'll keep trying, though, I'll keep trying! Anything.'

He was off, striding away through the misty drizzle, a huge figure. Terrible as an army with banners, thought Doran, though of course that was the Shulamite, and it didn't really mean terrible . . . it was a relief to think of something biblical other than that fearful malediction she had heard in church.

There was no sign of Rodney. Doran drifted back towards the people emerging, curious to hear their reactions. The journalist, a tall spotty youth, was darting from one to another, notebook open and pencil flying. Marcia was talking to him animatedly.

'Wonderful experience, wasn't it! What a comfort in these loose days to hear such a condemnation of wickedness. You can say I – yes, Miss Fawkes, do spell it properly – say I heartily approve of the vicar reviving a fine old service so much needed in these shocking times. . . .'

Helena was laughing outright, hobbling on Nancy's arm while Nancy struggled to hold her up and push the wheelchair with one hand.

'Wasn't Daddy great?' she was saying, well within the journalist's hearing. 'I've never heard him like that before. Don't you think he could have been an actor?' The journalist had turned hastily from Marcia and was scribbling down Helena's words.

'It was all about that man Mumbray,' she was babbling, 'the one who took me up to the castle and tortured me and said horrible things. I think he deserves comminating, don't you? Nancy said people like that ought to be put down, didn't you, Nancy –'

'Do hush, dear.'

But the journalist was shorthand-writing fluently, visualizing the headlines. 'Vicar's daughter names target of hate ritual. Accusations of torture in Abbotsbourne. Man made suggestions to young girl, she says.' It was going to be a lovely juicy story.

He moved on to the two tall sisters walking together. Rhona was silent but Vi prattled. 'Well, I didn't understand all of it, but my sister here lost her little girl all through Mr Mumbray, and if you ask me there's nothing too bad you could say of a man like him. I used to work for him, you know, and I've always said, haven't I, Rhona. . . .'

Doran wandered off through the wet long grass, between rain-darkened gravestones rough with lichen, leaning crookedly their carved swags of memorial flowers, skulls and crossbones, cherub heads and pious words. Here in sure and certain hope of resurrection lies Susan, wife of John Peacocke . . . Elizabeth, aged VII months . . . Matthew *aetat LIX anni* . . . Some of them had stood in St Crispin's in their time, paling and shuddering at the dreadful words of malediction, wondering if the priest were including them among the fornicators and adulterers, covetous persons, idolaters, slanderers, drunkards, and extortioners, whom he was dismissing to Hell. 'It is a fearful thing to fall into the hands of the living God: He shall pour down rain upon the sinners, snares, fire and brimstone, storm and tempest; this shall be their portion to drink.'

Doran looked at the church, from which everybody had now drifted away, down the path, through the lychgate. The door of the porch still stood open. It was kept locked when the building was empty, so Rodney must be still there. She moved towards it, then stopped, and turned away.

Four days had passed since the Sunday of the Commination Service. Very little had been said about it – too little to be healthy. It was as though they were all waiting for something; perhaps for the edition of the local paper in which the spotty youth's report of the occasion would be published. It was due out on Friday. Mumbray remained unseen in his fortress. Vi discovered that a large order for goods had been telephoned ('from a pay-phone, seeing there isn't one in the house') to the grocer and the greengrocer, to be delivered at the back door of The Oaks, and that these had duly been sent and taken in by Mrs Butcher, with hardly any exchange of words. Bob Woods had been seen stalking the lane leading up to The Oaks. Nobody knew whether the sale of the cricket field had been completed, because Eastgate Council refused to answer inquiries.

Nothing sinister, on the face of it; yet Doran felt curiously uneasy, unable to settle. It was the evening of 21 October,

Trafalgar Day, the day that saw Britain victorious, Nelson dead, Bonaparte beaten. Doran meditated on that, but it failed to cheer her up. Bell House was empty but for herself, Rhona spending the evening with Vi, as she often did. Creaks and cracks came from the old woodwork, the fire burnt sullenly low. Doran slammed down the book she was trying to read, stoked the smouldering logs, and went upstairs to get out her fan collection.

They were her collector's passion, delicious painted toys of silk and feathers, paper and lace and ivory, microcosms of the times which had seen them new. There was an eerie pleasure in touching the delicate sticks, which had so long outlasted the fingers that had held them, with one's own warm living fingers. A faint musky perfume still clung to some, others still bore the names of their dead mistresses: Anne, Caroline, Charlotte, and a date, often a year in the eighteenth century whose small people danced or courted on the fan's leaves.

She lifted them one by one from the long drawer where they were stored, each wrapped in an old pillow-case with a package of silica gel beside it, to register any damp, and carried an armful of them downstairs to the warmth of the drawing room. There she opened them and spread them against the back of the sofa and in the armchairs, kneeling on the floor to admire the play of the firelight on them. Old sequins dulled with years sparkled silver again, ghostly cupids smiled on tiny lovers, a cloudy Japanese Nanga landscape was suddenly sharp and clear.

The bell rang, startling Doran into immobility. Surely not a repeat visit from Bob Woods. She hesitated, remembering the number of people reported in newspapers as having opened their doors to night callers, then been struck down and robbed. But unable to resist the temptation to know who was there she went to the door and opened it on the chain.

'Only me,' said Rodney's voice from the darkness.

'Good gracious. Come in.'

He followed her into the sitting room, where she removed fans from the two easy chairs. Rodney was in civvies, a heavy camel coat and a thick Aran sweater. Settling in a chair, he took off his glasses and polished them. Doran thought he looked ten years older than usual, and infinitely weary.

'Trouble?' she asked.

'You could say that. Pretty, your fans.'

'Yes, aren't they. What's the matter?'

'This.' He produced a letter from his pocket and tossed it over. It was immaculately typed on fine notepaper and bore the signature of the Bishop of Barminster. Doran read it slowly, then scanned it again.

'How absolutely awful, Rodney.'

'Not nice, is it – not the sort of letter calculated to lift the heart and send a man singing on his way. Here are a few of the unpleasantest words that ever blotted paper. Seems they've had their eye on me for some time: no regular use of the ASB, too much of the tongue that Shakespeare spoke and not enough of the jargon of the board meeting. Too many Matins when we all know the Establishment hates 'em and would rather David hadn't bothered to write the Psalms – use of the King James Bible for the Lessons instead of Easy Scripture for Beginners, or whatever they call it, flippant remarks from the pulpit. There is no health in me, in fact. And now this.'

'Which seems to have been the last straw.'

'That's right. "An obsolete and contumacious service said without permission from the Bishop's Palace." To which I'm summoned next Monday. To be given, if I read the signs right, either a stern telling-off or the news that I'm to be suspended from my duties until the matter's been referred to Lambeth.'

'Oh, Rodney. I'm sorry. So sorry. But, you know, I told you something horrible would happen if you went ahead with that Commination. I *knew* it would. That man brings evil on everyone he touches.'

'Of course – because he's evil himself, an embodiment of evil – the nearest thing I've ever met to an actual devil. I know one's supposed to fight evil with good and forgive one's enemies, but that's not to say one ought to forgive other people's enemies. So that's why I thought I had to hold that service. It was a priest's weapon, and I used it. But I suppose, looking back, I really did it out of pride. Vainglory. Even superstition,' he said bitterly.

'You mustn't say that, you must never say it!'

After a pause, he said, 'No. Of course not. Thank you.' He leaned back in the deep chair and closed his eyes. 'This is one of the nastiest things that's ever happened to me, after Benny dying, and Helena's illness. Ever since that letter came I've been trying to come to terms with it, and myself, what it showed me about myself, without discussing it with anyone – then I felt I wouldn't sleep at all if I didn't come and tell you.'

'I'm glad you did.' Doran felt painfully inadequate. On the sofa, the eyes of a peacock's-tail Art Nouveau fan winked as a flame sprang up from the logs.

'If they chuck me out, what am I going to do? Come to that, what do I do now? What have I done today? After that letter came I went and prowled round the garden. Then I went in and paid some bills. Old George called round to say another pane of glass had been smashed in the Ascension window, so I went round and had a look at it and picked up some beer bottles and Coke cans the smashers had left. I think we had lunch after that, but I wasn't hungry so I don't remember a lot about it. This afternoon I took the Sacrament to Mrs Fitchett. She talked for hours and I made us some tea and drifted back home.'

'What's the matter with all that?'

'Anyone could have done it, that's what's the matter. I've wanted to be a parson since I was about ten, but perhaps I was wrong. Perhaps I ought to have trained for teaching and exploited my capacity for using other men's words in a prep school.'

'You'll feel better in the morning.'

'Oddly enough, I feel better now, probably because I'm here.'

Doran went across and sat on the arm of his chair. They looked long at each other, and suddenly his arms were round her and his head against her breast and she was deliriously happy, holding him tightly, bending to him, and giving kiss for kiss. Their first kisses, blotting out all she had given or

140

taken before. Short-breathed, she said, 'It's nearly midnight. I heard Rhona let herself in at the back door. By now she'll be in bed.'

'I wish we were.'

'Then stay! Nobody's going to know. Nancy won't worry. She'll think you've met a parishioner who needs you – actually, you have, because I do, most dreadfully.'

Rodney said, 'Darling', for the first time not in his Noël Coward voice.

'It isn't wrong – it can't be. We're both single, we need each other a lot. Whatever happens later, I want this to remember. Having you. Being yours.'

He held her away from him, searching her eyes. 'I want it too, more than I can say. I love you so much, Doran.'

They were shaken by the utterance of what had been unspoken between them for so long, gagged and in chains from which it was now exultantly free. Doran whispered, against his hair, 'I love you. I want you. Tonight's perfect. Will you stay, then?'

'Yes.' He got up and held her close, dropping on her face small light kisses, from brow to mouth.

'I always wondered,' she said, 'what it would be like kissing you. Whether your glasses would get in the way. They don't, do they?'

'No, but it would be nicer with them off. And everything else.'

'Then let's go upstairs.' She drew him towards the door, switching off the table-lamp as she passed it. The fans sat watching, twinkling away to themselves.

' "Lovers, to bed, 'tis almost fairy time," ' Rodney said. 'How sweet you smell, like new hay.'

The telephone rang.

Doran said, 'Blast.'

'Leave it.'

'Yes, I will.' But it rang insistently, so loudly in the quiet house that Doran knew Rhona would hear it in her light sleep and come down. Cursing under her breath she switched the lamp on again and snatched off the receiver, snapping, 'Yes?'

A blurred Welsh voice said, 'That you, gal? There's glad I am, been tryin' to phone you half an hour, all the bloody phones from Eastgate to here have been vandalized. Thought you wasn't in.'

'Oh, God, Howell. What's the matter? Where are you?'

'Just down the valley, outside the pub, Half Way House you know. Listen, I'll be with you in ten minutes, quarter of an hour. That OK?'

'No, it isn't OK. What do you mean, with me? I'm not expecting you, and what's more I don't want you, it's not convenient –'

'Now then, gal, don't be like that. I'm in a terrible way, in a shockin' state I am, had the hell of a row with Andrew, over Georgiou, you know, that boy we met in Crete, I told you, seems he's coming to London and Andrew said he could stay. Well, I said not, and Andrew flew at me, said I could get out if I felt like that.' He sniffed damply. 'So I been chucked, nowhere to sleep, no one to be sorry for Howell. . . .'

'You're drunk. What do you mean by ringing me? You've got plenty of pals in Eastgate. Go and doss down with them.'

'Ah, but they're all bastards, see? They all take Andrew's side, so I can't go there, can I, now? No, I thought of you. . . .'

The pips went. Doran put the receiver down.

'You got all that?' she asked Rodney.

'More or less. Howell in a mess, coming here.'

'I can't stop him. He'll be here in ten minutes, if he doesn't crash his car, but that's too much to hope for. Oh, darling. What a time to choose.'

'What a time. . . .' They were not touching each other, for it was dangerous now. Rodney reached for the coat he had discarded and put it on. 'I could say a lot of words nobody's ever heard me say. But my cloth, you know, my cloth. I nearly forgot it just now.' He laughed bitterly.

'I'm so sorry. I don't know what to say, and there's nothing I can do, except turn him away at the door, and then he'll make an uproar in the garden – I know him.'

'You can go to bed and forget about it. I'll try to. Good-night.' He kissed her gently on the cheek, and was gone.

142

Doran dropped heavily down in the chair he had sat in and put her head in her hands. She had not stirred when a car door slammed in the distance, and a maudlin tenor voice grew louder as its owner reeled up the path.

'Minnau ar y mwyth obennydd,
Yno yn breuddwydio'n ddedwydd,
Am yr un wy'n garu beunydd,
Ar hyd ye nos.'

Doran marched to the front door and flung it open.

'*All Through the Night* – just what I needed. Come in, and let me tell you for a start I was never less glad to see anybody.'

'Now *cariad*, is that a nice thing to say? Whass matter?'

'Nothing. Absolutely nothing. Yes, everything.'

11

After the high drama of the Commination, the Crispin Service held on the following Sunday fell a little flat. Rodney's mind was on his summons to Barminster, so that he lacked the verve to make his usual entertaining observations on the transit of St Crispin to Kent. The cake, too, lacked verve, and, indeed, almost everything else except a high degree of stodge. So many different ingredients had gone into it that they could hardly be expected to combine perfectly, and few of them were of high quality: many parishioners regarded the Cake as a kind of levy, yet another gentle form of church extortion.

Doran, whose kitchen had contributed ground almonds and a miniature bottle of brandy, found her slice uneatable and pocketed it in a tissue for Ozzy's elevenses. She observed that quite a lot of pocketing was going on, though some were eating heartily, feeling agreeably wicked – after all you only got wafers in church, usually. There was some competition for the decorations, Vi's own fanciful version in piped icing-sugar of the saint at his trade of shoemaking: it was capable of several interpretations, depending how one looked at it. The Sunday-school children who had pointedly stayed on for the ceremony inclined to the view that he was killing rats with a hammer.

Doran and Rodney exchanged only formal Sunday greetings. Both knew that the situation which had come about on Trafalgar Night would never happen again in just that way, and neither would try to force it. The moment had gone by.

But it had had its effect. Doran, with that sensation of delicious pain which is like no other emotion, knew that she was for the second time in her life deeply and passionately in love. Their first kisses had freed it, sent its glory blazing over them: the Dayspring from on high hath visited us, she had said so often in church, not knowing how that would be when, miraculously, it happened. But in having Rodney as she wanted him, fully and completely, she would destroy him. There would be newspaper stories: 'Vicar leaves parish, rumours of affair with 26-year-old member of congregation. The Reverend – said to be not available for interview, Miss – staying with friends.' And still, after all the sordid fuss, they would not be able to share a home, because of Helena. She, Doran, would wander on from man to man, doing what her body told her but her heart denied.

She had been home from Eastgate on Monday only a few minutes when the telephone rang. Rodney's voice said, 'My jailers let me go.'

Oh good, so he could be flippant again. 'How was it?'

'Well. A bit like a job interview when the employers are determined you shan't get it. Two of them, on the other side of the biggest desk outside a TV finance sitcom, countenances more in anger than sorrow to start with. *Two stern-faced men set out from Lynn.* . . .'

'Don't recite, get on with it. What was it really like?'

'Not as drastic as I feared. The letter was a frightener. The interview was more of a homily, an exhortation, a solemn warning.'

'What's going to happen, then?'

'Nothing much, until the next time. I can have Matins twice a month, as a great concession, so long as I bring the time forward and have it at half-past nine, which will mean almost nobody will come. I'm to use the revised Service of Baptism, no more Devil and all his Works and carnal desires of the flesh . . . sorry.'

There was a pause at both ends of the conversation.

'I'm to involve myself a lot more in the Eastern Aid movement and have talks with the diocese about pulling down that nice coffee-pot obelisk near the corner of the south transept and having a Youth Therapy hut built.'

'A what?'

'What, indeed? They'd find the money for that, but not for

146

repairs to the vicarage roof, and the estimate I sent them for damp-proofing to the kitchen seemed disproportionate. They suggested I find a good handy-man and pay him myself, seeing that my benefice is such a very desirable one, with two other parishes thrown in – but I ought to bear in mind the possibility of both Elvesham and Henbury churches being closed, which would make quite a difference to my stipend. No threats, just hints.'

'Oh dear,' Doran said. 'At least you haven't been sacked.'

'No. I almost wish I had. At this moment I feel extraordinarily like joining the Foreign Legion. But I don't suppose they'd have me because of my glasses.'

Doran was thankful that she had brought the VAT books home with her. Howell was much better at such things than she was, but not to be relied upon to get them done swiftly and the end of the three-month declaration period was near. It would be a good task to wrestle with after dinner, an effective way of taking her mind off other matters. And nobody would interrupt her.

The pile of invoices was slowly dwindling, the calculator tapping out yet another percentage. From a cassette came vintage jazz played on a piano: Doran did not particularly like it, rather the opposite, but it filled the spaces in one's mind without awakening any unwanted echoes, its controlled jangling and exaggerated syncopation a welcome irritant to the senses.

The bell rang. 'Oh, no,' Doran said aloud, 'it can't be.'

Rhona appeared. 'Sam to see you.'

Sam Eastry looked apologetic. 'Sorry to intrude on you, Doran.'

'Don't apologize.' Her tone was laden with sarcasm. 'Anything I can do for the police or you personally? Here I am, night in, night out, at the public service. All problems dealt with smartly and in depth. Free estimates, send no money.' At his puzzled look she laughed.

'Sorry, Sam, I'm not snapping at you, just letting off a bit of steam. Truly, I seem to sit here night after night, thinking I'm safe, getting on quietly with my life, and in comes one after

147

another with their troubles, wanting me to sort them out –
why they imagine I can, you tell me,' she added bitterly.

'Now, now. If people come to you for help it's because they
know you're interested in them, and because you're a nice kind
girl. Listen, Doran, this is a bit urgent. There's something
rum going on in the cricket pavilion, and I want your help.
Ben saw it on his way home from Scouts and fetched me.'

'Rum? What sort of rum?'

'Miss Meeson. In there praying or something, with lighted
candles. We don't much want the pavilion burnt down, do
we, even if they are going to demolish it. But the awkward
thing is, she's got nothing on.'

'Again?'

'Pardon?'

'Never mind. So how can I help, Sam?'

'Well.' His hand went to his pocket for the pipe he must not
smoke on duty. 'If it was just a case of a streaker, someone casual,
I could whip a coat round them and cart 'em off, but seeing as
she's a villager and, well, a lady. . . . I did speak to her and
advised her to put some clothes on and go home, but she just
stared and gabbled something at me. If Lydia'd been in I could
have got her home and given her something to change into, but
she's round at her mother's, and with just Ben there. . . .'

Doran was amused. 'I see. You want a chaperone. I doubt if
the sight of Stella in the raw would give Ben ideas, but let's
not take chances. I've got a big coat I could put round her,
then I'll take her home in the car. Right, I'm with you.' She
switched off the cassette.

'You're a sport, my dear – I can see you're busy.'

In a few minutes the Volvo stopped by the top gate of the
cricket ground. The night was dark, moonless, with a touch of
frost, and the lighted windows of the small pavilion were bright
as film screens. Sam, who scored for his team when available,
shook his head. 'Bit different from summer days. Wouldn't
mind going back to those times – a good match, curried egg
sandwiches and cakes for tea, then down to the Feathers for a
pint and a pipe. Don't suppose they'll ever come again, those
days, eh?'

148

Doran put a hand on his arm. 'Ssh.' They were within full view of the front of the pavilion. The door, which was normally kept locked, stood open: inside, in a cave of soft light, Stella knelt beside a chair. On the seat of it Doran recognized two of the articles she and Rodney had seen through Stella's bedroom window, the chalice, the black-handled knife, and other, smaller ones. Doran caught her breath at the timeless picture, the slim white kneeling body and bright ethereal hair, catching the light in its silver strands. It was a dream-scene by Fuseli, a detail from a witches' Sabbat of the Middle Ages, hypnotically beautiful.

Sam whispered, 'Come on. She'll catch her death of cold.'

They advanced quietly. On the pavilion steps Doran said quietly, 'Stella.'

The kneeling figure started and turned its face to them, the eyes blank and staring. Doran moved nearer, noticing that the white skin was goose-pimpled. She put her hand on Stella's shoulder. It flinched away from her; awareness came to the eyes. The voice, when Stella spoke, was remote.

'Don't touch me. I am consecrated. My names are Selene, Ishtar, Binah and Hecate.'

'You can't stay there, you know. It's bitterly cold.'

'We must be sky-clad for spells.'

Doran's mind whizzed round collecting possible explanations for the word. A dim memory of a television feature about witchcraft brought up the image of a high priestess solemnly justifying her uncomely coven's nakedness. Sky-clad, clothed with air.

'Well, you can't be sky-clad in our cricket pavilion, I'm afraid. Come along. Here's a nice warm coat I'll put it round you and then we'll go.' She gently raised Stella, whose limbs seemed almost inanimate, and got her arms into the sleeves, while Sam tactfully melted into the shadows. The objects on the chair would have to be moved, unsuitable as they were for their surroundings. Doran decided to put them in a corner until she could come back and tidy up. Distastefully, at arm's length, she moved them – knife, chalice, a small basin of blood (horrible) and a crude doll, obviously male, made from

149

what looked like toy-modelling clay. Stella watched passively while Doran removed them.

'You should say the Rune when you touch my ceremonial tools.'

'Yes, but I'm afraid I don't know it.'

'It's *Eko, Eko, Azarak,*
   Eko, Eko, Zamilak. . . .'

'Never mind now. Come along. Sam Eastry's here – you know him, don't you? Take her arm, Sam, she's a bit unsteady.' Between them they propelled her into the back of the car, Sam beside her. She was shivering now, words filtering from between her chattering teeth.

'The v-vicar came to see me – your f-friend, you know. He gave me quite a lecture.'

'Oh. He didn't tell me.'

'But I said, I have to use my powers, I swore that.'

'Ah. And what were you using them for just now?' Doran asked, over her shoulder.

'The c-cricket field – I have to save it. Really, I should have waited till Thursday – Hallowe'en, you know – but when one's dealing with Brethren of the Left-Hand Path there's no time to lose, is there?'

'No. Here we are.' The lighted window of Laburnum Cottage must mean that Marcia was still up. She was, with the television set flickering in the corner. Doran was pleased to see a coffee-pot and a cup on the table beside it, and no sign of a bottle.

Doran and Sam ushered in the muffled form of Stella, who by now was shaking convulsively.

'Oh Stella, at it again!' said Marcia sadly. 'Where did you find her this time?'

'In the cricket pavilion,' Sam said. 'Does she do this sort of thing often, Miss Fawkes?'

'I thought she'd given it up, I must say. Oh dear, not a stitch on. Come along, let's get you upstairs and into bed. Thank you for bringing her home, both of you. I'm sorry she's been such a nuisance.'

Outside, Sam said, 'I reckon someone up at the psychiatric

150

unit ought to take a look at Miss Meeson, don't you?'

'If she gets pneumonia a doctor will have to take a look at her anyway, and he'll probably refer her to somebody else. It looks to me like a nasty case of possession.'

Sam was shocked. 'By the Devil?'

'How should I know? Might be a case for bell, book and candle, or therapy or drugs – but it certainly needs taking in hand. I don't think she ought to be on the loose with that knife – which is stolen, anyway.' She told him of her suspicion.

'You mean Mumbray stole it for her? You reckon they're in something together, then? You ought to have told me all this before, you know, Doran. Apart from anything else, it's not safe for you to be playing about with such matters, all on your own. I did warn you not to get too deep into things.'

Doran took her eyes off the road to face him. 'I'm not "getting into" anything. I'm curious, inquisitive, if you like. I fancy myself as an amateur detective, maybe, but I never seem to get round to doing any actual detecting, not in time to stop anything happening. Remember what Holmes said? "It is a capital mistake to theorize before one has data", and there haven't been any data to get hold of.'

'That's right. No trout in the milk.' Sam laughed, pleased with himself. 'But seriously, Doran, do leave things alone. I know it was me got you into tonight's bit of bother, but I'd rather you spoke to me before you take anything else on.' They were outside the police house, the Volvo stationary.

'Then, just before I let you out, I'll speak to you about something else. Marcia Fawkes was being blackmailed by Mumbray and nearly died from alcoholic poisoning – but you knew about that, because you arranged for a WPC to go to East-gate Hospital with her. Well, she's completely over it, judging by tonight – not just the poisoning, the worry. For the first time I've seen her since all this started she hasn't got a thing on her mind. What does your faculty of deduction make of *that*?'

Sam was silent. Then he said, 'I don't know. Except that the blackmail's stopped. Or she's come to terms with it.'

'Exactly. She wasn't even stroppy with Stella for being brought home like that, and time was when she used to rave

151

about her mate's magical goings-on. Well, I just thought I'd tell you. Goodnight.'

Lydia Eastry was setting the table for her son's tea: bread and butter, some of the fruit loaf he was so fond of, their own raspberries from the freezer, a seed cake of her own making. As she clattered pots she sang. Ben, changing his shoes, looked up with a frown.

'What a rotten song, Mum. Do you have to?'

'What's the matter with it?'

'I dunno – all on the one note, or something.'

Lydia paused, her hands on the table, and repeated the verse, more clearly. Yes, it was more of a chant than a song.

'A soul, a soul, a soul-cake –
Please, good missus, a soul-cake.
An apple, a pear, a plum or a cherry,
Any thing to make us all merry,
One for Peter and two for Paul,
And three for Him that made us all.'

'I wonder what started me off on that, now? I suppose it was seeing 2nd November on the calendar, and then cutting the seed-cake. . . .'

'What's that got to do with it?'

'Don't talk with your mouth full. In the old days people used to go about asking neighbours to pray for the dead, say Masses, you know, and they got given cake at the door. . . .'

'Why cake?'

'I don't know. And they used to sing that "Souling Song". Sometimes they had a Hodener with them, a man dressed in a white sheet with a horse's skull on his head, jumping and dancing about.'

'Cripes. Was it a real skull?'

'Yes, quite real. And don't ask me if they killed a horse specially, because I don't know.'

'Did you go round with them, Mum?'

Lydia laughed. 'Heavens no – how old do you think I am? It must be a hundred years or more since people went Souling.

My grandmother remembered her mother telling her about it, in Cheshire where she was born.'

Ben was picking fruit out of the bread and eating it separately. 'Will you and Dad pray for Jane's soul today?'

After a moment Lydia answered, 'We do that every day. But not quite the way the Soulers meant. Get on with your tea.' She was not going to worry Ben with the thoughts that went through her head when the bells, Sam's Ladies, chimed on a Sunday morning, their melodious voices floating high above her daughter's grave. Jane, annihilated by a thirty-ton Continental transport as it skidded and mounted the pavement. . . .

A knock at the door brought her back to the present.

'I'll go!' Ben was off in a flash. She heard his voice at the door, then he was back. 'A lady to see Dad.'

'Who is it?'

'Dunno. Oldish, sort of.'

Lydia did not recognize the woman who hovered on the garden path. She was small and nondescript, with faded hair under a headscarf, a reddened nose-tip and a lined face. She stared at Lydia, a hostile stare, or perhaps one that came of shyness.

'I wanted to see the policeman.'

'I'm afraid my husband's not in. He's over at Eastgate. Can I give him a message?'

'It's urgent.'

'Won't you come in and tell me about it? Then as soon as he comes in he can deal with . . . whatever it is. Perhaps you'd like a cup of tea. There's one made, my boy's just having his. . . .' She ushered her visitor into the kitchen with a running accompaniment of chatter, ending with her usual, 'Do sit down.' But the woman remained standing, darting nervous glances about her like an animal herded into an unfamiliar environment. Lydia gestured to Ben, who was eating cake and taking a keen interest in the stranger. After he had gone she asked, 'You're Mrs. . . .?'

'Mrs Butcher. The Oaks. I work for Mr Mumbray.'

'Yes?'

'He's gone. Disappeared.'

'Oh dear. When?'

'Five days.'

With relief, Lydia heard her husband's key turn in the lock. She went to meet him at the door, and gave him a swift breakdown on Mrs Butcher's news. Sam was tired. He disliked Eastgate on a Saturday, disliked being on duty at all on a Saturday. The seaside traffic had been heavy and his superintendent irritable. It would have suited him very well to sit down and watch what was left of the afternoon's televised sport. Instead he nodded, removed his leather jacket, and went into the kitchen.

Mrs Butcher would neither sit down, accept tea, nor loosen her coat. It was all Sam could do to get information out of her, a bit at a time. She had last seen her employer on Monday evening, before she went to bed very early with a violent cold: he had made her go because he said she was infectious. He had seemed quite ordinary in manner, not disturbed. ('Bothered in his mind' was how she put it.) He must have had a visitor whom he let in himself, because she heard the bell ring – it might have rung twice, at different times; she was not sure, with her bad cold and the medicine which made her drowsy. No, she had not heard him come upstairs to bed, but then he was very quiet. And in the morning, no sign of him. Gone.

'You'd be very upset, of course,' Sam said. (Had she been? She showed no sign of emotion, but a muscle at the corner of her mouth jumped continually.) Yes, she had wondered at first, then she saw his car wasn't in the garage and she thought it was all right, because he liked to drive about very late at night. Where? She had no idea.

'Wasn't it a bit odd that he should stay out all night, at this time of year?' Mrs Butcher shrugged. She had not been really concerned until another night had passed without him coming home.

'Why on earth didn't you let us know then?' Sam asked.

'I didn't want to make a fuss. He'd not have liked it.'

'So you let yet another night go by . . . Oh, well, best get some details down. Will you come into the sitting room, Mrs Butcher, please.'

Within a few minutes he had taken down a description of Mumbray's car, its number-plate, the clothes he had been wearing when last seen. And that was about all. Sam had never, so far as he could remember, encountered such an uncommunicative witness, many as were the cases of missing persons in his experience. As he said to Lydia afterwards, it was as if she had not wanted to report the disappearance at all, and having done so was determined to give not a fraction more information than was absolutely necessary. And yet underneath her tight-lipped manner he sensed some emotion: what, he could not define. He wished Lydia had been in the room to listen. He wished still more that Doran had.

When Mrs Butcher had gone he telephoned Eastgate. The desk sergeant chuckled fruitily. 'More shock-horror at Abbotsbourne, Sam? Crime centre of the world, you are. Y'know, there used to be a song on the radio when I was a lad – something about "Here we are, ready an' willin' To strangle yer mother-in-law for a shillin' ''. Sounds like your manor.'

'That's right, it was called "Dirty Work at the Cross-roads".'

'*Crossroads*? Never seen it, but the missis is an addict. What d'you think's happened to this missing person, then?'

'Your guess is as good as mine,' Sam replied cryptically.

'Can't I investigate just the least bit?' Doran pleaded with Sam.

'Sorry, nothing doing. Detective-Inspector Ogle's in charge, and he won't want anyone under his feet. I'd keep out of it if I was you, Doran.'

'You always say that. . . . Oh, all right.' But she was inwardly determined not to be kept out of this most interesting mystery. The best way to find out anything was to ask people. In the shops, at the mobile library, in the Rose, she raised the question of Mumbray's disappearance and invited theories. The answers she got were in the main cautious, as though nobody quite liked to commit themselves. Bob Woods said, 'Good riddance, whatever's come of him,' and changed the conversation to Barbary's health. Marcia, caught in the hairdresser's, seemed far from anxious to talk, and Stella was not to be seen. Doran hung round The Oaks until Mrs Butcher emerged one morning with a rubbish-sack, and could be questioned. She stared inimically.

'No, I've heard nothing. No, I haven't got any ideas. Are you from the police, then?'

Doran said hastily that she was not, just a neighbour.

'I know you. You've been here a few times, haven't you? With that parson.' She dumped the plastic sack outside the gate and vanished indoors.

Rodney said, 'Keep out of it, Doran, for pity's sake. It really has nothing to do with you. And do we want the man found, anyway? Can't we just accept his absence, and be thankful?'

'No, because I believe there's something behind it. I think he's gone away for a reason, to work out something else awful to do to us. *Reculer pour mieux sauter*, as it were. He'll come bounding back like the Demon King, you'll see, and I swear a lot of other people think so too, from the cagey answers I got.'

'I don't think so.' Helena was trundling herself into the room in her new self-propelled wheelchair. 'I think he's somewhere in a field, all scrunched up with agony, staring up at the sky with a terrible expression on his face and dead, dead as anything.'

'Be quiet, if you can't say anything pleasant, Helena,' said her father. 'You know nothing about it.'

Once again, only months since the vanishing of Debbie, the district was being combed by police, but this time the woods yielded no body. Mumbray's car had not been found: he might have driven to any part of the country. Detective-Inspector Ogle was disinclined to follow a trail that led nowhere, and anxious to get back to more rewarding work than looking for a guy nobody seemed to want found. 'Wasting police time, if you ask me,' he told Sam.

That day came news: Mumbray's car had been found abandoned in London, on an old bomb site in Hackney, its wheels and other fittings missing. Of its owner there was no sign, nor any clue to his whereabouts. The mass of fingerprints on the steering and body-work was worse than useless. Just another vandalized car: the search was no farther forward, the mystery unsolved and likely to remain so until Mumbray came forward of his own accord.

Which he did, a full three weeks after his disappearance. A shepherd, rounding up sheep on Romney Marsh, noticed on the surface of one of the deep dykes which drain the marshlands something that floated. At first he took it for a figure cut from some advertisement, a hoarding poster torn down and dropped in the water. Then he looked closer, cried out and ran, scattering his sheep, flying from that miasmic horror to the road where his car waited.

12

There was no doubt that the corpse was Mumbray's. Immersion in the dyke, and the attentions of various interested creatures, had made it hideously unrecognizable, but enough remained of the clothing, and a wallet contained plastic credit-cards and a still-legible driving licence. Such was the state of the body that Mrs Butcher was only shown the jacket of the suit at Eastgate mortuary. She identified it, then went into some kind of convulsion and had to be removed to hospital and put under sedation.

At police headquarters, Detective-Inspector Ogle was put in charge of a murder incident room. The autopsy had raised doubts in the mind of the pathologist.

'I thought at first,' his report read, 'that it was a case of asphyxia, since the signs were present and death had obviously not occurred by drowning. I then observed the extreme inflammation of the stomach walls, which suggested to me bacterial poisoning, caused by the intake of bad food. But tests on a portion of the membrane suggested otherwise, and at this point I decided that samples should be sent to the Public Analyst.'

The PA's verdict was that the cause of death had been aconitine poisoning. There was insufficient evidence to show how it had been administered, the remains being in such an advanced state of decomposition.

'So what's all that mean?' Ogle asked the pathologist, who was reading the report with interest while puffing at his pipe. Understandably, he favoured a strong brand of tobacco. 'Could have been suicide?'

'Could have, but it seems funny stuff to choose. *Aconitum ferox* is a root, bit like horseradish to look at. Its common name is monkshood, by the way, genus Ranunculaceae, and it's quite pretty. If he didn't absorb it in its natural state, and why should he, it could have been taken in medicine or as a liniment. The tincture dose is very small, not more than five drops a time. Better find out if he was being prescribed anything of the kind.'

Ogle, who had been going to, frowned irritably and scribbled. 'What's it prescribed for?'

'Feverish states – depresses the action of the heart. Severe bronchitis, tonsillitis, laryngitis – cardiac hypertrophy, in the right cases, but it's dicey. The liniment's used for sciatica, any kind of neuralgia, sore and painful bruising. You'll find it in the stuff they treat cricket injuries with on the field.'

'And you don't think a suicide would pick it?'

'Frankly I don't, not for choice, though it's been known. The liniment would cause a feeling of paralysis in the mouth, fairly alarming, and the tincture would bring on a very nasty burning and tingling sensation that I'd think would make the party concerned put it down quick and decide on something pleasanter, like a barbiturate or even phenol, which tastes a bit like Benedictine if you don't think about it too much.'

'Thanks, I'll stick to Benedictine, or I would if I could afford it on my pay packet. So would you say aconitine was a popular poison?'

'Used to be in Bengal, once upon a time – they were always knocking each other off with it, according to the records. The Victorians didn't know a lot about it until Whatsisname, Lamson, poisoned his young brother-in-law in 1881 for the boy's Four Per Cents and Consols – but then Lamson was a doctor.'

Derek Ogle was a man who liked to do things in his own way, and proposed to climb the police ladder without undue help, but in the case of Mumbray, Deceased, he thought it well to talk developments over with Abbotsbourne's village bobby. He knew of Sam Eastry's reluctance to be promoted, and found it incomprehensible, remembering what he

160

thought of as the boring small-town character of Abbotsbourne and the infinite desirability of almost any move upwards; but Sam had been neither resentful nor obstructive during his earlier involvement in the case, and Ogle recognized honesty when he saw it, not to mention a thorough acquaintance with the place and its people. He drove back up the valley.

'Something told me last time I was here,' he said, as they strolled in the well-tended garden of the police house, 'that the corpse wasn't exactly the most popular man in the parish. Am I right?'

'Perfectly right.' Sam was being careful, though helpful.

'Why was that?'

'He rubbed people up the wrong way. Or that's how it seemed to me.'

'Which people?'

Sam dead-headed a faded flower which had escaped his notice. 'Well, hard to say. There was the business of the cricket field.' He explained it. 'Upset a lot of people, that did.'

'And does that go on, or has his death knocked it on the head?'

'It comes to a halt. The contract hadn't been signed, and as no will's been found the whole thing's in abeyance.' Sam omitted to add that he had learned this from Doran, who had taken the trouble to telephone the council's solicitors, and come to him with the glad news.

'Mm. So it looks as though the death has done Abbotsbourne a bit of good. Right, what about individuals? Anyone have a particular down on the late Mr M.?'

Sam was reluctant to sell any of his fellow-villagers down the river, for the gratification of this sharp-nosed, sharp-eyed personage. He said, 'I couldn't put my finger on anyone in particular. There was just a general feeling. Mr Mumbray kept himself very much to himself, and that's not much liked in a place as small as this. His didn't mix, you see – didn't go to church or any of the pubs, or belong to the Gardeners' Society, that sort of thing. Didn't take an interest, you might say.'

161

Ogle shot him a sharp look, conscious that he was being fobbed off and not liking it. 'All right. I'll have to do some interrogating myself, on top of what I've done already. Can we check names and addresses?'

Doran was alone in Bell House. She had never been more alone there, for Rhona was gone. On the day that the discovery of Mumbray's body was made known she had come to Doran, solemn-faced.

'I don't like having to tell you this, Miss Doran, but I'm leaving. I can't stay here any more.'

'Rhona! But why? I don't understand.'

'Well, it's a bit hard to explain. But all this business – that man missing, and police all over the place, and then finding him, and the nasty atmosphere. . . . I don't know, it's all been too much, too like when I lost Debbie, even though it was so different really. I ought to be glad he's dead, and I am, but it's upset me.'

'Don't you think you might get over it in time?'

'I might. But I don't think so. It was ever so kind of you to have me and Debbie here, and don't think I'm not grateful. But since she went it's not been home to me, and I'd be happier away.'

'Yes, I see. I do understand. Have you any idea where you'll go?'

'Brighton. There's a cousin of Jim's there. I always got on with her. I phoned her and she says there's Christmas vacancies in the big shop where she works, and she's sure I could get one, and then perhaps something in the domestic line, seeing I'm a bit long in the tooth for a shopgirl.' She smiled faintly.

'I'm sure you'll get something easily, Rhona. Someone's going to find a treasure in you – lucky them. When do you want to leave?'

'Soon as possible – Saturday, I thought, if that's all right with you. Then I can settle in over the weekend and go to Billington's for an interview on Monday. I'll leave everything straight here for you.'

'Yes, thank you. I'll manage.' Never mind about notice, never mind about an employer left alone in a big house that whispered and creaked and sighed at night. Never mind that there was probably a murderer loose in the village, one who, however justified in the present case, might decide to repeat his or her success. Rhona had made up her mind, and that was that. On the Saturday, accompanied by Vi, she accepted impassively Doran's parting kiss and left in a taxi with a quantity of luggage. It was surprising how little different in appearance the house was without her, as though she had breathed nothing of herself into it.

And yet her going left a void, which rang and echoed. That evening Doran applied herself furiously to the cleaning of a box of miscellaneous silver and plate, to the accompaniment of *Belshazzar's Feast*, played at top volume. Thou art weighed in the balances, and art found wanting. . . . A pretty Georgian spoon, restored to its old soft lustre, winked up at her, grateful, perhaps. Inanimate objects did not let one down. Doran talked to it, watching her face diminished and lengthened in its concave bowl.

A scatter of snow fell during the night. She telephoned Rodney, catching him in the rush between morning services.

'Please, could you bring yourself to come for a walk before lunch? On the downs or somewhere, I don't care. But of course you couldn't, you're too busy. Silly of me to ask, on a Sunday.'

There was a pause, then: 'Why not? I've just got to slip round to Mrs Fitchett. Half-elevenish?'

Rodney's little car was climbing up the valley, through fields speckled with the white of snow and the dull ochre of browsing sheep. Away to the south rose the green velvet humps of Bronze Age barrows, under which urns and ashes, and the older bones of mammoth and elk and little wild horses, lay undiscovered. Doran contemplated them in her mind's eye with a certain satisfaction. How clever of Keats to see one's fancy burrowing like a demon mole beneath grave-mounds . . . exactly what it did. Rodney cast a sidelong glance at her.

'Mrs Fitchett was having one of her good days. She said,

"It was that there Condemnation Service of yours that did for that man, Vicar, and no mistake." I shook my head modestly, but I rather think I agree, little as I want to. A Condemnation Service was just what it was.'

'Nonsense. You didn't mean to kill him.'

'I don't know. Perhaps I did. I think I was carried away by a feeling of power, the wrong sort of power.'

'Well, you certainly didn't mean to influence someone to poison him.'

'Is that what happened? Let's stop here, shall we.'

They began to walk towards the fragment of abbey ruin that broke the skyline. The short-turfed ground was hard beneath their feet, the air crisp as broken ice; Doran began to feel better, scuffing her feet through dead leaves and breathing the air from a distant bonfire.

'Yes, that's what happened, so far as I can gather from Sam. He didn't mean to tell me anything, but I called in with some winter cabbage, because Ozzy *will* grow too many, and we got talking, and I sort of read between the lines. The coroner's jury favoured Murder by a Person or Persons Unknown, because of the type of poison, it seems, and Detective-Inspector Ogle's after clues like a ferret down a rabbit-hole. Sam's out of it now, of course. Ogle and his side-kick are going round interviewing everybody who might have – have had anything to do with it.'

Rodney broke off a withered branch and swished the air with it. 'Including me, and my household?'

'Doubtless. Sam hasn't named names, just given him a list of people who had contact with Mumbray. Everyone except tradesmen and the garage and the postman, I suppose.'

Still swishing with the stick, Rodney murmured, ' "I know not what she saw or heard, but fury filled her eye, She bought some nasty Doctor's-stuff, and she put it in a pie." '

'Yes, seemingly somebody did, and good luck to them.'

Very casually, Rodney said, 'It wasn't you, I suppose?'

'No! What a dreadful thing to say.'

'I just wanted to shock you from your Sabbatarian gloom. Didn't really think you were Nell Cook *redivivus*. And I suppose you'll contrive to find out what Ogle gathers from his victims – get talking, and read between the lines, as you did with Sam? Just be careful, Doran, that's all. Nell Cook also had a strong investigative streak, and finished up as a fleshless, sapless skeleton within a horrid well. Wouldn't like you to do that.'

'You have a diabolical memory,' Doran said tartly. Then, suddenly, stopped in her tracks and whispered, 'Don't move. Look!'

Some ten yards ahead of them, under a low bank fringed with snow, was a family of foxes. The dog, handsome in the pride of his russet winter fur, watched as three young ones tumbled and scuffled over the outstretched paws of their mother, bright-eyed, seemingly boneless, cuffing and nipping each other. One staggered to its feet and was instantly floored by its sibling, rolling over against the vixen, who graciously bent her head and licked it. Innocent, beautiful, utterly oblivious to the threatening presence of the two humans, they seemed a Holy Family of their own kind.

'God damn all huntsmen and pink coats,' Doran whispered.

'Amen.' Rodney's hand had found hers and held it fast. Stillness and peace wrapped them: for a long moment there was no one in the world but themselves and the foxes.

Detective-Inspector Ogle liked to think of himself as a twenty-four-hour policeman. It had effectively ended his marriage, not much to his regret: he was content enough in his Eastgate flatlet, with the prospect ever before him of a large and handsome desk at a window facing on Victoria Street, and the best carpeting Scotland Yard had to offer beneath his well-polished shoes. With future commissionerhood in his mind, he allowed nothing to come between him and the execution of his duties.

With his acolyte, young Detective-Constable Warrash, he arrived in Abbotsbourne early on a bright cold morning. They parked the police car in the square, Ogle's keen gaze noting other cars which were improperly parked or looked as though they belonged to owners who would leave them over the time limit. He proposed to conduct his inquiries on foot, thus promoting the circulation of the blood and stimulating the brain between interviews.

'You take it from me,' he told Warrash, 'somebody here knows something. Last time around I got the message loud and clear, most of the late Mumbray's neighbours hated his guts. Let's see who hated 'em most. How's your shorthand?'

'Not bad, sir. I do keep practising, all the time.'

Ogle grunted. 'I'll know if you leave anything out – my memory's photographic.' A rude reply occurred to Warrash, to the effect that there was no need for him to take bloody notes, in that case. He refrained from uttering it.

The surgery was their first call. The receptionist, timidly smiling, showed them into Room One, Dr Levison's own. He was there, by appointment, half an hour earlier than his usual time. Tom Fullathorn, in Room Two, waited to take any urgent calls and the first appointments if police time overlapped them.

Eli Levison's eyes were wary, his manner stiff, verging on the brusque. With just such an air might Spaniards of his race have waited for the heated irons and pincers of Torquemada's inquisitors.

Yes, he agreed, Leonard Mumbray had been a patient of his. For something very minor, a pain in the upper arm which Mumbray had feared might be a symptom of heart trouble.

'And was it?'

'No, just a rheumatic twinge – quite common at his age.'

'And you treated it with – what, Doctor?'

'I gave him a prescription for an embrocation.'

'Which he used?'

'I couldn't say. Presumably the trouble cleared up, as he didn't come back.'

'Can you let me have a copy of that prescription, Doctor?'

After the slightest pause, Levison said, 'Certainly. I'll have the case-notes brought in.' He pressed a bell. For the first time he was able to take his eyes from the detective's, but already Ogle had read in them fear and guilt. Not, he fancied, guilt for murder, or fear of what the prescription might reveal. No, there was something else, some tie between Levison and

166

Mumbray. That would come out in due course, and meanwhile Levison would be left sweating blood.

'Right,' Ogle said as they emerged. 'That's him taken care of first, like we promised him. On to The Oaks.'

They had been there before, to the ugly quiet house, before the body had been found. Mrs Butcher waited for them, watchful and guarded. Some housekeepers would have resented their search of the kitchen, its cupboards, refrigerator, drawers, oven, but she stood aloof, while Ogle poked and pried. All was clean and decent, but no savoury scents haunted the air from garlic, herbs or spices, and the only recipe book was a pedestrian, well-thumbed one which belonged to the gas cooker. Warrash, newly-married to an enthusiastic young wife, thought it was as though nobody had cared much what was prepared in that kitchen or eaten in the house. What kind of man had Deceased been? Ascetic, frugal, fonder of eating out than eating in? He would not have fancied Mrs B. as a cook himself – too stringy, not the figure for a woman who enjoyed her own cuisine, and with a look to her of one who could have a nasty temper once she had let her face slip. A bit mad, even.

Ogle found her hard to interrogate, since she volunteered nothing and seemed to be challenging him silently to get more out of her than she wished to give. Yes, she had been with her late employer a long time, twenty-one years. He had very simple tastes, just plain food, preferring sweets to savouries, and what he ate she cooked herself, not liking bought stuff and mixes. As to drink, he didn't care for it – just kept a bottle of brandy in the house. Asked to produce a specimen of this, she handed over a bottle, almost full, for Warrash to take away for analysis.

The rest of the house yielded nothing helpful to the inquiry. There were hundreds of books in what might be called a study or a library, law books, dictionaries, uniform volumes of Dickens, Trollope, and similar classics, all looking equally unread. The owner had not been a man to inscribe his name or use book-plates. It was as unrewarding a room as Ogle had ever seen.

The bedroom presented a rather different picture. Its

furnishings were as plain and ugly as those of the rest of the house, as impersonal as those of an old-fashioned hotel might be. But in a deep, walk-in wardrobe Ogle found more books, on shelves behind a front of hanging garments. He looked, read, flipped pages and passed on a volume to the constable.

'Not sure but what you're too young for this sort of stuff.'

Warrash too looked and read, before, very pink about the cheeks, he handed the book back.

'Nasty, eh?' Ogle was working his way along the shelves, sampling here and there. 'I reckon we'd impound this lot if we found 'em in a shop. I knew it, I could have told you, there's something here not what it ought to be, and here's the evidence of it.'

'Somethig nasty in the woodshed,' Warrash offered helpfully.

Ogle's mind was a literal one. 'Not much use looking out there. It's a man's bedroom tells you what he is, you remember that. Well: sadism, stuff about witchcraft, a history of torture and execution, abnormal psychology, volumes of what they call curious prints, and just plain filth. Not a bad little haul. Start loading up, will you? There's a couple of suitcases on the wardrobe. Then you can go and fetch the car.' He began to remove the volumes from the shelves. Warrash eyed them distastefully.

'Have we got to?'

'Yes, we have. Why? Don't you fancy handling 'em? You'll see worse than that if you stay in the Force, my lad. Come on, heave ho.'

As Warrash filled the suitcases with their unpleasant burden Ogle went downstairs for a final prod at Mrs Butcher.

'Didn't mix much then, Mr Mumbray? But I expect he got to know some of the locals. Who, now? Just give me a few names.'

'I don't know, I'm sure.' Her face was tight shut against him. 'Some of them called, but I didn't take note.'

'You must have told him their names if you answered the door.'

'I didn't take note, I tell you.'

Under Ogle's penetrating stare she proffered uneasily, 'There was the vicar. And that crippled child of his. And that girl who sells furniture, her at Bell House. And a big young man, plays cricket, shouts a lot. Oh, and a woman with a subscription list.'

'Who was that?'

'I can't say, I'm sure, only that she got nothing.'

I'll bet, thought Ogle. Gleefully he stored up names he already knew to dictate to Warrash when they got back to the car.

Eli Levison was not pleased to receive another police visit just before the end of his surgery.

'No, I will *not* supply you with a list of patients for whom I've prescribed medicines containing aconitine. The dead are one thing, the living something else.' His hand hovered over the bell.

'I can find out, you know.'

'Then find out. And make sure you get every detail of their complaints – however confidential.'

'Got a lot of VD round here, have you?' Ogle's expression was innocent. The doctor's palm came down sharply on the bell.

Ogle had not expected a warm welcome. 'Come on.' He jerked his head at Warrash. 'We're going to talk to everyone Mrs Butcher mentioned. First the parsonage.'

Rodney was out when they arrived. Nancy, after hard scrutiny of Ogle's warrant card, admitted them with the enthusiasm she would have shown towards a pair of man-eating tigers. 'The vicar's got enough to worry him as it is,' she informed them, to Ogle's interest.

'Now what might his worries be?' he asked rhetorically of Warrash, when they were alone in the study. 'I'll look forward to finding out what makes a reverend tick.' He walked round the bookshelves, perusing. 'Mm . . . not too many religious books, not as many as you'd expect. Lots of poetry, and novels. Very fond of P. G. Wodehouse, seemingly. Works of Dickens. Life of The Rev. R. S. Barham. Lewis Carroll – that's kid's stuff. And a whole shelf of books about cricket. One of these hearty parsons is he?'

Rodney, when he at last appeared, looked not in the least hearty. He had just come from a deathbed, and was not in the mood for anything other than solitude and a cup of coffee, but settled down resignedly to answer questions. Yes, he had met the late Leonard Mumbray, socially, at a cocktail party. Later they had met twice, he thought. He had called on Mumbray in connection with an episode involving his daughter. Briefly he described it, Warrash writing busily and Ogle's eyes gleaming like twin green traffic lights.

'So you weren't able to prove this charge the little girl brought, sir?'

'Not prove, exactly, but there was no doubt in my mind.'

'Not given to fancying things, is she?'

'No more than most children.'

'She's an invalid, your daughter, sir?'

'Badly crippled. It's a progressive muscular disease – incurable, I'm afraid. Dr Levison will tell you more about it if you want to know' (though I don't see what business it is of yours, his tone implied).

'Oh, so Dr Levison treats her, does he? Er, might I have a word with the little girl, sir, if it's not putting you out? I'd just like to get her version of this story about Mr Mumbray.'

'I'd rather you didn't, Inspector. She's easily upset.'

'It would be most useful, sir. I won't be hard on her.'

Rodney went to the door and shouted for Nancy, who appeared a few moments later hovering protectively over Helena and her wheelchair. Helena, far from being upset at the prospect of police interrogation, was excited and forthcoming, turning sharply from her father to Ogle and answering questions almost before they had been asked. Warrash squirmed: he thought he had never met a nastier little girl.

'Oh, yes, it was him, the same man,' she was saying. 'Daddy took me to see him, and Mr Eastry came as well, and I knew him perfectly well but he said he'd never seen me before. I was frightened and Nancy gave me some of my new medicine when we got home, didn't you, Nance.'

'Ah,' Ogle said thoughtfully. 'So you can't have liked Mr Mumbray much, after that bad experience.'

170

'I *hated* him,' she spat out. 'He said horrible things, I wouldn't like to tell you what.' She looked so ready to do so that Nancy said warningly, 'Now, dear!' with a hand on her shoulder. But Helena rushed on. 'He was evil, you see, pure evil, Daddy said, one of the Devil's people. Daddy held a special service to get rid of him, did you know that? It was such fun, terrible curses and calling down God's anger on sinners and things, fire and brimstone and storms and rain – "this shall be their portion to drink", I remember it said that. And then that man died.'

Ogle was fascinatedly taking in the vicar's tense face, Nancy's frantic anxiety: pondering on the sentence of Scripture which had remained in the child's mind – why? He nodded slowly.

'Bit unusual, a service like that, sir, wasn't it?'

'It was a Service of Commination,' Rodney said tersely. 'It's not often used. I thought it appropriate.'

'Very strange, Mr Mumbray dying afterwards, like he did. Quite a coincidence. Somebody did give him a portion to drink, you know – or eat, possibly.' He watched all three faces, Helena's gleeful, Nancy's angrily defensive, Rodney's drawn, troubled.

'*Not* a surfeit of lampreys, then,' murmured Rodney wildly.

'Pardon, sir? Well, I think that's about all. Oh, just one thing – this medicine Miss Helena takes, could I have a drop or two of it in a small bottle?'

Helena frowned. 'What do you want my medicine for? It's nasty. I don't like it.'

'Just a sample. For our analyst to take a look at.'

13

Rodney said after a shocked pause, 'Go and get the bottle, Nancy. And then I think it's time Helena had her lunch.'

'What about yours, Vicar?' Nancy snapped.

'I shan't want any. Just coffee.' She went, glaring at Ogle, leaving the door a crack open.

Helena scowled. 'I'd rather stay here and talk to the detective.'

Ogle mentally rubbed his hands: and so you shall, my dear, so you shall, if I've anything to do with it. Then, aloud, 'That's a very smart chair you've got there – up-to-date model, is it?'

'Oh yes,' Helena told him proudly. 'It's the latest thing, the new power sort. Daddy paid ever so much for it, didn't you, Daddy? I can get all over this floor by myself and quite a long way outside, even up kerbs, it says on the advertisement, but Nan won't let me cross roads yet. Shall I show you how it works?'

'No, that's all right, thanks. It must be nice for you to get about so easily. How far have you been, outside?'

'Well – round the square, and the churchyard, and Cow Lane because there isn't much traffic. Dr Levison says I've got to get all the exercise I can because my muscles need it –'

Nancy returned, tight-lipped, with a medicine bottle and a smaller, empty one. She handed them to Ogle. 'Here, fill it yourself, then you'll be sure I'm giving you the right stuff. If you want a funnel there's one in the kitchen.' But he was pouring neatly, with a practised hand, then placing the sample bottle in an envelope before giving it to Warrash. Helena was all sharp-eyed interest.

'Why are you doing that?'

173

'Just routine, just routine.'

'Go along,' Rodney said. 'And you, Nan. If the inspector's finished with you, that is.'

Helena sped out, knowing a certain tone in her father's voice which meant his patience was at its limit. Nancy turned at the door, her eyes on Ogle's. For such a small spare person she had a formidable air, reminding him of a great-aunt who had never considered him a nice boy.

' "Whoso," ' pronounced Nancy, ' "shall offend one of these little ones, it were better for him that a mill-stone were hanged about his neck, and that he were drowned in the midst of the sea." '

'Well!' Ogle said after the door had shut, 'was that a bit out of your special service, sir?'

'Actually no. An observation of Our Lord's to His disciples. You must excuse Nancy. She's very defensive of Helena – and me, for that matter. We're all the family she has.'

Ogle was embarrassed. 'Quite. Yes, well. Coming back to Mr Mumbray, sir, what do you yourself, personally, really feel about his death, considering that you knew him slightly, and bearing in mind things you've heard from your . . . from people round here.' Surely one didn't talk about a parson's flock these days.

'For myself, Inspector, I thought him a very evil man whose actions deliberately brought a great deal of trouble upon this village. As a priest, I can't exactly allow myself to rejoice in the death of anybody. I can only trust that he's – how can I put it – changed for the better. Does that answer your question?'

'Very neatly, sir. Well, thank you for your time. I hope the little girl wasn't upset.'

Over Real Ale, breaded scampi and chips, in the Feathers, he laid his deductions before Warrash. 'I'm not inclined to think the Rev. had anything to do with it. These religious types can get a bit wild, of course, ranting and raving texts like that nurse or whatever she is –'

'I think it's called Speaking with Tongues, sir.'

'You can think again. That's something quite other, I had a

174

very nasty case of it once, man cut his wife up in pieces. . . .' The recollection was interfering with Ogle's scampi. 'No, as I said, I don't think the Reverend Rod's the violent sort. But the kid – *what* about her? Ever see a meaner little face? How a nice guy like that comes to throw such a vicious little runt, well, it beats me.'

'She's ill, sir, and diseases like that change people. I expect she's very frustrated and takes it out on her dad – you could tell he's got a lot to put up with.'

'You stick to your shorthand and leave the psychology to me. Who's next, then? "The girl who sells furniture" – that's Miss Fairweather, and she's out all day. "Big young man, plays cricket", Robert Woods, works in Eastgate – better leave both of 'em for the evening. "Woman with a subscription list" – that would be Miss Marcia Fawkes, Laburnum Cottage, well-known do-gooder and pillar of society. Lives with another woman, also a Miss. Two of *those*, I wouldn't be surprised. Lot of it about these days, though how they. . . .' His speculations brought a blush to Warrash's young cheeks. 'The other one's a nutter, according to what Eastry said, or what he didn't say – plays about with voodoo, magic spells and stuff. Let's go and have a shufty.'

Marcia and Stella were both at home. They were sitting by a good fire, Marcia embroidering a church kneeler, Stella nursing two kittens, a tabby and a black. In the fireplace alcove the television cackled and quacked as a forties film comedy ambled on its way. Marcia received the police graciously. Stella smiled vaguely, crooning to the kittens that nice uncles were coming to see Tommy and Grizel. Ogle asked politely whether the television might be turned off.

'Of course, officer – I'm afraid I don't know what I ought to call you. Oh, Inspector, thank you. We weren't really watching, were we, Stella, though I do think they're so restful, these old films, the girls all with the same hair-dos, long at the back and rolled up at the front, and shiny red lipstick. But it's all so innocent, isn't it, compared with the things that go on today.'

'Oh, very. Speaking of which, how well did you know the late Mr Mumbray, Miss Fawkes?'

She looked him straight in the eye, a tactic which he had learned to distrust. 'Hardly at all, really. We met at someone's house – once, I think.'

Ogle reached for the constable's notebook and flipped its pages ostentatiously. 'Yet the local paper's reporter says that you spoke out very strongly against him after the Commination Service. He quotes you.'

'Oh. Yes, well, I did know how our dear vicar felt about this man, and other people did too, what with practically abducting little Helena and taking the cricket field away from the village, and then that dreadful business about the Selling girl – he must have been a very bad man.'

Warrash scribbled. 'But you had no personal quarrel with him, madam?' Ogle asked. Marcia's face, as she returned an emphatic 'No', was as complete a blank as a human face could be; too blank. He decided to investigate her, since she was not going to give anything of her own accord. He turned to Stella.

'Miss Meeson. What terms were you on with Mr Mumbray?' Out of the corner of his practised eye he saw the warning look Marcia gave her. Stella stroked a sleeping kitten from its head to the tip of its tail.

'Terms? I don't understand.'

'You had met him, I believe.' Necessary to spell it out to this dumb character. 'Socially?'

'Oh yes. At the Haydon-Trees' – before he banished them. I knew him at once for Chorozon.'

'Sorry, madam, you've lost me. Who?'

'Chorozon.' Her tone implied that police officers were woefully uneducated not to recognize a household name. 'The demon, the Dweller in the Abyss. He controls the unconscious, you know, and makes people subject to his will. That's why all these bad things have happened, because he willed them to. He was a very powerful magician. But I was too strong for him, wasn't I, Marcia?'

'Yes, dear, you were.'

'Could you spell the name for me, madam, so that we can get it down in writing.'

Stella spelt it out, making a sign with her finger as she did

176

so. 'The usual way of overcoming Chorozon,' she said chattily, 'is to employ a magic sword. Well, of course I haven't got one, and it would be rather difficult to get hold of one without borrowing one from a museum of magic. (There are several, did you know?) But I guessed that an *athamé* would do, and I actually found one, so I took it. I knew they'd never miss it because they had so many knives and things.'

'I don't think the inspector quite understands what it is, Stella,' Marcia said gently.

'Oh. Well, it's a knife with a black handle – a special kind. If it's killed in the past, so much the better.'

'I see, madam.' Ogle was now as convinced as the scribbling Warrash that they were dealing with a dangerous lunatic. 'And you attacked the deceased with this knife? Perhaps there was something, er, poisonous on the point of it?' (What a brilliant deduction, he thought, one that would explain everything.)

Stella's eyes opened wide. 'Oh no! That would have been *quite* useless. I used it in spells, very powerful spells, and at last I defeated Chorozon. Doran Fairweather and the constable stopped me, but the charm had already worked. You know, when I first met this man he was dwelling in I was quite excited, because I saw a great challenge in him. I'm a white witch, you see, and he was a black magician. . . .'

'Stella,' Marcia said, 'I'm sure these two gentlemen would like some tea. Would you go and put the kettle on?'

'But Tommy and Grizel are so comfortable . . . oh, well, if you like.'

When she had gone Marcia said hurriedly, 'I know that all seemed very strange, Inspector, but you mustn't take it too seriously. Stella has these fancies, and I must say I don't care about it myself, she makes such a mess in the kitchen boiling up herbs, and I don't like some of the books she keeps in her room – some by that terrible man Crowley, I expect you've heard of him. But I do assure you that since – Mr Mumbray died she's been much better, quite ordinary, really. I think she believes she did it herself by magic. You won't – do anything about her, will you?'

'I can't say, madam. We have to pursue our investigations in every direction. To go back to you yourself – are you sure you had nothing personal against the deceased, nothing that would, say, give Miss Meeson the idea that she ought to get rid of him to help you?'

Marcia's eyes snapped once, and her mouth tightened. 'I've told you, nothing. I hardly knew the man.'

Back in the car, Ogle asked, 'Got all that? Right. Head back to the cop-shop. I want to talk to Eastry.'

'Think she did it, then?'

'The nutter? You tell me. It's the other one I'm interested in.'

Sam Eastry, hating himself, felt obliged to tell Ogle about Doran's revelation to him that Mumbray had been black-mailing Marcia. Yes, it was all hearsay, but his source was a very reliable one. Pressed, he named Doran. He confirmed that Stella had been seen performing curious rites in which a black-handled knife had been featured, and added that the knife had disappeared from the Haydon-Trees' drawing room. Reluctantly, he parted with the address of the Haydon-Trees' solicitors, and mentioned Marcia's bout of alcoholic poisoning. Life grew fairer by the minute for Ogle. Eagerly he dashed off to the Rose, found himself at its doors before opening-time and went round to the back, thundering insistently at the door to the accompaniment of the Bellacres' dogs' frenzied barking.

Rosie Bellacre, putting the finishing touches to her appearance before her evening duties, was not pleased to see him, but had no choice but to ask him in.

'Yes, Miss Fawkes did pass out that morning. It was the first time she'd done it, but she'd been in quite a lot recently, and drinking more than she ought to. Not that we're stuffy landlords, at all, but we don't like scenes, and I was getting a bit worried until Doran came in and sorted her out. Doran Fairweather, Bell House, friend of the vicar's.'

That girl who sells furniture. Ogle purred. The name was cropping up in every inquiry, and he was impatient to meet its owner. Did Mrs Bellacre, he wondered, have any ideas about why Miss Fawkes had taken to drinking heavily?

Rosie hesitated. 'Well. Win . . . my husband and I thought she had something on her mind. She'd changed a lot the last few months, came in often, whereas we never used to see her at all, and I know she was buying bottles of sherry and whisky at the off-licence in Chapel Street, because they mentioned it to me and said, joking-like, we were missing out on a good customer. Miss Fawkes used to be so prim and proper, you'd never have thought she'd take to . . .' She glanced at the clock. 'Will you excuse me? We open up in five minutes.'

The boy who had reported the Commination Service was not at home, his mother said, but Ogle tracked him down easily enough to the art shop at the end of the High Street, where a small exhibition of a local artist's works was having its preview that evening. As the shop's owner laid out wine-glasses and made last-minute changes to the hanging line, he was collecting titles of paintings and making up his own descriptions of them, which when his paper came out would astonish the artist. Delighted to be called on by police, he responded eagerly to questioning. Ogle hoped not to catch his awful cold.

'Oh, you read my piece, did you, officer? Now that was a very interesting job, very much out of the usual run – I get to cover a lot of weddings and funerals, of course, but a Com . . . a service like that's quite something else, isn't it? I must say I thought the vicar went a bit far –'

'Miss Fawkes. You reported her as talking to you quite violently.'

'Oh yes, very wound up, she was, quite excited.'

'Did she mention Mr Mumbray's name?'

The reporter thought. 'Sorry, can't remember.' He blew his nose long and sonorously. 'But the vicar's little girl did. She said –'

'I know, I've got your report here. So you think Miss Fawkes had some good reason for being so much in favour of the service? Yes, I see. Right, thanks.' He rushed Warrash out into the fresh air, stared after by local landscapes, abstracts, and flattering portraits of Abbotsbourne children, already bought for forty pounds each by their fond parents.

Warrash was very tired. He had been note-taking all day; he had had some nine hours of his superior's company, had walked and driven miles, and eaten so hurriedly that even his youthful digestion had suffered. He had been just a little frightened by Stella Meeson, more than a little sickened by Mumbray's collection of books. At home, in the suburbs of Eastgate, his wife Alison would be back from work and busy preparing the evening meal he had promised he would be home in time to eat.

'Is that it, sir?' he asked, hoping against hope that Ogle, too, had had enough. Even detective-inspectors must sometimes feel human exhaustion and hunger and general fed-upness with the job.

' "It"? No, that isn't it. We've got to catch this Fairweather number' (rather good, that, sort of Sam Spade word) 'as soon as she gets back, before she's had time to go round asking too many questions. Very snoopy type, from what I can make out. Back up the High Street, turn left, down a bit of a hill, then I think I know where it is.'

Doran was struggling with a casserole. She was heartily sick of grills, quick but boring, never up in time to prepare food before she left for work, but the previous evening she had forced herself to put some diced beef into a marinade of red wine and dried herbs. By now it should be tender, delicious, just right for frying up with onion and mushroom. Instead it was of the texture of boiled plastic, and an unappetizing grey in colour. Eating fragments of onion, she cursed it, thought bitterly of Rhona, now doubtless living on hearty meals prepared by her husband's cousin, and read snatches of a new thriller from the mobile library, propped up against a mixing bowl.

The bell rang. Doran paused, seriously considered having it disconnected and the knocker removed, then answered the door.

Ogle presented himself, then his constable, and had a foot in the hall before Doran had had time to take in the information on his warrant card.

'Yes, right, come in. It'll have to be the kitchen.' There was

180

only one chair in it, so she dragged another in from the hall and herself stood, stirring the surly casserole, which was now trying to burn itself to the bottom of the pan. Ogle sat upright, his eyes everywhere, as possible clues started out at him from the kitchen implements on their wall hooks, the grocer's calendar, arrays of cups and jugs neatly hanging with handles facing the same direction, the vase of dried flowers and the bowl on the floor lettered PUSSY to attract the stray cat Doran was trying to tame. Warrash drooped over his notebook.

'Miss Fairweather.' Ogle believed in beginning by terrorizing females, according to the gospel of the late Alfred Hitchcock. 'I've been given to understand that you made several visits to the late Mr Leonard Mumbray.'

'Yes, I did.' The female seemed not at all terrorized; disappointing. 'I suppose you want to know why. I called on him three times, once to deliver a bookcase he'd bought from me, then in connection with his having frightened Rod – our vicar's daughter, and then about the cricket field. I expect you know about that. I don't think there were any other times.'

Ogle muttered something under his breath to Warrash. It was meaningless, but would sound portentous to her. 'I see,' he said aloud. 'And what were your relations with him?'

'Relations? What an odd word. My attitude to him, if that's what you mean, Inspector, was one of great dislike. I thought he was a bad man who was trying to do bad things to as many of us as possible.'

'A black magician, perhaps?'

Doran frowned. 'What? No, of course not.'

Ogle let a silence fall: usually a telling manoeuvre, but his victim merely crumbled a stock tablet into boiling water and added it hopefully to the pungent mess in the pan. He studied her: attractive in what he could only call an airy-fairy sort of way, like one of those model girls who look glamorous in spite of having, apparently, come indoors out of a high wind wearing no make-up and assorted rags. Lovely figure, a bit thin for his taste, pretty hair, big eyes. Certainly the best-looking female he'd met in Abbotsbourne, so far. He pressed on.

'You know Miss Marcia Fawkes well?'

'Not really. Only as an acquaintance.'

'But well enough to hear from her that she was paying black-mail to Leonard Mumbray.'

Doran dropped a spoon with a clatter. 'Who told you that?' But of course, it could be only one person, Sam. So confidences were under the axe; what would come out next? 'Well, never mind where you got it from – yes, she did tell me that.'

'And told you the reason for the blackmail, too.'

Doran set her lips tight. 'It was something in her past, an indiscretion that Mumbray found out about – he'd been a lawyer, you know. More than that I won't tell you, because it's not my secret. Ask her yourself.' She watched him muttering to Warrash, and the constable underlining something heavily.

'Then there was the matter of Helena Chelmarsh. You were convinced that it was Mumbray who took her away from home and . . . maltreated her?'

'Well, of course. Aren't you?'

'I interviewed the vicarage household at some length this morning, Miss Fairweather. It seemed to me very strange that nobody, nobody at all, should have seen Mumbray pushing the little girl in her invalid chair, all the way to the ruins and back. My constable and I drove up there this morning, and it's quite a distance. All a bit odd?'

'It was just his luck. He would have got away with giving a firework display on Margate front and not being noticed, if he didn't want to be. The devil's luck, that's what he had.'

'Ah! So you *do* think he practised black magic?'

'No, I don't, and why do you keep saying that?'

'Somebody else's testimony. Returning to Helena Chelmarsh, whom I gather you know very well, would you describe her as a pleasant-natured child?'

Doran felt herself beginning to blush: the questions were getting nearer home. 'No, I'm afraid I wouldn't. She has a lot to try her, what with being nearly helpless from her illness, and often in pain. One couldn't expect her to be quite like other children.'

'No. She struck me as what I might call vindictive. Enough to take revenge on someone who'd upset her badly?'

Now he saw shock register on Doran's face. It was a moment before she answered. 'I could never believe that for a minute. Surely it's one thing to be sharp-tempered, and another to. . . .'

'Commit murder? It's been known. Some juvenile crime, especially in recent years, has included deliberate homicide for revenge. And I'm told the new invalid chair's made her pretty mobile. Given the sort of luck you were mentioning, and a bit of cunning on her part, which wouldn't surprise me, it's possible, I'd say.'

The shock was there, all right. Ogle followed up his blow. 'Her father's very protective of her, I take it – enough to have gone round with PC Eastry to face Mumbray with charges of assault, and got a flat denial. So wouldn't he have been capable of taking reprisals into his own hands? That housekeeper or nurse or whatever quoted a pretty violent bit of the Bible – what was it, Constable?'

Warrash read back from his notes the passage from St Matthew's Gospel to a listener whose cheeks were now pale. She answered, in a voice that trembled a little, 'I never heard anything so ridiculous. The vicar is quite incapable of injuring anybody.'

In her reaction, Ogle had his cue to pursue a line of inquiry suggested to him by various hints he had picked up that day: not conscious hints, merely overtones his sharp ear had caught from the way in which people had mentioned Doran. He appeared to switch away from the sensitive subject of the vicarage.

'I heard from Mumbray's housekeeper,' he said conversationally, 'that you'd called there several times. Oh yes, we'd confirmed that, hadn't we? Now, Miss Fairweather, I have the distinct impression, and correct me if I'm wrong, that you had your own reasons for disliking Mumbray, quite apart from the ways in which he'd upset the community. I wonder what they could have been? Had he made any accusation against you?'

'No.' The pale cheeks were a deep, painful scarlet now, the blush spreading. She put her hands to her throat, hiding its colour. Warrash, who had taken a warm fancy to her and was hating his superior more every minute, was visited by the memory of a romantic story concerning some lady of old days whose skin was so delicately transparent that when she drank red wine it could be seen visibly coursing down her long slender throat. Possibly Mary, Queen of Scots, also a victim of brutality. He tried to comfort her with a sympathetic look, but her eyes were turned away from him.

'Come now,' Ogle said sharply. 'Don't tell me Mumbray didn't say something to you. Defamatory, was it? Slur on your character? You might as well come clean, because I can find out anyway.'

Words poured through Doran's mind, uttered in the sneering highish voice she remembered too well: the sacred roof of the vicarage, the woods, a spare cassock, I wonder if you practise. . . . and then the rest of it. The casserole pan distracted her from horror by giving off a plume of smoke proceeding from burnt onion, charred underdone meat, and wine which had de-alcoholized itself so effectively that it was merely a smear. It completed the ruin of her appetite. She switched off the burner and tipped the contents of the pan into the sink-basket, thankful to have something practical to do.

'Mumbray made an insulting suggestion to me,' she told Ogle, 'which was complete invention and the sort of thing that would occur to a mind like his. It's not worth repeating to you. And it certainly has nothing to do with his death. Satisfied?'

Ogle was not. But he had gleaned enough. He made some specious inquiries about the antique trade, apologized for having interrupted her supper, then suddenly appeared to remember an important question.

'Your live-in housekeeper, Mrs – Selling. Know where she is nowadays, do you? Oh, Brighton. Right. My constable will just take down the address before we leave. Felt very bad about her little girl, I expect. PC Eastry gave me a fair overall picture – widowed mother, only one child, no men friends. . . .'

'Rhona would never bring herself to attack anyone physically. I think you've been given an exaggerated idea about people in Abbotsbourne, Inspector.' If Sam had betrayed her, and all of them, as he seemed to have done, she would be utterly disillusioned, utterly bereft (or not quite bereft, so long as Rodney was true). Somehow the interview was over, the smug Ogle and the yawning Warrash being ushered out of the front door.

Doran gave a hasty tidy-up to the kitchen, flung the pan and used dishes into cold water in the sink, and retreated into the sitting room. There she poured herself a large whisky, drank it too quickly, and without in the least intending to break down began to cry.

Ogle was saying to Warrash, 'Very interesting. Ve-ry interesting. Quite a tough young lady. But not tough enough, eh? Gave away more than she thought she was doing.'

'I like her, sir. I'm sure there's nothing wrong about her. She's just very concerned for other people.'

'That's what you think, is it, Constable? I don't believe I asked your opinion. Here we are, Wicket Lane. That's the cottage, Old Thatch.'

Bob Woods was at home and answered the door, looking gigantic, with an expression to match, a giant who smelt the blood of an Englishman. He listened grimly to Ogle's introduction.

'I can see you for five minutes. In the hall. My wife's not well, and I'm just about to ring the doctor. Right, get on with it.'

Deeply affronted and antagonistic, Ogle put his questions. Yes, Bob answered, he had thought Mumbray's conduct had caused his father-in-law's death, directly or otherwise. Yes, he had made suggestions to Bob's then fiancée, which she was too innocent to understand. He had most certainly been responsible for the proposed use of the cricket field as a building site. Bob was not sure when he had heard that the sale had fallen through; probably after the news of Mumbray's death. Asked what medicines Dr Levison had prescribed for his wife, he referred Ogle to the doctor, adding some crude reflections on the timing of police procedure which caused Warrash to agonize in silent hysterical mirth.

Ogle said little in reply, but stored the remarks in his bosom, trusting fervently that he and Woods would come up against each other again presently, and that he would by then have some ammunition against one whose natural weapon would seem to be a bludgeon or butcher's cleaver, but might in some circumstances have been poison.

* * *

It could have been an hour, or more, or less, after the police had left, when Doran forced herself out of her lethargy. There had been nothing to cry for, only a policeman's questions that probed tender spots. Mumbray was dead, Abbotsbourne was free. They could never make a charge stick against Rodney or Helena. Rhona was gone and the house unnaturally quiet, but one would get used to it. With a surge of cheerfulness, she realized that she was hungry.

The kitchen still smelt as if an infant class had just taken its first cookery lesson there. The worst of the effluvia came from the pedal bin, containing the ruin of the casserole. Outside, near the front gate, a dustbin waited for its contents to be collected next morning. Doran tied up the plastic bag and went out, slamming back bolts and rattling the chain to create some noise in the silent hall. The night was cold and still, dampness in the air, the beams from a distant street-lamp foggy, like the light of a rain-boding moon.

She lifted the dustbin lid, moved a couple of bottles to make room for the new contribution.

Out of the moist gloom came a something rock-hard and violently wielded. It struck her across the back of the head and sent her spinning against the dustbin, lights exploding behind her eyes and sickening pain blotting out her consciousness.

14

A blur of white dissolved slowly into a blur of green. The green blur grew vertical lines as it began to move sideways. A very much smaller brown blur came closer and closer, and resolved itself into a face.

The face was female, and contained two dark beautiful eyes gazing down anxiously.

'Hello,' croaked Doran and a soft voice said, 'Thank God.'

'Two lovely black eyes, Oh what a surprise,' Doran murmured dreamily. 'Can't 'member any more.'

'Well, just don't you try, honey.' The face disappeared behind the green curtain and came back with another face, male, over a white coat. There was some muttered conversation, then something was put to Doran's lips. She drank whatever it was thirstily, tried to apologize when it ran messily down her chin. Then she was asleep again.

The next time she woke was to extreme discomfort and an ineffable scent, a blend of American cigarettes, varnish, clothing overdue for the cleaner's and a sickly-sweet aftershave. It told her who was sitting beside her bed.

'How are you now, then?' asked Howell. Doran turned her head with extreme difficulty.

'Hellish. I seem to have broken all my bones. The top ones, anyway.' She added a muffled shriek.

'No, you just got a nasty bash, they said, nothing broken at all.'

'You could fool me. What are you doing here, anyway?'

'There's nice and grateful, when I come to see you special, instead of goin' to Machynlleth to my mam's like I'd meant.

187

They sent for me, see. That copper friend of yours got my address from your phone book.'

'What cop . . . oh, Sam. Oh God, my head aches, and my shoulder.'

'Should think it bloody does – take a look at it.'

She managed to twist her head further, and gasped. A huge bruise spread down below the short sleeve of the hospital nightdress, a Joseph's-Coat bruise of black, purple, green and blue.

'You'd better tell me what happened, hadn't you.'

'Sure. All right if I smoke in here?'

'No. And I shouldn't think there's any drink in that locker you're eyeing hopefully. Just get on with it.'

She had been found, Howell said, by the milkman about six o'clock in the morning, lying unconscious beside her dustbin. He had intelligently telephoned both ambulance and police, and she had been brought to Eastgate Hospital. Sam had alerted everyone who might even remotely have known anything about what had unquestionably been a murderous attack, but no clue to it had emerged. With Ogle, who had been called in, he had searched Bell House; nothing appeared to have been taken, and there was no sign of disturbance. What the police called a motiveless crime. She had lain unconscious for two days and nights, heavily concussed, but X-rays had revealed no brain damage, despite a minute depressed fracture of the skull.

'You mean it – whatever it was – actually did break my skull?'

'That's what the medics say.'

Doran shut her eyes and shuddered. It was painful to shudder.

'Well, you don't need to worry yourself,' said Howell cheerfully, noting that the clock in the ward, visible beyond the curtains which surrounded her bed, indicated that visiting time was almost up. 'The shop's OK. Andrew's helping me out nicely, learning the codes, he is, and talking ever so intelligent to the trade. He brings grub in for us, too.'

'What a love. Don't you think you'd better be going now?

188

Not that I'm not pleased to see you, but my head aches so much I think it will fall to pieces unless someone brings me a soothing draught or preferably a Mickey Finn. You might mention it to any passing nurse.'

'Sure. By the way, all right if I take twenty pounds from the petty cash? I seen something I fancy down town, you know that little shop where the guy's selling up, well, he's got a tarted-up table that I bet's good burr walnut under all the gunge, so I thought if I offered him around fifteen. . . .'

'Bug off,' said Doran.

By the next morning she had ceased to feel like an animated pain. The aches were more localized, the hospital staff pleased with her interest in food. On the stroke of eleven, the beginning of visiting time, the curtains parted to admit Rodney.

Doran was instantly aware that her face was scratched and cut from contact with the gravel of the front path, that her left cheekbone and eye were swollen and blackened, and that the bruise which covered her neck and shoulder had crept up to peer coyly round her ear. She was also conscious of a burning blush suffusing these features.

'You look wonderful,' Rodney said. He took her hand and held it fast, gazing down at her as though he could never gaze enough. 'I suppose it would be silly to ask how you feel, like a tele-reporter on the scene of a tragedy.'

'Not at all. I feel like Tom after Jerry's put him through a mincer and thrown him through a plate-glass window. But compared with when I woke up, absolutely super. How have you been keeping?'

'Tolerable. I've dropped in before, after it first happened, but they wouldn't let me see you.' He had spent a night and a morning in Eastgate, only going home when it was fairly certain that she was out of danger. Now he sat down, changing over hands so that he could still hold hers. There were lines and droops of tiredness on his face. The little coloured nurse had seen them as he entered the ward; when she popped in and offered him a cup of tea he accepted it gratefully. He had not noticed mealtimes much in the past three days.

189

'I know what happened,' he said, 'or at least what seems to have happened – someone blipped you on the head, like Bad Sir Brian Botany. But who, and why? Nobody seems to have the least idea, neither our Sam nor Dectective-Inspector Ogle, though I'm sure he'd love to prove that I did it myself. Can you throw any light, now that you've got over the worst?'

'Not a lot. Nothing, really. Someone scrobbled me proper and I didn't know a thing about it until whatever it was hit me. Except . . . you're not supposed to remember anything at all when you've been knocked out, but I have just the very faintest idea that I heard something either when it happened or a second before it happened.'

'Like what?'

'A voice. A word. A sort of hiss. That's the nearest I can get to it, a sibilance, like a word ending in a sharp s sound.'

'S. Ess? A feminine ending, as it were traitress?'

'Why should anyone call me that? There are lots of others. Actress, authoress, sempstress. . . .'

'Ogress, princess, duchess, peeress, priestess. . . .'

'Murderess,' Doran said suddenly. Their eyes met. 'But why? Nobody could possibly think I killed Mumbray – except Ogle, and he wouldn't be hanging round my gate with a truncheon or a Penang lawyer, waiting to blip me. It's in his interest to keep me alive and prove his case, and get made Chief Constable of all the Isles or whatever he's aiming at. Oh, well, whoever it was and whatever the reason didn't hit hard enough, or there'd be yet another corpse in the case with a sad swell'd face.'

Rodney did not, as he would normally have done, cap this by observing that a Medical Crowner's a queer sort of thing. Instead he gripped her hand so tightly as to drive the blood out of it and said, 'Shut up. Don't even suggest that. Sorry, did I hurt you? But while we're on the subject, why was the injury no worse?'

'They say that the cosh, or length of piping, or whatever, just missed the bit at the back of my head where it would have been fatal, because my shoulder took the worst of the blow – I suppose I moved as the thing came down on me.'

He shivered. 'A big assailant, then. Tall, strong.'

'Perhaps.' Both knew the other was thinking of Bob Woods. 'Never mind. I've got to stay here another week, and then take it easy at home with the district nurse dropping in.'

'Right. I'll send Nancy round to give a hand. And Vi will be only too willing to oblige. You'll be all right – I'll see that you are. If I hear of you trying to go out I'll put myself on picket duty at the door. That'll give the bishop something to think about. Can I put my arm round you, or will it hurt too much?'

'I don't care if it does.' She lay against his shoulder, in a state as near to peace as she remembered. He put his lips to her hair.

'You smell of carbolic. My favourite – *Fleurs de Phénique*. Doran, I have to tell you. I had a talk to Helena last week – well, it developed into rather more than that, raised voices and flashing eyes. Nancy came in to see what the row was, and I told her to stay, because it concerned all of us. Helena's turned thirteen now, technically a woman, not a child any more. It's time she learned to control her tantrums, and particularly her attitude to you. I've been too soft with her in the past, and so has Nan, and we've both got to take a stronger line, if she'll do her bit and make an effort to behave. Think it'll work?'

'It might.'

'If it does – would you give it a try – give *us* a try? If she could get used to you, by degrees, get into the habit of being civil to you and accepting you, then we might be able to make a go of it . . . a permanency.'

'Get married?'

'Yes.'

She sighed. 'I daren't even think about it, in case it's all a pipe-dream of yours. You see, it's myself I'm afraid of. Antagonism makes me cringe, and wilt, and bolt for refuge. Daft, but there it is, I am very comptible even to the least sinister usage.'

'I pass on that one.'

'Viola. *Twelfth Night*. I think so, but then I'm not thinking very clearly just now. Never mind Viola. If you'll work on

Helena, I'll try very hard to toughen myself up and grow a carapace, laugh and sing when she's rude to me. Just pray it works for both of us. All of us. Oh, darling. . . .'

Nurse O'Brien put her head round the curtain, which she had kept drawn out of respect to a clerical collar. The embrace she witnessed caused her to squeak with shock, for she was a girl reared to take the celibacy of the clergy for granted.

'Excuse me, Your Reverence, sorry to interrupt, but time's up.'

Rodney disentangled himself. 'Right, Nurse. 'Bye, love. See you tomorrow, same time, same place.' When he had gone Doran stared at the enormous bouquet of expensive out-of-season flowers.

'Where on earth did that come from?'

'Sure, His Rev . . . that gentleman brought it. Isn't it a treat for sore eyes? Don't tell me you never saw him bring it in.' She had not, for her eyes were full of him.

Nurse O'Brien giggled. 'Don't laugh now, but when I saw him at first I thought Holy Mary, she must be feeling worse, she's sent for a priest. And all the time it was your boyfriend.'

'Yes,' said Doran thoughtfully, 'my boyfriend.'

Ogle leaned back in Vi Small's best armchair and crossed his legs comfortably. He approved the pin-neat little front parlour at Castle Cottages, the present-from-Ramsgate type ornaments dotted about among photographs of family and friends, the fluorescent orange carpet with its shrieking geometric pattern. It was just the sort of room he preferred for interviewing the innocent, and Vi headed his list of innocents. She reminded him strongly of his mother and her contemporaries in Beckenham, where he had grown up. And she was the kind who would tell the truth, because nothing could stop her flow of eloquence, and the truth might be somewhere in it.

'This cake, Miss Small, Crispin Cake, I think you said.' He glanced at his constable to make sure the name had gone down correctly. Warrash's place had been taken by Bill Reece, whose complete disregard of grammar, syntax and spelling was a byword at his station. Reece nodded reassuringly. He had written it as Krisping, from a vague association of cake with oven-cookery.

'That's right.' Vi was sitting very upright, wearing her best blue polyester dress and eyeshadow to match. She was being a Very Important Witness, whose words would be reported in all the papers.

'You made it yourself, I believe, here, in your own kitchen. So, as you had collected all the ingredients personally, you knew exactly what went into it.' He consulted a list. 'Flour, sugar, butter, margarine, dried fruit, nuts, eggs, spice, pre-served cherries. . . .'

'Glassy.'

'*Glacé*, exactly. So nothing could have got into it without you knowing it.'

'Nothing at all. Like I told you, I weighed up all the quantities, there was a lot too much sugar so I left some out, and two of the eggs looked none too fresh to me so I put in two of my own. . . .'

'*Unless*,' said Ogle with an air of cunning, 'something had been mixed into one of the ingredients which was invisible. Into flour or sugar, for instance, or even the dried fruit? It has been known.'

Vi sniffed. 'Not likely. I've got a way of sensing them things, and it wouldn't have got past me, you can bet on that. They don't look right, if you know what I mean, there's a sort of something. Besides, I tasted the mix myself, always do. When our Debbie was a little thing she always used to like to scrape out the bowl for me when I was making cakes. "Auntie," she'd say, poor little mite. . . .'

'Ah, yes.' Ogle signalled to Reece to stop writing. He had taken the trouble to inspect an aconite plant: its tough dark root might well be cut small and inserted among candid peel and dried fruits. There had been fatal accidents when some-one had mistaken its root for horseradish and died of roast beef with poison sauce, but who would put horseradish in a cake? Besides, inquiries of the health authorities had shown that no ill effects had been reported among those who would have shared in the cake.

'I know what you're thinking, Inspector,' Vi said. 'You're thinking that man could have eaten some of my cake and that's what killed him. Well, you can forget about that, for he never set foot in church nor chapel neither, and from all I've heard he'd have worshipped devils and idols if anybody, which I doubt. Oh, he liked sweet things, puddings and that, all right, daresay he'd have lived on treacle pud if I'd served it up every day when I was cooking for him, which I wish I never had, because if I hadn't Debbie would never have gone to that house and been murdered, and. . . .'

Ogle rose briskly, glancing at the imitation carriage clock on the mantelpiece, which Vi had got from a mail-order offer. There was no point in questioning her further. As he was trying to extract himself at the door Vi said, 'Oh, I forgot to tell you. There *was* something else I was given for the cake. Miss Fairweather gave me a little bottle of brandy, one of them miniatures, real brandy, not the cooking sort, which I thought was very good of her. . . .'

Doran was back home. Far from resenting her house imprisonment, she was only too glad to rest and be idle, stiff and bruised as she still was, and more than a little shocked to know that the delicate citadel of her skull had been breached, even though they promised there would be no permanent harm. The saying about needing some ill-fortune like a hole in the head took on a new meaning.

Her visitors were frequent. Rodney came every day, sometimes more than once, letting himself in with the spare key. Others who only called to make kind inquiries gave her the trouble of getting herself to the door, sometimes from the sofa by the fire, sometimes from bed. She admitted Ogle with a sinking heart. It was not easy to answer probing questions with a permanent headache and the woolliness that came of pain-killers.

'The brandy was perfectly innocuous,' she told him. 'Just an ordinary miniature that I got from the off-licence. Of course I hadn't opened it – you don't open a bottle and then give it away, do you?'

'I've no proof that it wasn't opened, madam, have I, since the bottle's long since been thrown out.'

'Then you'll have to take my word for it. Are you suggesting that I poisoned the brandy?'

Ogle smiled. 'Well. . . .'

'In that case, would you mind telling me why nobody was affected by it, except Mumbray, assuming that he somehow got hold of a piece of the Crispin Cake, which seems most unlikely?'

Ogle was perfectly aware of the problem, and irritated to have no smart answer to it. 'I thought perhaps you could tell me that,' he said.

Doran caught her breath. 'Are you accusing me of murder?' Young Reece's hand paused, arrested in shock, over his notebook.

'I'm not accusing you of anything, madam, naturally, since no proof exists against anyone, nor is it even absolutely certain in law that the deceased didn't take his own life. I merely think you know more about this case, and the people involved in it, than anybody else, and that you could give me valuable information if you chose to be helpful instead of obstructive. Possibly you're protecting somebody. Perhaps you don't want the killer to be found.'

Doran shut her eyes, tired of Ogle's inquisitor's face, tired of stupid pointless questions. 'Do you know the common names of aconite, Inspector? You see we all know what the poison was, even if the police think it's a deadly secret. Things get around in a place like this. Well, one of its names is monkshood, and the other is wolfsbane, possibly because a few centuries ago wolves used to eat it and complain of being unwell. Now, it seems that this particular bane was somehow administered to one particular wolf, a wolf who preyed on our little fold. *I* think that person who administered it was a gamekeeper, not a murderer. Work it out. Please would you go now? I really am very tired.'

She was aware of indignant huffing noises and something that sounded like a vague threat, then of retreating steps and the door slamming. Perhaps it had been unwise to answer him back like that. He could hardly haul her off to gaol, but he could make things even more unpleasant for her, by harassing and bullying. But she was glad she had said it: Mumbray's killer had done a public service, from whatever motives, and nobody really wanted the person found.

Yet the itch of curiosity would not go away, the desire to know who among them had dispatched the wolf: and she would find out at any cost.

'I don't know why,' she told Rodney. 'Perhaps it's just morbid interest, but it might be defensive – a sort of "where will the next bomb fall?" question. It might be you, or me, or any of us. They say killing whets the appetite, and this must have been a very satisfactory killing, a really piquant starter. Don't *you* think we ought to know?'

'Not personally. I hate the whole thing. I'm afraid of it, especially since you were attacked. The person concerned is still around and doesn't like you, doesn't want you making inquiries. It could happen again.'

'But whoever it was called me "murderess". I think. That means they, he, she or it, didn't kill Mumbray. So who did? Because I know I certainly didn't, in spite of Ogle and his miniature of Three Star.'

'I don't know. Oh God, and I say that advisedly, I wish I had the right to look after you, to be with you always, instead of this nonsense of you being in one house and me in another. It makes me feel a complete helpless twit. I deserve to be preached to death by wild curates.'

'You what?'

'The Smith of Smiths. Seriously, drop it, my love. Rest and get better, and don't talk to too many people. Are you being looked after properly, by the way?'

'More than. Vi can't keep away and talks my unfortunate head off when she's here. Sweet Lydia walks all the way from the police house, and Sam pops in far oftener than he should. Wasting police time, I think it's called.'

'I told Nan to call and see if you wanted anything. Did she?'

'Yes, thanks. She brought me some things from the chemist.'

'Did Helena come in with her?'

'She stayed at the gate. How are you getting on with your – campaign?'

He shrugged. 'Hard to say. It'll be easier when you're about again, and we can talk at home. Has Bob called?'

'No. Why should he, anyway? I don't know him that well. I hear Barbary might have had a miscarriage but didn't, so that's all right.' The same unspoken thought occurred to them, that if the baby had been lost, and if Bob had been Doran's unseen assailant, he might have called, with ill intentions. Yet she had done him no harm, had done nobody harm.

Rodney said, 'Look, why don't you go away, as soon as you're well enough? It would take your mind off all this, and you'd be so much safer. You've got friends you could go to, haven't you?'

'Friends? People I used to know, if that's the same thing.' Old people in North Oxford, neighbours of her parents, not likely to welcome her as a guest. Students of her year, scattered now to various professions and homes, probably remembering her only as the girl who had made a fool of herself over a good-looking jerk, and gone slightly potty and thrown away her degree. There had been a Mary and a Siobhan who had been on her wavelength, and fun at the same time, but to seek them out now would be a foredoomed failure.

'You could go to an hotel, somewhere peaceful, the Cotswolds, the Dales, Bath. You'd like that, wouldn't you?'

'With you it would be heaven. On my own – I expect I could get agreeably caught up with ruins and museums and the local trade. I could go to Stow-on-the-Wold and Moreton and Cirencester and Bristol ... yes, you interest me strangely.' But how much more wonderful it would be to set off together, driving westwards towards the low winter sun, finding themselves at small hotels built of stone the colour of pale honey, in bedrooms looking out on quiet gardens where late roses bloomed, walking in country towns with all the day their own. And all the night.

He got up. 'That's all right, then. Now I feel better about you, and I shall go away and take a confirmation class with a new spring in my step and heavenly rhetoric in mine eye, and on Sunday I shall preach a sermon that'll stop them reading the epitaphs on the walls. All because you're going away and

197

you'll be safe. How's that for heroic detachment? I don't want to lose you but I think you ought to go. Abbotsbourne isn't the place for you just now, the walls are hung with velvet that is black and soft as sin, and little dwarfs creep out of it and little dwarfs creep in.'

'I do hope not. Rodney, please go, or I shall get weepy when you do, and I can see Vi coming up the path.'

It was a Saturday afternoon, crisp and cold, when Bob Woods loomed up outside the trellis gate which separated the back garden from the front. Doran, tidying up shrubs Ozzy had neglected and picking out the occasional aggressive weed, felt her heart jump. But she drew the bolt and let him in. He was so huge, so strong, and she had more than once visualized those big hands, which needed an outsize bat, with a length of iron piping between them. He was smiling sheepishly.

'Thought you might like to know Greta's over the worst. She took Ravi's death very hard, but she seems to have got a lot of strength from somewhere since.'

Doran thought of various wise things to say about Christian fortitude, said none of them, and merely remarked that she was very glad.

'What's even better, she doesn't want to go back to Willow Cottage, even though they're not pulling it down now.'

'Aren't they? Is that definite?'

'Absolutely. The sale of the field's off. Mumbray's will left everything to Mrs Butcher and there's nothing in it about buying up property, so it stays as it is. Isn't that great? We're finalizing next season's fixture list now. But what I started to say was that Greta's coming to live with us. There's bags of room, that sort of granny-annexe at the back. She's going to look after the baby when he comes, let Bar have plenty of rest, and stay on as a sort of nanny to the next ones. She loves kids, you know, and she lost all hers. Couldn't be better.'

'I'm very pleased, Bob – for Mrs Singh and both of you – or all three of you. It's going to be a he, then – you've decided?'

'Well. I reckon I could get a little lad started on the game pretty soon – matter of the eye and the hand, that's what it is, and growing up in the atmosphere.'

'I'll try to find him a *Wisden for the Very Young* or *With Bat and Ball in a Sandpit*. By the way, if it's a girl I suppose you'll let her score?'

'Here, you're not one of these libbers, are you?'

'Most definitely not, Bob. Man, man, man, is for the woman made . . . sorry, I talk to myself sometimes at the moment, don't mind me.'

'Got over your accident, then? You look a nasty bang, didn't you?'

'Yes, more or less over it, thank you, and it wasn't an accident. Somebody had it in for me.'

He shook his head. 'Take care. We don't want to lose you.'

She watched him go, half-frowning. He must be all that he seemed, an open book, too hot-tempered and outspoken for his own good, but surely with nothing against her personally. It could not have been his hands that wielded the weapon of attack. Far weaker ones could have done it, given the occasion and the motive.

While they had talked the first shades of dusk had fallen, lights sprang up in other houses, while she must go alone into her own dark one.

The latch of the trellis gate rattled. A figure stood beyond it. Bob, returned? Reluctantly, Doran drew the bolt. Outside stood Marcia Fawkes.

15

Heavily muffled, wearing a high-crowned hat with a scarf tied over it, booted and fur-gloved, Marcia looked strangely bear-like. *How easy is a bush supposed a bear*, and how much more easy by dusk to suppose a person a lowering grizzly, advancing slowly, as Marcia was advancing, to enfold one in a death-hug. Doran found herself retreating, step by step, as the menacing figure moved forward.

'My dear child! I'm very glad to see you out and about.' Well, that was friendly, anyway. 'I meant to come before, but you know how it is, committees and bazaars and things, so many near Christmas.'

'Oh, don't apologize. I've been keeping myself rather quiet.'

'Of course, quite right.' The beady eyes were scanning her – why? 'But I felt I really had to know how you were.'

Doran was conscious of a strong reluctance to be trapped indoors. 'Marcia, I'm so sorry, I can't ask you in – I haven't lit the fire yet and the house is stone cold. Ozzy's cut me some kindling and logs but I've got to cart it in and stack it and. . . .' She was babbling, and all the time Marcia's eyes were darting about.

'Oh, don't worry, my dear – I'd just as soon be out in the fresh air.'

With a lurch of the heart Doran realized, for the first time, that the weapon her attacker had used had probably been a heavy garden tool. Ozzy was notoriously careless about locking the tool-shed: had the Someone found his wood-chopper or the short-handled spade? It seemed more and more likely, and here she and Marcia were, only a few steps away from the shed. Which was open, because she had taken the secateurs from it only an hour ago. Her hand clenched on them – they would be something to fight with, at least.

But Marcia was very close now, breathing out an aura of strong peppermints. 'I just wanted to tell you what's happened. You've been *so* kind to me and Stella.' (Well, I thought I had, Doran mentally replied, that's why I wondered. . . .) 'That awful policeman came back to the cottage last week. It seems he wasn't satisfied, he thought I knew more than I said about Mumbray's death. Thought I had a personal grudge against the man. Somebody, and I wouldn't be surprised if it was those publicans, had been gossiping to him about me having had a few drinks now and then, and some other busybody had told him what I said after the Commination Service, and he'd put two and two together and made five. So he sent Stella out of the room and put me through the most dreadful interrogation. My dear, you can't imagine some of the questions he asked me – I didn't know where to look. Then, because he could see he was getting me upset, he said he'd found some evidence that Mumbray was blackmailing me.'

That was a lie on Ogle's part, Doran decided. It was Sam who gave it away. Very unethical behaviour.

'So at that I'm afraid I broke down and told him the truth, what Mumbray knew about me and the threats he'd made. He told that young constable to write it all down, and I really, well, felt the handcuffs closing, isn't that what they say in the thrillers? Then he made Stella bring out all her dried herbs that she'd used for spells, and took samples of them away.'

'And?'

'He came back a few days later and said there was no trace of aconite in them. That was what he thought I'd given Mumbray, though what chance I'd have had, well, what a ridiculous idea. I thought he seemed a bit disappointed.'

'I bet he was – he'd lost a suspect.' Relief was flooding Doran: the bear had become only a bush again. But something niggled.

'Marcia, that night Sam and I brought Stella home from the cricket pavilion, there was something odd about you. You

202

seemed quite different – calm and happy, as though you'd got something off your mind. Was I right?'

Marcia smiled, a broad smile. 'Quite right, my dear. You see, I'd just had a wonderful experience. I'd been to a meeting in Barminster, and driven home by the marsh road. A few miles from here I saw a car standing by the side of the road with its lights on. I hooted, but nothing happened, so I stopped in front of it and saw it was empty. Then – I don't know what made me look, but right at the other side of the meadow, by the edge of the next dyke, I saw a figure moving, somebody in a light coat. I've got marvellous eyesight, you know. It was moving in a funny sort of way, sort of weaving about – then suddenly it fell, and rolled out of sight, over the edge of the dyke. And something made me look back at the car, and I saw that it was Mumbray's.'

Doran gasped. 'And what did you do?'

'I waited,' Marcia said calmly. 'About a quarter of an hour. He didn't come out again. I knew the dyke was full because we'd had so much rain. So I went and switched off the lights – the car wasn't locked and the keys were in it – and drove off. I knew it must be him, you see, and I knew retribution had overtaken him.'

'How did you suppose it had done that?'

'I've no idea, but I imagined the Commination must have worked. I've always had a very strong faith, since I was a girl.'

Doran was chilled, revolted, fascinated. 'Did you tell Inspector Ogle all that?'

'Naturally not, dear. What do you take me for? Isn't it all quite wonderful, turning out this way? And the best of it is, Stella's given up all that magic nonsense, at last. She thinks it worked, you see. We get on quite splendidly now – I'm very, very fond of her, you know.'

I'll bet, Doran thought. That's putting it somewhat mildly. But never mind, she hasn't murdered anyone – not actually murdered. It was just that she didn't strive officiously to keep alive. *Who saw him die? I, said the fly.* Thank Heaven. Marcia was saying a fulsome farewell, shutting the gate behind her. Doran collected firewood, went into the house, locking and bolting the back door, flicked every light switch she passed, and made a roaring fire in the sitting room. Then she crouched in front of it, holding her hands to its comfort. She was very, very cold, and not merely from the night air.

Ogle was indeed a disappointed man. His investigations were getting nowhere, and his superiors were about to take him off the case and write it off as a suicide. He had lost his best candidate in Miss Fawkes, the Fairweather girl was obviously out of the running. He had been very interested in Dr Levison but had found it absolutely impossible to prove that he had administered poison to Mumbray, even though aconitine had been an ingredient in the embrocation prescribed for the dead man's arm. The same prescription had been made up for Bob Woods during the cricket season, for a bad bruise on the leg, but even Ogle found it hard to believe that the hot-tempered young giant would have had the cunning, skill or patience to choose poison as a weapon against an enemy. There was aconitine in Helena Chelmarsh's calmative medicine, but here again common sense told Ogle that juvenile cripples, unpractised in the manipulation of an electric wheelchair, do not normally travel three-quarters of a mile to polish off a person they dislike, even fear. There had been no developments about Mumbray's car, which the police assumed to have been stolen and abandoned.

Ogle confessed himself baffled, a Watsonian attitude which Sam Eastry encouraged every time they met. 'If it can't be proved, leave it alone,' was his resented advice. 'If anyone's done it, and got a death on their conscience, that's punishment enough, isn't it?'

Too much, possibly, Sam felt, in the case of such a victim as Mumbray. He was beginning to be his cheerful self again, now that his beloved village was no longer under an evil shadow, and even the shadow of the sword of judgement seemed to be passing away from it. Mumbray had been buried in Eastgate Cemetery, very quietly, only Sam himself and a leaden-eyed Mrs Butcher in attendance. That, surely, must be the end of it. He let his mind return to the hyacinths he was bringing on for flowering exactly at Christmas, and the problem of finding a suitable present for Ben, who was quite definitely not going to get the BMX he had clamoured for insistently for months.

'You don't want this 'ere, do you,' Ozzy stated, rather than inquired, indicating the object he was just about to pile into the back of his battered van, along with a lidless saucepan and a few bottles, and some logs he had decided would not fit neatly into Doran's sitting-room firegrate.

'Indeed I do!' Doran seized it from him. 'Don't you dare take it away – or anything from outside the back door.'

'But it's only an ole table, ain't even got no varnish on. What d'you want that for, miss?'

'I want it because it happens to be an eighteeth-century turned-oak joint-stool, and it's worth about seven hundred pounds, if I get the right buyer.'

'Oh. Got the worm in, you know.'

'Yes, I did know. They're dead.'

Ozzy scratched his head beneath its woollen tea-cosy cap. 'Funny things people want. When I worked for that Mrs . . . the Colonel, *you* know, them what flitted – well, one day I see that Miss Whatsit . . . the lady with the white 'air, a bit mental, I always thought – I see her comin' out of their French window with an ole knife. Wasn't even a proper kitchen knife, bits o' fancy work on it. Now what would she want with a thing like that?'

'Black-handled, was it? About so long?'

'That's right. I expec' they give it 'er because she ask. Not that they give much, judgin' by what I got paid for good work.' Morosely he watched Doran put the jointstool behind her where he could not possibly get at it again.

So Ozzy had actually seen Stella take the *athamé,* the Italian dagger, and had said nothing about it. What else had he seen? She questioned him closely, but he put on his mulish look and returned only vague answers.

'I gotta go now, miss. They're removin' down The Oaks and I might pick up a bit of somethin'.'

Doran pondered. It was early in the day, not lunchtime yet. The vans might not have left. She resolved suddenly to go and see if she, too, could pick up something: information, before the only person who had known Mumbray well vanished for ever from the neighbourhood.

A van was still outside, two men loading a rolled carpet into it. Empty windows stared like blind eyes. At the end of the path which led down the side of the house Ozzy was rooting through a pile of rubbish, transferring objects from it into a sack. The front door stood wide open. Doran went in calling, 'Mrs Butcher! It's me, Doran Fairweather.'

She was standing in the stripped kitchen, whose bare walls showed marks where the cooker and refrigerator had been; a small shrunken figure. Like someone left on deck when the ship was going down, Doran thought. The woman took no notice of her entrance, continuing to fasten the buttons of her drab coat, slowly, as though it were an effort. Doran touched her arm.

'Mrs Butcher. Are you all right? You're cold. Would you like to come home with me and have some tea before you go?'

'No, thank you.' The voice was as dull as the gaze. Doran was filled with overwhelming irrational pity.

'I do think you should. You don't look well to me. The stuff's nearly all out now, isn't it?'

A nod. Doran went into the hall and glanced into each room. Nothing was left, only tatters of newspaper on the floors where carpets had been, a dead pot-plant and a rusty all-night stove standing in a hearth.

'Well then, you don't need to wait,' Doran said briskly. 'Give me the keys, and I'll ask the foreman to lock up and drop them in at the estate agent's. It's Dixter and Wylie's, isn't it?'

'That's right.' The foreman was happy to oblige, particularly with the addition of a pound coin, and his team whistled appreciatively at Doran. She went back to Mrs Butcher, who was standing obediently in the same spot, and together they left the grim empty house. Who would live there next, Doran wondered, and would they feel the emanations of past cruelty and horror?

Mrs Butcher said nothing in the car. Doran was aware of faint mustiness about her, as though no perfumed preparations of any kind touched her skin. Her coat and headscarf were clean but looked oddly as though they belonged to somebody else, the garments of a refugee. In Doran's kitchen she sat down when told and unfastened her coat, also as instructed. It was obviously the way to deal with one used to obeying orders. A faint look of interest came into her face as she gazed round the kitchen with its beamed ceiling, dresser where Staffordshire figures cheerfully mingled with commonplace china and good porcelain, its Minton tiles over the sink painted with plump Victorian elves and fairies.

'It's pretty,' she said suddenly.

'My kitchen?' Doran poured tea and surreptitiously slipped an eggspoonful of kitchen brandy into her guest's cup. 'I'm glad you like it. I feel one should be surrounded by nice things even in kitchens and bathrooms. After all, why not? What pleases the eye pleases the mind, doesn't it? Don't you think that print's rather jolly? My housekeeper thought it was a bit naughty, but I told her she had to put up with it and it was really very innocent, just a bit of late-Georgian fun.' She knew that Mrs Butcher was not taking in a word of all this chatter, but a very faint tinge of colour was creeping into her sallow face and the tight, thread-thin mouth was relaxing. The cup finished, Doran poured her another, with a further nip of spirit. She hoped it was not a case of getting the witness drunk in order to extract a confession, but somehow she had now reached a point where this forlorn woman was not a witness so much as a person in need.

'Mrs Butcher. . . .' she began.

'Not Mrs Butcher. Mrs Mumbray.'

Doran dropped her teaspoon with a clatter. 'Mumbray?'

'That's right. We was married over twenty years. I used to be a cleaner in the office where he worked. I was quite pretty then. I'm younger than I look, you know, miss.'

'Yes, I – I'm sure you are. I mean – you've been through a lot.'

The brandy was doing its work. 'I was pure when he married

me – I think that's why he picked me, he said it was important to have a virgin for his experiments. He wanted to be a magician, you see, like a Mr Crawley or some such name. He had a lot of books about it, with pictures in – I couldn't look at them at first. This is very nice tea, I expect it cost a lot. He used to tell me to do things that I didn't like, well no nice girl would, and some of the things he did to animals were awful, I used to cry. But he had such a way with him, miss, you can't imagine. I lost my dad when I was little and I reckon I'd always wanted a man to look up to. If Mr Mumbray told you to do something, you did it. But I was a disappointment to him, he couldn't bring off any magic tricks with me. And I was a bit ill and not so pretty, my hair went quite grey, the way it is now. That's why I'm still pure, because he wasn't interested in me no more. He just kept me as a servant.'

Doran made a choked sound, and poured herself a slug of brandy neat. 'Go on.'

'I never did really understand, but I think he found out he couldn't be a real magician, not like Mr Crawley, who could raise the Devil and all sorts. So he made up his mind to follow the left-hand path – that's what he called it, doing bad things to people on purpose.'

'Evil for evil's sake.'

'That's right. We moved here when he gave up his business because he'd found out a couple of people lived here that he knew something wrong about. One was Dr Levison, he'd had an affair with a patient and Mr Mumbray had found out, and kept sending him letters saying he was going to report him to some council and get him stopped from being a doctor.'

'And the other was Miss Fawkes, I suppose.'

'Yes. I remember her when she was quite young and came to the office.'

'And Barbary Miles? What was all that about?'

'Well, she was pure, you see, and he thought he'd try again, like he did with me. But he had a bad argument with her father, and . . . he'd learned how to upset people very badly.'

'He must have upset Major Miles quite a bit – he died.'

'Yes. Then I think he found out that Miss Miles's boyfriend

had moved in with her, so she wasn't no more use, and he started on that little girl – something to do with you, wasn't you?'

'My housekeeper's daughter. He wanted her for the same thing?'

'At first. Then he took against her, said she'd no apt . . . something.'

'Aptitude. So he tortured her mentally until she hanged herself.'

'Did he – was it that? I never really knew, I didn't talk to her much. Poor thing. Funny, I can say that now, I didn't feel anything much at the time, only what he felt.'

'And . . . the vicar's daughter? Was that the same thing as well?'

'Oh no, he said that was just a joke, she was an ugly child and what he called a natural devil's plaything. He used to tell me all about what he did, of an evening. He was proud of it. Once upon a time he'd have liked to be a great lawyer, and he'd a lot of brains. This was a way of . . . I don't know how to put it.'

'Having power. The power of life and death. Omnipotence.'

'If you say so. You're clever, too, aren't you, miss. Yes, that's why he was going to buy that field, to make as many people miserable as he could. He *was* going to get at the vicar, said he'd make him pay for that service he took, and it was something to do with you, miss, but he didn't live long enough. Oh, and I forgot about those people at Lily Lawn. He hadn't got nothing on them except he guessed the Colonel wasn't what he seemed, and he went to London and looked up the Army Lists, and then started on them, and they got scared and left.'

'I thought it must be something like that. Mrs B . . . Mrs Mumbray, can you possibly remember anyone who came to the house that night before your husband – disappeared? Or any other time? It's important.'

'Well. Not that night, no, I had a terrible cold and I stayed in bed. I heard the bell ring a couple of times. No, I couldn't hear voices up there. That woman with the white hair, she'd been, more than once, and I know they had a row, all over this magic – might have been her that came, or that young man, very big, fair hair. It was him give Mr Mumbray a black eye once, before we went away last summer. That's why we went. The furniture was all over the place.' The animation began to die away from the small withered face. 'I've been talking a lot, haven't I? Don't usually talk this much. I didn't say anything I shouldn't, did I, miss?'

'No, of course not, not at all. Have some more tea. No? Then I'll run you to the station, shall I? Where will you go?'

With an effort, Mumbray's widow remembered that she had booked in at a private hotel in Ealing, a place she had once known, now under different management but still taking in guests. Then she would have to find somewhere to live permanently.

'They say I'll have a lot of money now. Seems funny, doesn't it? Dunno what I'm going to do with all that – there's no one to tell me now. He always used to, you see. Everything.' Blank eyes, blank mind. Perhaps some initiative would come back to her as her master's influence faded, but she would never be a whole person again.

Doran felt drained when the London train had gone, as though she had lived Mrs Mumbray's dreary life vicariously. Over and over again, throughout the evening, she reviewed the woman's story, interpreting it, embroidering it.

In bed, sleep would not come. She tried her usual recipe for insomnia, a cup of hot tea from the friendly machine by her bed, accompanied by a few pages of a book which could excite no passions and propel no flights of imagination. But tonight Scott's *Tales of a Grandfather* failed to bore her gently to sleep; she snapped the light off again and went back to musing.

She realized now that Mumbray's housekeeper had hovered in the background of her mind, the only shadowy figure in Abbotsbourne's gallery of characters. Now that the truth had come out it was possible to deduce that she might have killed Mumbray out of revenge for her wasted life. But that was nonsense. The woman had been a drained useless thing, useless as Mickey Mouse playing at being the Sorcerer's Apprentice. Just a human tool, handmaid to a devil.

Over and over in her memory she played back the conversation in the kitchen. 'He was going to buy that field to make as many people miserable as he could.' What had come next? A specific target for malevolence. Words came back, and the flat tones. 'He was going to get at the vicar, said he'd make him pay for that service he took.'

And, connecting by a startling bright link, other words, Doran's own to Detective-Inspector Ogle, words of which she had been rather proud at the time. Something about wolfsbane 'administered to one particular wolf, a wolf who preyed on our little fold . . . I think that person was a game-keeper, not a murderer.'

Gamekeeper. A gamekeeper's function is to protect threatened creatures, 'Hart and hind and all beasts of venery . . . partridge, pheasant, woodcock, quail. . . .' Into her mental eye came a Victorian scrapbook which had been among the lots at a country-house sale. Doran had seen, and been tempted to tear out and destroy, a yellowed photograph of a gamekeeper's gallows, a fence hung with the victims of his gun and traps: stoat, weasel, magpie, jay, rosy-breasted bull-finch, domestic tabby cat, owl and squirrel, grisly and pathetic in death, fur and feathers bloody, bright colours gone drab. Execution Dock, Tyburn gibbet. *I wonder we ha'n't better company Upon Tyburn Tree. . . .*

Better company would have been a human predator like Mumbray, and somebody had finished him not by gun or trap but by poison. What game was that particular keeper protecting? It was all growing clearer, as the dawn-light crept through the curtains. Mrs Mumbray had said: 'He was going to get at the vicar, make him pay for that service he took.'

Without breakfast Doran went to Early Communion, seven o'clock. Only three or four others were there, devout parishioners who never missed. The great impersonality of the rite lay between her and Rodney, his hands offering her the Bread and Wine, his voice pronouncing the Blessing. After it was ended she felt a little cleaner, and completely

211

resolute. Rodney took her hand at the church door, his eyes searching hers.

'All right?'

'Yes.'

'You've found something out.'

'Yes, I have, but I don't want to say anything now.'

He nodded. 'I'll be out all afternoon – Advent service at Elvesham, the children's Nativity play, then tea with Lady Pryce. Behold me like Mr Collins, my air grave and stately and my manners very formal, no doubt dispensing little delicate compliments. See you this evening, perhaps. Are you sure you're all right? Good morning, Mrs Lewes, keeping well?'

In the early afternoon Doran was ringing the bell of the vicarage. Nancy answered the door.

'Good afternoon, Miss Doran. I'm sorry, the vicar's out. Gone to Elvesham.'

'Yes, I know. But may I come in?'

The house was quiet, Helena's wheelchair standing empty in the hall. 'She's resting,' Nancy said. 'Does her good, having a sleep after lunch, 'specially this weather. She feels the cold, not being able to exercise like other children. Er, did you want to leave a message for the vicar?'

'Well . . . could I have a word with you, Nancy?' Doran was finding her mission hard, wishing she had gone for a walk and thought the thing through. But she had done that already. Nancy was leading the way into the drawing room, where a fire smouldered behind its wire guard, and Helena's toys and books lay scattered on the sofa. Doran took a fireside chair, Nancy perched straight-backed among the litter of objects, not compulsively tidying because they were her charge's possessions. Suddenly she leapt up.

'Not too early for tea, is it? I could do with a cup myself.' She was off to the kitchen before Doran could answer. It was certainly not too early for tea, to one who had had no lunch. The whole purpose of Doran's visit was beginning to feel silly. She sat, glad of her lined boots, still in her loden coat, gazing round at a room which was Rodney's and yet not

Rodney's, planning a room which would be wholly his – and hers.

Nancy was back with the tea-tray, stirring the pot, then pouring. She was of the milk-in-last school, very correct. There were slices of lemon in a small dish.

'I expect,' she said, 'you want to know about Helena's Christmas present. Well, if you ask me, and I know better than anybody else, she'd like one of these games where you answer questions like how many American presidents have been shot. She's getting ever so interested in things, reading her father's newspaper after breakfast. Now I think that's a good sign.'

'Actually, Nancy, it wasn't that,' Doran said in a rush. 'I have to know this for my peace of mind, it's not that I intend to do anything about it. I only want to get things absolutely clear. Just – do you know anything about Mr Mumbray's death? Anything special, I mean, that other people don't know.'

Nancy stirred her tea. 'What a funny question, Miss Doran.'

'I just thought. . . . Nancy, you're very fond of the vicar and Helena, aren't you. I mean, so fond that you'd do anything for them?'

The nurse's eyes were expressionless as she answered, 'I was a Barnardo's girl – did you know? They found me in a slum in Walsall, in a room with my mother. She was dead of drink. Nobody knew who my father was. Just one of her men – she had a lot, she wasn't married.'

'Oh dear. I'm sorry.'

'Somebody told me all about it, when I was older, out of spite. It upset me, I can tell you. I've never got over it, really.'

'I can understand that.'

Nancy sipped her tea. 'I settled down in the end, of course. I had a lot of different places, doing nursing and that. Then an agency sent me to Mr Chelmarsh – that was when he had his first parish, up in the Midlands. Mrs Chelmarsh was dying and Helena had just been taken with this dreadful trouble. I looked after them all, till Mrs Chelmarsh died and afterwards.'

'Yes. You must feel you belong to them.'

Nancy's eyes met hers. 'I feel they belong to me, Miss Doran, that's how I feel.' Helena's hideous monkey-toy was on her lap, grinning up. She stroked its livid orange fur. 'Drink your tea, it'll get cold. There's lemon if you want it.'

'Thank you.' Doran was not fond of black tea with lemon, but her cup obviously was cooling. She put in a slice, and drank thirstily, Nancy watching her. The fingers stroking the monkey were still. The tea was quite hot but faintly unpleasant; Doran wondered whether Nancy had changed the brand she bought, or whether the lemon had been kept too long and was sour. A curious tingling sensation was in her mouth. She spooned out the lemon and drank again. The tingling was stronger, decidedly unpleasant now, affecting her tongue and throat. She licked her lips.

'Don't bother to talk,' Nancy was saying. 'You won't be able to for long, anyway. That stuff makes your mouth numb, then it goes all over your body. I looked it up in one of the Reverend's books and I know just what it does. It killed that Mumbray, and it'll kill you, very soon. Too smart for your own good, you are – I guessed you'd come and tackle me. So did you think you could get away with it, Miss Doran – pinching my home and my family, moving in? I worship the Reverend, you know. He's not going to have any wife that'll come between us and upset my Helena. She's to be a good girl for her new mummy, is she, and we're all going to be cosy together? Well, I've put a stop to that – I tried to, before.' She laughed, the comfortable laugh of a nanny. 'Did you hear me call you "adulteress", when I hit you? I know all about your goings-on, you see, him over at your place. Pity about that night. You moved too quick for me. This time you won't be able to move.'

But Doran still could. The taste in her mouth was acrid, the icy numbness was growing, and her heart seemed to be slowing down. It was now or never. She was on her feet, making a dash for the door, was through it, turning the key. She stumbled to the hall telephone – thank God it was there, not in the drawing room.

214

If only she could get the words out. Dial 999. The first time she mis-dialled, then got it right. In the drawing room Nancy was moving noisily, perhaps unlocking the French window to get into the garden.

'Which service do you require?' asked an impersonal voice.

'Ambulance,' she croaked. 'Abbotsbourne vicarage. Fairweather. Been poisoned. Tell police. Quick!'

She made for the front door, but fell, and lay helpless. The sounds from the drawing room had stopped. Nancy must have got out, and would now be coming round the house from the back garden, intending to get in and finish her off. If only she could get to a bathroom, find an emetic. . . . There was a tiny room off the hall, where coats, boots and general clutter were kept. By an enormous effort she crawled to its open door, and inside, and kicked it shut.

She lay among boots, garden tools, baskets and cans of floor polish, windscreen de-icer and paint. Soon their odours faded and there was nothing in the world but numbness and a burning pain all over her body.

Someone was shaking her, lifting her, asking, 'What the hell's happened to you? Poison, they said. What poison?'

She could not speak to tell Eli Levison that it was aconitine, the poison that had killed Mumbray. She would never recall how Eli and a young man with him carried her to Eli's car, and drove her the two-minute journey to the surgery. On the way the young man, excited and eager like a healthy puppy, told her that he was a medical student attached to the group practice, and that they were in the doctor's car because the ambulance service had very intelligently telephoned the surgery's emergency number. She heard nothing of his explanation of this, or of how they smashed a window to get into the vicarage.

At the surgery Eli subjected her to a stomach-pump, which was horrible but effective. On his examination couch she began to come back to full consciousness. 'That was . . . extremely disagreeable,' she whispered, trying to wipe her streaming eyes.

'Less disagreeable than dying,' he snapped, rolling her

sleeve up and jabbing her arm with an injection. His brow was covered with beads of sweat, she noticed idly. The young man was smiling, clearing up the surgery. At least someone was happy.

'You'll be all right now,' Eli told her. 'You'll be pleased to hear that alcohol and warmth are recommended at this stage, so I'm going to take you into the house where Esther will give you some brandy. Then we'll put you to bed at home. Finish up here, Terry, and I'll come back and give you some notes.'

'Thanks, Doctor.' The boy's eyes were shining with an almost holy enthusiasm. 'Never thought I'd be in on a poisoning case as soon as this. Wonderful, how things turn out, isn't it?'

'Wonderful,' Doran whispered.

She was in bed at home, warm and drowsy, empty and sore. Somebody was pouring water from a jug and urging her to drink it. She noted that the jug was one that usually stood on the window-sill, Coalport hand-painted with wild flowers. She had taken it from stock because it had a hairline crack, and she was particularly fond of it. She tried to tell the someone to take it away and bring a kitchen jug, but the words seemed reluctant to come out.

Rodney was sitting by the bedside, watching her face. She managed to croak, 'You look like Hamlet on a bad day.' He smiled, a wincing smile, and picked up her hand. Vi was in the room, too, hovering anxiously. Eli stood at the foot of the bed, shaking a thermometer. She reflected that they must all look like a Victorian narrative painting, the dying girl forgiving everybody. Only she wasn't dying now.

Downstairs, Rodney and Sam Eastry talked, together with Sam's superintendent who had driven up from headquarters. Sam told them how Nancy had been found, wandering in the garden, shouting that she must get in and see to Helena. Sam and young Glen Lidell had arrived on the scene in response to a call from the surgery, and closed in on her before she could get into the house; she seemed to have forgotten how. They

216

had called a neighbour in to stay with Helena, telephoned Rodney at Elvesham, and driven Nancy to Eastgate, where she was interrogated. 'She said straight out,' Sam told them, 'that she'd tried to kill Doran, as though it was the most natural thing in the world. And that she'd killed Mumbray, because he'd frightened her poor baby – Helena – and asked nasty questions about the Reverend.'

'But how? How did she get the stuff to Mumbray, and what was it?' Rodney asked.

'Easy. She put a whacking great dose of Helena's medicine, which Dr Levison says was based on aconitine, into the piece of cake she'd saved from the Crispin ceremony. Helena's prescribed dose was a small teaspoonful – the cake must have held about a cupful. She said, rather proudly, she'd boiled it down to reduce the volume. Then she went round to The Oaks that night and begged Mumbray to stop threatening her dear vicar. Quite a little actress, she must have been.'

'She was,' Rodney said grimly.

'The clever bit was giving him the cake. She said the little girl had sent it to persuade him not to worry Daddy. She knew about his sweet tooth – Vi had told everybody. Well, it seemed he couldn't resist the bait, and stuffed it into his mouth.'

'And went haring off into the marshes?' the superintendent said sceptically.

'Driven desperate, I should think, sir – trying to escape from the thing – not thinking straight. Or perhaps wanting fresh air. Who's to know? Must have been tough, according to what Dr Levison says about the speed that poison moves at, to get as far as he did. And then to die in the water – he'd have asphyxiated, anyway.'

The superintendent asked, 'And you'd never seen anything suspicious about this woman before, Eastry? No reports of odd behaviour? No? And you, Vicar, you'd no idea that she was manic?'

'Not the least. Think I'd have kept her, if I had? I knew she was passionately devoted to Helena and me, of course. But I could never have guessed she'd carry it that far. She went on a lot about Mumbray, after what he did to Helena, and then seemed to have forgotten about it. Obviously she hadn't.'

'And her attitude to Miss Fairweather?' the superintendent asked. 'You didn't realize that she resented your desire to, er, bring her into the family?'

'No,' Rodney said shortly. His hand went to the little crucifix he wore unseen. Life without Nancy was a grim prospect; life without Doran would have been something he dared not envisage.

Sam asked, 'How d'you think Helena's going to take this because Nancy won't be coming back?'

'Badly, I'm afraid.'

Helena took it so badly that she brought an old-fashioned attack of hysterics on herself, and played it for all it was worth, becoming apparently so ill that an agency nurse was called in to look after her. Some of it was real, including the black depression that followed, for she had lost a surrogate mother who would never come back to her; Nancy was in custody, undergoing medical tests, and her solicitor was hoping for a verdict of Guilty but Insane when she was ultimately tried.

Helena's father took up the burden of her. If she had been demanding before, she was furiously possessive now, greedy of his presence at all possible and some impossible times, flying into infantile tantrums when thwarted, levying upon him moral blackmail and delighting to interfere with his parish duties.

'Put her into a home,' suggested Eli Levison, that good Jewish father who adored his own daughters, revered the institution of the Family, and had never before come across so bad a case of juvenile tyranny. 'They'll know how to sort her out. She's mentally disturbed, at least enough to be admitted to the right sort of place.'

'I can't. She needs me.'

Eli shrugged. 'If that's how you feel. Then I'll ask about for a woman to look after her permanently. It'll cost you.'

'I know that,' Rodney answered shortly. 'I don't care. The only thing I care about, apart from her welfare, is that she hates Doran. Really hates her – seems to think she somehow caused the whole thing. Jolly prospect, isn't it? "This looks not like a nuptial." '

'Martyrdom's said to be very good for the soul. *Mazel tov.*'

Doran and Rodney leaned on a stile and contemplated the January fields, under a carpet of white starred with black skeleton trees. The tips of their noses were pink with cold. Their hands, in thick gloves, were not touching. These days holding hands was like looking into a shop window full of goods one couldn't buy.

Rodney said, 'I've always hated January. Gate of the year, indeed – more like a blasted concrete roadblock. It's running nicely to form this time. The Dean of Barminster's preaching here next week and I can't stand him, great prosy twit. Mrs Binns thinks she's dying and wants me to read *Pilgrim's Progress* to her every morning.'

'Cheer up, it might be *The Lower Depths* or *Jessica's First Prayer* or last year's Booker Prize. Same with me, January.' Doran sighed. 'I bought a lovely Art Deco figure at an auction last week, ivory and gold on a marble base – cost a fortune. When I got it to the shop and was gloating over it Vic Maidment dropped in and pointed out that it was a very good fake – said I wanted my eyes testing. He knows about Deco. I drove straight back with it but the owner's gone abroad, and anyway, they'd say they advertised it in good faith in the catalogue. Oh, and I've found dry rot in the kitchen and a fox took my stray moggy. All next week, *East Lynne.* Sometimes I yearn for the bad old days of the Abbotsbourne Crime Wave.'

'Cheer up yourself, they might come back – with luck, something a bit less nasty next time. Barratry? Simony? No, that's ecclesiastical preferment, not at all what we need.' Glancing down at her, he gently flicked back a curl which was falling over her left eye. 'You look like a spring Dryad lost in winter.'

'I feel like one. Rodney, what are we going to do – about us?'

'Wait. See what the year brings. Hope on, hope ever. . . . My darling girl, I talk an awful lot of nonsense, but I will say this seriously: feel free. If you find somebody else who'd be right for you, and I'm still – tied, go and be happy and don't give me another thought. I'd hate it, but if you were happy I could stand it.'

'That's said to be a definition of true love.'

'Perhaps it is. There's a certain well-known Thirteenth Chapter of Corinthians . . . No, I'm not going to quote. For once. Come on, let's go for a long healthy tiring walk. There's a pub not more than two miles off where they do strangely good pies and fantastic soup, scalding hot. *Soup of the Evening, beautiful beautiful Soup*. . . .'

Singing, he handed Doran over the stile and led her down the narrow icy path between the fallow cornfields.

THE END

Disposal of
the Living
by Robert Barnard

'Sharp, sly and funny portrait of local rivalries and obsessions
confirming Barnard as one of our most original and versatile
blood-spillers'
The Times

'A pacey, entertaining read, with plenty of chuckles and
cunning plotting'
Police

'Smart updating of village mystery, with Mr B. displaying a
wonderful eye and ear for snobbery, malice, and other small-
town delights'
Scotsman

'One of the wittiest comedies of manners'
Punch

When the women of Hexton-upon-Weir decided to band
together to block the appointment of a new vicar who was not
only unacceptably High Church but also — oh horror! —
celibate, they managed to create merry hell. As the town was
riven by faction and counter-faction, Helen Kitterage, wife of
the local vet, tried to remain aloof, but finally, during the
town's fete, the ill-will and plotting degenerated into murder, a
murder that affected Helen more than anyone else.
Somewhere among the secrets of this female dominated town
was a key shame that someone was prepared to kill for.

0553 131296

The Complete Steel
by Catherine Aird

Ornum House was open to the public on Wednesdays, Saturdays, and Sundays. Mrs Fisher, dragging her unwilling family around the Stately Home had never intended to go down to the dungeons and armoury, but when her son Michael went missing she knew that that was where he was likely to be. She caught him just in time, struggling to open a standing suit of armour.

'Look, Mum,' he shouted, wrenching at the vizor, and at that moment he managed to lift it.

A face stared back. It was a modern face, a twentieth century face the face of Mr Meredith, Librarian of Ornum House. And he was dead.

0552 127922

Wycliffe and the
Peagreen Boat
by W. J. Burley

Tragedy seemed to stalk the Tremain family. Sidney Tremain had hanged himself for no obvious reason. His son, Morley, had had the misfortune to fall in love with a girl who slept around — and get convicted of killing her. And now Cedric Tremain was charged with murdering his wealthy father by blowing up his boat.

Chief Superintendent Wycliffe knew something was wrong, knew that the apparently cut and dried case wasn't what it appeared to be. Carefully he cast his bait — and waited for the real killer to surface.

0552 12804X

A SELECTION OF CRIME TITLES AVAILABLE FROM CORGI BOOKS

THE PRICES SHOWN BELOW WERE CORRECT AT THE TIME OF GOING TO PRESS. HOWEVER TRANSWORLD PUBLISHERS RESERVE THE RIGHT TO SHOW NEW RETAIL PRICES ON COVERS WHICH MAY DIFFER FROM THOSE PREVIOUSLY ADVERTISED IN THE TEXT OR ELSEWHERE.

☐	12792 2	THE COMPLETE STEEL	*Catherine Aird*	£2.50
☐	12793 0	HENRIETTA WHO?	*Catherine Aird*	£2.50
☐	12794 9	A LATE PHOENIX	*Catherine Aird*	£1.95
☐	13128 8	POLITICAL SUICIDE	*Robert Barnard*	£2.50
☐	12804 X	WYCLIFFE AND THE PEA GREEN BOAT	*W. J. Burley*	£2.50
☐	12805 8	WYCLIFFE AND THE SCHOOLGIRLS	*W. J. Burley*	£1.95
☐	12806 6	WYCLIFFE AND THE SCAPEGOAT	*W. J. Burley*	£2.50
☐	13232 2	WYCLIFFE AND THE BEATES	*W. J. Burley*	£1.95
☐	13231 4	WYCLIFFE AND THE FOUR JACKS	*W. J. Burley*	£2.50
☐	10275 X	BELIEVE THIS, YOU'LL BELIEVE ANYTHING	*James Hadley Chase*	£1.95
☐	11096 5	THE DEAD STAY DUMB	*James Hadley Chase*	£1.95
☐	09648 2	HAVE A CHANGE OF SCENE	*James Hadley Chase*	£1.75
☐	11309 3	HAVE THIS ONE ON ME	*James Hadley Chase*	£1.75
☐	10715 8	I HOLD THE FOUR ACES	*James Hadley Chase*	£1.95
☐	10765 4	MALLORY	*James Hadley Chase*	£1.75
☐	11817 6	TRY THIS ONE FOR SIZE	*James Hadley Chase*	£1.95
☐	11457 X	YOU HAVE YOURSELF A DEAL	*James Hadley Chase*	£1.95
☐	11308 5	YOU MUST BE KIDDING	*James Hadley Chase*	£1.95
☐	12021 9	RUMPELSTILTSKIN	*Ed McBain*	£1.50
☐	13240 3	A HELL OF A WOMAN	*Jim Thompson*	£2.50
☐	13242 X	RECOIL	*Jim Thompson*	£2.50

All Corgi/Bantam Books are available at your bookshop or newsagent, or can be ordered from the following address:

Corgi/Bantam Books,
Cash Sales Department,
P.O. Box 11, Falmouth, Cornwall TR10 9EN

Please send a cheque or postal order (no currency) and allow 60p for postage and packing for the first book plus 25p for the second book and 15p for each additional book ordered up to a maximum charge of £1.90 in UK.

B.F.P.O. customers please allow 60p for the first book, 25p for the second book plus 15p per copy for the next 7 books, thereafter 9p per book.

Overseas customers, including Eire, please allow £1.25 for postage and packing for the first book, 75p for the second book, and 28p for each subsequent title ordered.